"Was he a friend of yours?" the police officer asked as the lead paramedic examined Donald.

Maggie wished the officer would evict all of their customers from the pie shop, even if that meant losing some business. She didn't want to discuss her aunt's boyfriend in front of everyone they knew.

"He and I have been dating," Aunt Clara confessed, large tears rolling down her cheeks. "He was such a wonderful man. I can't imagine who would want to hurt him."

"Unless it was someone who knew one of those five women he allegedly killed." Professor Simpson's loud voice overtook the rest of the sound in the pie shop.

Praise for

Plum Deadly

"A well-constructed plot and lively dialogue. . . . Fans of Joanne Fluke's Hannah Swenson series and other culinary cozies will be satisfied."

—*Publishers Weekly*

"Cuddle up and lose yourself in the cozy Pie in the Sky pie shop with Maggie, Aunt Clara, and the rest of the gang . . . a charming little mystery that kept me entertained until the very end."

—*Rainy Day Ramblings Book Blog*

Other Novels by Ellie Grant

Plum Deadly

Treacherous Tart

Ellie Grant

POCKET BOOKS

New York London Toronto Sydney New Delhi

Pocket Books
A Division of Simon & Schuster, Inc.
1230 Avenue of the Americas
New York, NY 10020

This book is a work of fiction. Any references to historical events, real people, or real places are used fictitiously. Other names, characters, places, and events are products of the author's imagination, and any resemblance to actual events or places or persons, living or dead, is entirely coincidental.

First Pocket Books trade paperback edition November 2014

For information about special discounts for bulk purchases, please contact Simon & Schuster Special Sales at 1-866-506-1949 or business@simonandschuster.com.

The Simon & Schuster Speakers Bureau can bring authors to your live event. For more information or to book an event contact the Simon & Schuster Speakers Bureau at 1-866-248-3049 or visit our website at www.simonspeakers.com.

Interior design by Leydiana Rodríguez-Ovalles
Cover illustration by Jesse Reisch

Manufactured in the United States of America

10 9 8 7 6 5 4 3 2 1

ISBN 978-1-4516-8956-3
ISBN 978-1-4516-8958-7 (ebook)

We'd like to thank our son,
Christopher Lavene,
who makes the best "pies" in the
world, for his help with this project.
You are the best!

Treacherous Tart

One

"Is there any way this could be a different Donald Wickerson?" Maggie Grady asked as she and Ryan Summerour sat drinking coffee. "One who doesn't seem to kill the women who fall in love with him?"

It was the Christmas season at Pie in the Sky, a pie shop near the Duke University campus in Durham, North Carolina. Temperatures had dipped obligingly low for holiday festivities and shoppers. A snowstorm had added a powdery white dusting to rooftops and trees. It was a perfect Christmas-card scene.

Except for one thing.

Maggie's Aunt Clara seemed to be smitten with a man who might be responsible for the deaths of each of his six wives.

"I don't think there's any mistake. I've done my research."

Ryan owned and operated his family's business, the *Durham Weekly* newspaper. He'd first received a tip about Donald Wickerson from a friend in Georgia about six months ago. Since then he'd followed other newspaper stories about the man they'd dubbed the Black Widower, who had now moved to North Carolina.

He'd known about Wickerson long before Aunt Clara had met him at the library a few months before. He just never expected her to meet and fall for the man.

Maggie shook her head in frustration. Her short brown hair flew around her pretty face. She closed her green eyes—the same color as her aunt's.

"I can't believe it. Just as I get my life settled, Aunt Clara goes off the deep end for some 'black widower.' It's crazy."

"Give her a break. She's been alone for a long time. She's looking for someone special in her life. My father would be the same way if he met someone who was interested in golf and didn't mind him trumpeting his political views every five minutes. I don't know how my mother lived with him."

Ryan ran his hand through his dark-blond hair. Instead of calming it down, the gesture made the ends curlier. He squinted at a stack of old newspaper articles from around the state, selecting one from the top, and holding it an arm's length away from his blue eyes. He was in his forties, and fighting the need to wear glasses.

"You're going to have to give in and get glasses." Maggie watched him with a smile. "If you hold papers any farther from your face when you read, you'll go cross-eyed."

Maggie and Ryan had only been a couple for a few weeks—they'd met after Maggie moved back home to Durham earlier in the fall. It had been a difficult transition settling back into small-town life since she'd spent the past ten years working in New York, but meeting Ryan had helped.

It was a good relationship, after they'd worked out the kinks. They'd met under unfortunate circumstances. Ryan had wanted to write a story about her for the *Durham Weekly*, but it hadn't been very flattering given that she'd come home in a firestorm after being fired from her job for embezzlement.

But they'd clicked soon after. They seemed to have a lot in common, despite the differences in their choice of work. They'd both graduated from Duke University. They'd both grown up here and had become part of family-owned businesses.

"Okay, let's just focus on what we can do to keep your aunt from being Donald's next victim."

"I thought you were going to write about him in the paper?" Maggie got up to start cleaning the pie shop. It was almost six, closing time.

There had been a flurry of activity earlier, before the snow had started falling. People liked to load up on extra food before it snowed. After the white stuff was on the ground, they wanted to stay inside, make popcorn, and drink hot chocolate. "I want to write about him, but I can't use his real name. After the first article came out in my friend's newspaper, his lawyer threatened to sue. I've been careful. I can't afford a big lawsuit. He has a lot more money than I do since he keeps inheriting from his dead wives."

He got up and took their coffee cups to the kitchen. Maggie followed him to get the mop. The dark-blue tile floor in the eating area of Pie in the Sky was excellent for hiding coffee stains from customers.

But she still knew they were there.

"Have you talked to Frank about it?"

Frank Waters was a Durham homicide detective who'd helped Ryan with a few other articles he'd written in the ten years he'd been running the paper. Frank was friends with Ryan's father, Garrett, who'd run the paper before him.

"There's nothing he can do." Ryan put the cups and other dishes he found into the dishwasher in the kitchen. "Technically, Donald hasn't done anything wrong. He's been investigated after each of his wives' deaths—they never find anything. All of their deaths were ruled accidents. Frank warned me about using Donald's real name. That's about it."

Maggie viciously rammed the mop into the wringer on the bucket. "Well, I'm not standing around waiting until Donald 'accidentally' kills Aunt Clara. I just got her back in my life again. I'm not losing her to some lucky serial killer who preys on women with a little money and property."

She'd been trying to find some way to broach the subject with her aunt to warn her of his intentions, but she still hadn't found the right moment, or the right way to go about it.

The front door chimed, letting them know someone had come in.

"Yoo-hoo!" Aunt Clara called from the front. "Is anyone here? I know it's closing time, but we'd like some coffee, please!"

Maggie peeked around the corner of the service window between the kitchen and the front shop area. "He's with her. We'll have to table this discussion until later."

"There you are!" Aunt Clara's merry voice matched the holiday decorations and the twinkling lights around the pie shop. "I was beginning to wonder what a person had to do to get some service in this joint."

Her aunt giggled as she held Donald's hand, which made Maggie cringe. Clara's wrinkled face was still pretty, with its slight blush and sharp green eyes. In her youth, red hair had flowed softly around her shoulders. Now that she was older, she cut and dyed her hair, making it a strange, orange-colored fringe of sorts that still framed her face.

"Well, some customers can be *very* annoying," Maggie joked, quickly shooting a pointed glare at Donald, who didn't seem to notice.

It was hard to keep from turning to Donald and accusing him of preying on her aunt, but it seemed she had no choice but to be amiable since she had no real proof that he'd done anything wrong.

At least not yet.

Maggie spared them a smile as she brought out two cups of coffee. "What are you two up to?"

"We're back from a wonderful program about the history of Christmas at the library. Donald said he wanted to try our Marvelous Mince pie."

Donald smiled and kissed Clara's hand. "That's right. Your pretty little aunt convinced me that her mincemeat pie is as good as my mother's used to be. I have my doubts. Clara can be quite persuasive."

Maggie wanted to slap Donald and tell him to keep his hands off her aunt.

But what if Ryan was wrong? What if Donald was her aunt's last chance at happiness?

Donald certainly didn't look like a killer. He was tall and handsome for an older man. He reminded her of a model for an ad selling flannel shirts and boots. He had that rugged, outdoor quality to him.

She couldn't ruin a possible chance for her aunt's happiness without hard proof. "My aunt makes a mean mincemeat pie. I'll be happy to get you a slice. Anything for you, Aunt Clara?"

"Yes, honey. I'll take a slice of the coconut custard. It's named after me. I feel guilty if I don't eat some once in a while. Not too much—I don't want to put on any weight."

Donald stared into her eyes. "You have such a trim little figure. I'm sure you don't have to worry about it, Clara. Now, me, on the other hand, I have to be careful or what's left of my muscle will go right to fat."

Maggie wished she were charmed by how cute they were together as he patted his flat stomach. Aunt Clara beamed at him adoringly.

It was hard to look at the two of them together without thinking about those other women who'd once thought he was charming.

Maggie hurried back into the kitchen to get the slices of pie.

"You have to tell her." Ryan had already dished out some mincemeat pie for her. "She has to know."

"What would I say? 'Ryan thinks the man you're dating is a killer'? She'd ask how you know. You don't really have that answer."

"We could show her the old newspaper clippings."

Maggie thought about it as she sliced Clara's Coconut Cream pie for her aunt. "Maybe that would work. I could *accidentally* leave your file open with the clippings on the kitchen table at home."

Ryan scoffed at that. "That's going to be better than telling her?"

"It would present the evidence you have at the same time as the accusation." Maggie closed up the pies and put them back into the refrigerator. She picked up a pie plate in each hand. "She doesn't know anything about this. She hasn't made the connection yet between your articles and Donald. I don't want to just blurt it out."

Ryan put a fork on each plate. "If you're going to do that, I think you should do it here. We could set something up like we're looking at the file when she walks in."

"How is that better?"

He shrugged. "It would be safer. I'm worried what her reaction will be, aren't you? She should know the truth, but I don't want her to run to him for comfort."

"And if she chooses to go out with him anyway and hates me for bringing the whole thing up?"

"She's not going to hate you for saving her life. She might not like it at first, but she'll forgive you later. I'll bet the women Donald killed would have wanted someone in their family to do as much for them."

Maggie rolled her eyes at the idea and took the pie out to Aunt Clara and Donald.

"Thank you so much, Maggie." Donald's smile

seemed warm and genuine as he took the pie from her. "Your aunt has told me all about you. I look forward to furthering our acquaintance in the future."

"Me too." Maggie moved away to continue closing down the pie shop for the night. She wished he wasn't trying so hard to be charming. It made it hard to dislike him. Either he was innocent or he had his act down perfectly.

"Sit with us for a minute." Her aunt pulled out a new dark-blue chair for her. "Everything looks so wonderful in here now that the remodeling is done."

The entire shop had recently received a much-needed face-lift, playing up Pie in the Sky's history, and its family ties to Duke University. The dark-blue school colors were echoed in the new seat covers, tile floor, and counter. The old, flat ceiling lights had been replaced by coffee-cup-shaped lights. Maggie had hung old photos taken at the school and at Pie in the Sky. It was a great touch.

Maggie didn't want to refuse her aunt. It was important to maintain her relationship with Aunt Clara through this. Even if she was worried about Donald, alienating Aunt Clara would be like handing her over to the man.

So she sat.

"Your aunt tells me you used to work in New York City." Donald carefully chewed his pie as he spoke.

He was certainly neat and had excellent manners—*all the better to snag the ladies and kill them*, she supposed.

Ryan had said that this man preyed on older women who were well off and alone. Maybe she could say something to warn him off, to make sure he understood how things were. If he was even *thinking* about killing her aunt to get her money and property, he needed to think again.

"Now that I'm Aunt Clara's *full* partner in the pie shop, it's nice to see some new things done around here."

"Yes," Aunt Clara chimed in. "Maggie and I work very well together. Of course, there's going to come a time when being here five days a week at five thirty in the morning might get to be too much for me. I'm glad I'll have her to take over."

Maggie was surprised by her aunt's words. "You've never said anything about retiring. Is something wrong?"

"No, of course not," Clara denied. "I'm only thinking about the future."

"Your aunt has worked hard her whole life, from what she's told me," Donald intervened. "You have to expect she might want a nice, long rest. Maybe in the Bahamas, or Mexico. It would be good to get away from these harsh winters near the mountains."

"Aunt Clara *loves* winter." Maggie mangled the dish towel she held. "She loves snow and ice. And she *loves* working at Pie in the Sky."

"You're absolutely right." Aunt Clara put her hand on Maggie's. "And I'm not talking about right now or even tomorrow. Just someday. I'm not the spring chicken who first opened this place before you were born."

Aunt Clara transferred her gaze and her hand to Donald with a sweet smile. "I've been learning about the fine art of enjoying life without working. One doesn't need to work hard all the time. That's why I took off early today. I deserve an occasional day off."

Maggie could hardly believe her ears. She'd never heard her aunt sound this way. It had to be Donald. He was already setting her up to depend on him. Next, he'd convince her to marry him and then he'd be trying to figure out ways to get rid of Maggie.

She had to nip this in the bud.

"Excuse me, but *I'm* not such a lady of leisure." Maggie got to her feet and tried to keep her tone light and airy. She didn't want to tip Donald off. "The pie shop won't close itself."

"Go right ahead, honey." Aunt Clara nibbled at her pie. "We'll finish up here, and Donald said he'll take us home."

"Ryan's here." He waved to Aunt Clara from the service window. "I'll have him take me home. You two take your time. I'll see you when I get there."

She took the dirty coffeepots to the kitchen to be washed.

When the door between the dining room and the kitchen had swung closed behind her, Maggie's anger boiled over. "That's it. You're right. We have to find a way to tell her."

Two

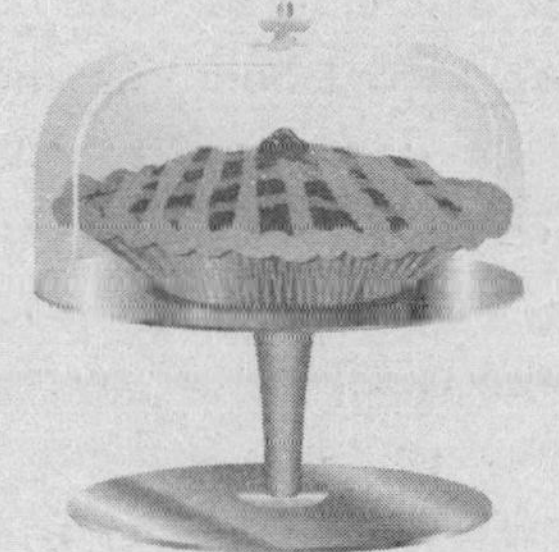

Maggie said good night to Ryan in the car. She was tired when she reached the house she shared with her aunt. It was the house Maggie had grown up in after her parents had died in a terrible car wreck when she was a child.

Aunt Clara and Uncle Fred had taken her in when she was five and done their best to make her part of their family. Her aunt and uncle had no children of their own, and Maggie had become like their daughter.

The house was an older, two-story red-brick that had mellowed in the hot sun to more of a pink shade. Maggie and her aunt had painted the faded shutters and doors to a sparkling white again since she'd come back home.

It had been hard for her aunt since she'd lost Uncle Fred, who had died of a heart attack one evening a few years before, after they'd come home from the pie shop. Maggie hadn't known how hard it had been until she'd moved home again. Between her and her aunt, they'd managed to settle into a new rhythm together, and tackle things that had been ignored for a long time.

The stubborn crack in the concrete stairs leading to the house wasn't one of them. Maggie sighed as she walked past it and opened the door. She went inside, hung up her coat, and took off her boots.

Of course, Donald was still there.

He was sitting back in one of the good chairs with his long legs crossed, holding a delicate cup filled with one of Aunt Clara's fragrant teas. He looked so much at home that Maggie gritted her teeth, quickly passing by the living room and going upstairs to her bedroom. She'd have to talk to Aunt Clara later.

She took a quick shower and bundled up in her flannel pajamas and robe after she was done. A new furnace was on her list for next year. The old one was electric and left them cold most of the time. She hoped to add a gas furnace and a couple of gas logs for the fireplace in the parlor. Just the thought of it made her feel warmer.

She was saving money for the upgrade, hoping not to have to draw the money from their savings. The pie shop was making enough money for them to survive but not enough for them to thrive. Plus, Maggie liked the idea of having a small cushion. She was a rainy-day kind of girl.

She thumbed through the pie shop trade magazines she received on a regular basis. She'd been surprised how many periodicals were dedicated to making pie. There were also some online groups that she belonged to that were very helpful in coming up with new ideas for pies and ways to promote the shop.

With Christmas upon them, Maggie had gone all out for the season. Not only were the festive decorations new, she'd also added some new recipes she and Aunt Clara had tried. Christmas had always been her favorite time of the year—it was something she and Aunt Clara shared. Maggie wanted her aunt to be happy, the same way Maggie was happy with Ryan. She wanted Ryan to be wrong about Donald even though she was afraid he might be right. The newspaper clippings were very convincing, even though there hadn't been enough evidence to arrest him.

Maggie looked out the window at the old tree

she used to climb down when she was a kid. It was dark, but in her mind's eye, she knew every branch and curve of that old oak. Uncle Fred had even assisted her mode of escape by adding various devices to help her get up and down.

The truth was that she had no way of keeping Aunt Clara completely safe. She could only tell her aunt what she knew and hope she would be wary of Donald. Donald was a black mark on the otherwise pleasant life she'd set up for herself since coming back to Durham. Though the beginning of that transition had been painful, it was completely worth it. She and Aunt Clara worked well together. The impact of their partnership was beginning to show results at the cash register. The future looked bright.

Except for Donald.

Suddenly she had a great idea.

Maggie opened her laptop as she heard Donald's hearty laugh from downstairs.

What if she could find someone who could steal Aunt Clara away from Donald? Sure, she and Ryan might be able to prove Donald was an evil opportunist who took advantage of older women, but where would that leave Aunt Clara? She'd be heartbroken and alone.

Before that happened, Maggie decided to register her aunt with a dating service. She was sure that she could find Aunt Clara a suitable match in no time. She went to the various online sites and looked through what they had to offer. She needed a site that had some older gentlemen who might be looking for a relationship with a wonderful older woman.

She finally settled on the Durham Singles group. They showed photos of older men and women from the area. Maggie paid the reasonable fee and joined for her aunt.

It took her a solid hour to fill in all of the required information—lucky she knew her aunt so well that she didn't need to figure out how to coax any necessary details out of her. She uploaded a photo of Aunt Clara looking particularly pretty in a red dress she'd worn for a Christmas party they'd attended last week at the Business Owners' Association.

Maggie fudged on a few items. Did they really need to know her aunt's *exact* age? She decided to make her aunt a few years younger. After all, Aunt Clara was *very* youthful, and had a sprightly attitude toward life.

She added all of her aunt's interests—pie making, running her own business, reading, being a strong part of the library. She also enjoyed music. She made sure it was clear that her aunt owned Pie in the Sky. Maggie felt like that part was very important. It would be wonderful if Aunt Clara could meet another dedicated business owner, even though that hadn't worked very well with Garrett Summerour, Ryan's father, who'd run the *Durham Weekly* newspaper for many years. Aunt Clara had declared that Garrett was too political for her tastes.

Maggie made a notation in Aunt Clara's profile for the dating service that she didn't care for politics.

There was a knock on the bedroom door. Maggie lowered her laptop cover even though her aunt never looked at a computer if she could help it. *Guilty*, she imagined.

Aunt Clara opened the door and peeked around. "Donald is gone. I didn't know if you were giving us time alone or if you were asleep, even though you never said good night. Do you want a snack before bed? I could use a little snack myself."

This was Maggie's perfect opportunity to tell Aunt Clara the truth about Donald.

"I *am* a little hungry." Maggie stretched and yawned as she got up from the bed, unable to resist her aunt's endless supply of delicious treats. "Maybe a *small* snack."

In truth, Maggie had gained ten pounds since she'd started working at the pie shop again. Funny, she'd worked there through high school and while she'd attended college without gaining an ounce.

She'd only been back a few months. If she kept gaining at that rate, she'd have to find a second job working at a gym to get rid of the extra weight. She wasn't a runner anymore, as she had been in her youth.

"I have plenty of hot cocoa and a slice of cheddar for the last piece of that new caramel apple pie we tried this week. It was good. What did you name it again?"

"Caramel Apple Without a Stick."

"That's it!" Aunt Clara clapped her hands. She loved new pie names. "It's a great name."

They'd already had a caramel apple pie at the shop. Maggie had added some nuts on the top and they put a pat of butter on each slice as it was served. It had become very popular.

Maggie agreed, and they went back downstairs. She could hear the old furnace gasping and wheezing. It tried its best but was too old for the job. She wished she could go ahead and retire it now, but her thrifty little soul begged her to wait.

"Did you and Donald have a good time?"

"Oh yes. He's such a dear." Aunt Clara took out the last piece of pie for Maggie. "He didn't like cheddar on his pie. That's odd, don't you think?"

There couldn't have been a better lead-in to what Maggie wanted to say. When the hot cocoa was ready, she sat down at the small kitchen table in the kitchen.

"There may be something else odd about Donald. I haven't wanted to say anything because you've been so happy with him."

"What is it, Maggie?" Aunt Clara sat across the table from her niece, the same table she'd once shared with her husband.

"Ryan found some information about Donald."

"He checked up on my boyfriend?"

"It wasn't checking up exactly." Maggie took a hasty sip of her hot cocoa. This was harder than she'd thought it would be. "Ryan had heard about him before you met him."

Maggie went on to explain about Ryan's research, Donald's reputation, and what they feared Donald might have in store for her aunt.

Aunt Clara was silent for a moment. She was clearly mulling over Maggie's words.

"That's crazy." She sipped her hot cocoa. "Ryan obviously has Donald mixed up with someone else."

"There are pictures of him. He's infamous. The police can't do anything because there isn't enough proof, but they've questioned him dozens of times. He's been in newspapers across the South."

"Maggie, you shouldn't dwell on this. There is some kind of mistake. That's why the police can't prove anything."

"I'm worried about it. I don't want to lose you."

"You know, many people thought terrible things about you when you came back from New York. They thought you'd embezzled money from the bank you worked for. I always knew it wasn't true. I'm telling you now that this isn't true about Donald either."

"But Aunt Clara—"

"Never mind." Clara's voice was stern. "Eat your pie. We have to get up early tomorrow."

Her aunt turned around and did something she never did—she went upstairs without saying good night and without waiting for Maggie to finish her cocoa.

She was angry. Maggie put her empty cup in the sink and threw away what was left of the uneaten pie. She'd lost her appetite. Knowing her aunt was mad at her was enough to keep her from enjoying the delicious caramel apple pie.

Maggie had known before she'd said anything that Aunt Clara's feelings would be hurt. How did she expect her to feel? Earlier that evening it had sounded as though her aunt was planning her future with Donald. How would she have felt if her aunt told her that Ryan not only didn't care for her but also planned on killing her?

On the other hand, she had to say *something*. Maggie hoped her aunt would forgive her. Even if she didn't believe Donald was a killer, she hoped the knowledge would make Aunt Clara more cautious around him.

In the meantime, Maggie would keep up her daily, not-so-subtle reminders to Donald that her aunt wasn't some lonely woman with no one who cared what happened to her. She wished the police would hurry and find some *real* evidence against Donald before this went any further.

Maggie turned off the lights and made sure both doors were locked before she went back upstairs to bed. It was going to be a long day at work tomorrow if Aunt Clara stayed angry with her.

Three

Despite Maggie's fears, Aunt Clara was as talkative and happy about getting up and going to work at the pie shop the next day as she ever was.

"I think you forgot to set your alarm again." She came into Maggie's room, completely dressed, at 4:30 a.m. to remind her that they had to be up by five. "I was up anyway. I thought I'd come in and get you going."

Maggie gazed bleary-eyed at her old Cinderella alarm clock on the bedside table. "The alarm didn't have a chance to go off. It's only four thirty-five. It doesn't go off until five."

"Well, you're up now. Might as well get ready."

"Thanks." Maggie fell back on the bed. She remembered times when Aunt Clara had been angry at her when she was growing up. Uncle Fred had been a straightforward person, telling her at once why he was angry. Aunt Clara had been quietly angry. She didn't talk much, and was devious about it—like now.

Maggie was more like her uncle in that regard.

Maggie switched on a small lamp and put on jeans and a white Pie in the Sky T-shirt. She'd purchased some new T-shirts so she could wear a different one each day. Months of wearing the same color with the pie shop logo had begun to grow tiresome.

Maggie entered the kitchen just as the toast popped up. Aunt Clara was humming as she poured orange juice. They'd devised a system between them. Whoever got up first made breakfast. This morning it was pimento cheese on toast. Aunt Clara handed the plastic container of pimento cheese to Maggie along with two slices of golden toast.

"I think we'll have Evie's Elegant Eggnog pie as our pie of the day. I have some whipped cream that I got from Mr. Gino at cost yesterday. We could add a dash of that to make it more festive."

Maggie yawned. "That sounds good."

Aunt Clara smiled at her niece. "Did you have

trouble sleeping last night, honey? You look *awful* this morning, bless your heart."

"Thanks." Maggie spread a little pimento cheese on her toast. It wasn't her favorite breakfast, even though her aunt's homemade variety was definitely better than the store-bought kind. "I think it was getting up too early."

"Oh. I thought it might be too much on your mind. Maybe a little guilty conscience?"

"I don't want you to be angry with me over what I said last night." Maggie hugged her. "I want you to have someone nice in your life. I have some doubts about Donald. Wouldn't you want me to know if there was something unusual about Ryan? Wouldn't you want me to be prepared?"

"I'm not angry." Her aunt sipped her juice. "I have no doubts about Donald. And if I had any doubts about Ryan, it wouldn't be my place to tell you."

"Why not? Would you rather Ryan killed me and left me in a trashcan?"

"No. I know in my heart that Ryan is a good person. I don't believe that will happen with Donald either. Are you ready? I'm going to put on my coat."

Maggie swallowed the rest of her toast and juice before she followed her aunt. She wished she'd had coffee, but they'd given up having coffee at home in the morning since she'd put in the espresso machine at the shop.

"I'm sorry. I knew your feelings would be hurt. I wish I hadn't said anything."

Aunt Clara sniffed. "That makes two of us."

The two women headed outside into a light snowfall with their hurt feelings intact. The dark sky was a perfect backdrop for the madly whirling snowflakes, illuminated by the streetlights. Snow already covered the stairs and the large holly berry wreath Maggie and Aunt Clara had hung on the front door.

"Beautiful!" Aunt Clara enjoyed the snow that was falling. "At this rate, we should sell a lot of pie today. There's no point in wasting time thinking about things that don't matter."

In other words, Maggie thought, *don't bother thinking about Donald and what he has in mind.* Her aunt's message was loud and clear.

Traffic was light that morning as they walked the short distance to the pie shop, as Aunt Clara had done for the past forty years. The Duke University campus was in close proximity to the pie shop, although when the old oaks were full of leaves, you could barely make it out. Thousands of pinpoint lights gleamed through the skeletal trees in the winter, and the old chapel tower was visible.

Students from the university usually showed up later in the day to study. Police officers and firefighters always came in for an afternoon slice of pie and hot cup of coffee. Several book clubs met at Pie in the Sky. The shop had a reputation for being clean, cozy, and comfortable, as well as serving great pie and coffee.

But it was more than that. Aunt Clara and Uncle Fred had always made everyone feel welcome and special when they visited. Maggie hoped she was doing the same now.

"I love this time of year." Aunt Clara's gloves were covered in snow as she made, and tossed, a snowball. "See how the snow makes everything like a beautiful Christmas village? It's never that way any other time. Even though the flowers are pretty in the spring, it's not as special as it is now."

Not wanting to continue their argument, Maggie agreed. "I like all the Christmas decorations too. Mr. Farmer at the corner has been using the same Santa, sleigh, and reindeer up on the roof since I was a kid. He must have grandkids that put it all up there now."

There were other houses with colored lights still glowing softly in the gray morning. Dozens of wreaths with bright red bows hung from windows and doors. The snow swirled around garlands, and tinsel hung from huge old fir trees too, making the holiday scene complete.

"Oh yes. Mike has several grandchildren, and I think one or two great-grandchildren. He has six children of his own. It's to be expected." Aunt Clara smiled as a few more snowflakes fluttered on her eyelashes. She blinked them quickly, looking child-like in the predawn light.

"That was the only thing that would've made mine and Fred's lives better, you know. We always wanted to have a child. It wasn't to be, however. Lucky for us, we had *you*."

Maggie smiled. "I'm very happy you and Uncle Fred were there for me. I couldn't have asked for a more loving family."

Aunt Clara paused to hug Maggie on the wet sidewalk. It was too warm for the snow to stay around for long. The weather forecast had predicted all of it would be gone by noon.

"Let's not fight anymore, okay?" Aunt Clara kissed her cheek. "Things always work themselves out, don't they? Have some faith. Everything will be fine."

Maggie agreed with her. She wouldn't throw Donald's past into her aunt's face again—at least not unless there was solid evidence to back her up.

They reached the pie shop with its lights twinkling in the dark morning and went inside to get busy. Five days a week, Maggie and Aunt Clara made dozens of pies by hand. In the warmer months, the fluffy, light cream pies like Chocoholic Cream, Clara's Coconut Cream, Popular Peach, and Killer Key Lime were in demand. They were cool and sweet for the customers who came in from the hot street after a long day.

With the holidays and the cooler weather, Fantastic Fig, Pumpkin Pizzazz, Caramel Apple Without a Stick, and Evie's Elegant Eggnog pies were what the customers craved.

Aunt Clara's Marvelous Mince pie had to be kept in stock too.

She used an old recipe her mother had created with molasses instead of sorghum, and apricot juice instead of beef broth. The pie wasn't so heavy even though it was laden with fresh raisins, apples, oranges, and pineapple.

Maggie hadn't even wanted to taste it—it sounded awful. But from the first bite, she'd loved it.

Aunt Clara would never sell a homemade pie that was more than a day out of the oven. She didn't like the way leftover pie tasted. It was part of the secret to Clara's success and longevity at the shop: everything was as fresh as it tasted.

Maggie didn't know how her aunt had kept up with all the work each day by herself. It was all both of them could do to get everything done. Even without the new customers, Maggie was astonished at how much her aunt had done for so many years.

Of course, that had led to everything else going by the wayside. Maggie hoped that they could manage, between the two of them, to keep the pie shop going and continue improving the house and yard.

Coffee customers always came in first, grabbing a quick cup on the way to work. Maggie had invested in the professional espresso machine with some of her severance pay. She'd really bought it for herself, but it had become very popular with the customers too.

It took a little more time than the coffee in the pot, but she thought it was so much better, thick and full-flavored. She sighed each time she sat down to drink it. Some customers thumbed their noses at the lattes and preferred the plain coffee. But Maggie relished the thick foam on top of her mocha latte, and she loved the hissing sound of the machine as it steamed the milk.

By six fifteen on that rainy, cold morning, dozens of people had stopped in for a hot cup of coffee and a cheerful "good morning." Some bought pies, either whole or by the slice, for lunch and later in the day.

By six thirty, fresh pies were coming out of the oven, golden brown and delicious. The heavenly smell of cinnamon, nutmeg, and fruit spread quickly through the shop before it wafted outside. Maggie turned on the Hot Pie Now sign as several of their regular customers came in.

Among them were Raji Singh and his wife, Ahalya, from the Bombay Grill, which was one of four shops in the same shopping strip as Pie in the Sky. Aunt Clara owned the property, and Maggie collected the rent each month. She was better with money and computers than her aunt.

"Good morning!" Raji's usual broad smile spread across his handsome face. "We would like some pie, please. A slice each of whatever you consider to be holiday pie."

"I think we'll have some Elegant Eggnog pie ready soon, but it's too hot to serve right now." Maggie consulted her whiteboard menu at the front of the pie shop. "We have some Pumpkin Pizzazz and definitely some Marvelous Mince. Any of that sound good?"

Ahalya smiled and nodded. "We'll both take a slice of each." She handed the rent check to Maggie.

"We're experiencing the holidays through food," Raji explained. "This is our first Christmas in this country. Yesterday we tried these delightful little cookies with colorful sugar sprinkles on them. We've also tried fruitcake this year."

"And what did you think?" Maggie smiled as she got them each a slice of mince pie from the new front cooler where the daily pies were kept.

"They were excellent," Ahalya told her. "We enjoyed them very much."

"Except for the fruitcake," Raji qualified. "Really, I wasn't fond of that."

"There are plenty of holiday foods to try." Maggie put two slices of pumpkin pie on plates. "Are you sure you want to eat all of this now?"

"Oh yes," Ahalya assured her. "The sooner, the better."

"It will be a while for the eggnog pie to cool." Maggie totaled up their purchase. "Mind if I ask why this sudden dive into holiday food?"

"Not at all. A customer came into the Bombay Grill yesterday and complained that we had no holiday food. No one has ever said that to us before. Ahalya was deeply offended. Now we must stuff ourselves with holiday food so we can decide what type we should serve with our meals."

Maggie had never cared for Indian food—until she started eating at Raji's restaurant. Now she loved it—the exotic spices and aromatic curries were like nothing she'd ever eaten before. She enjoyed the fabulous decor and ambiance there too. She couldn't imagine serving festive American cuisine there.

"Isn't there something Indian you could make that could be a special holiday food without veering too far from your culture's traditional cuisine?" Maggie asked while she waited on the man and woman who'd been in line behind Raji and Ahalya.

"We can't seem to find an equivalent holiday food to the things you eat here at this time of year."

Maggie didn't know a lot about Indian food except for the dishes she enjoyed. "Your food is so good, it doesn't need an equivalent."

Raji's dark eyes lit up. "Perhaps we can ask some friends who might have an answer. Would you be willing to try some holiday foods if we find some?"

"Sure. That would be great. I think Aunt Clara and Ryan would like that too."

"Thank you for your advice, Maggie. I'm going to eat pie now."

She laughed to herself as she saw her friends dig into their multiple slices of pie. She knew they didn't celebrate Christmas, but it would be interesting to see what they came up with.

"Good morning, Maggie." Professor Ira Simpson found a chair at one of the small tables. "I'll wait for the rush to be over. I dislike waiting in line."

Professor Simpson had been teaching at Duke University for as long as anyone could remember. He'd taught Maggie's mother, Delia, Aunt Clara, and Maggie. He was a kindly man, with white wings of hair at his temples and a constant twinkle in his brilliant blue eyes.

He seemed much younger than Maggie knew he was. It was possible that was why it wasn't unusual to see him with a pretty student or young teacher on his arm when he came in.

"I'll be right with you, Professor," Maggie promised.

"No rush." He pulled out his copy of the *Durham Weekly*.

Maggie had forgotten that this was Wednesday, the day Ryan's newspaper came out. It was a lot of work for him to do everything involved with it, but the paper didn't make enough money for him to afford hiring someone full-time. Ryan made do with a few part-time people who helped with photography, or the occasional article. He also had a few students who helped deliver the papers.

The newspaper was popular. Maggie hoped it could avoid the financial problems other newspapers seemed to be having.

Five other customers came in looking for pie and coffee. Maggie filled their orders and sent them back out into the cold gray morning. She took Professor Simpson's order and got him set up before she went into the kitchen to see how Aunt Clara was doing.

She didn't see her at first. Her aunt was crouched by the back door, which was swung wide open to the alley outside.

"Are you okay?" Maggie cautiously made her way to the rear of the kitchen. She'd had a few unpleasant experiences in the alley but was hoping to put them behind her.

Aunt Clara looked up with a big smile on her face. "She's starving. You can see her ribs."

Maggie peered around her aunt. There was a scrawny, ragged-looking cat with one ear almost chewed off. It was eating a slice of Marvelous Mince pie.

"Watch out!" Maggie warned her aunt. "It could have rabies or something. You shouldn't have let it into the kitchen. Now we'll never get rid of it."

"She won't come any closer. I've been feeding her for the last week."

"You've been feeding it pie?"

"We had it left over. I thought it was better than nothing. On the other hand, if you feel like I should pick up some cat food—"

"No. If you start feeding it cat food, that will be even worse."

"Whatever you say." Aunt Clara shrugged. "I'll keep feeding her pie. She'll probably gain weight faster than if she was eating cat food."

Maggie could see customers waiting in line at the front of the pie shop. "Let it finish eating and nudge it out the door. Whatever you do, don't try to touch it. They call these feral cats. They don't like humans."

"She seems friendly enough to me."

"Please, Aunt Clara, don't touch the cat."

Maggie left her aunt in the doorway and went back up front. The pie shop was completely full of people—some sitting down waiting for food and some waiting in line for to-go items.

"What can I help you with?" Maggie asked the first customer.

After a few minutes of filling cups and glasses and slicing pie, the line began to go away. Maggie tackled the customers at tables, getting their drink orders first and then coming back with the drinks to take their food orders.

"Pie and a big cup of hot coffee sounded so good this morning." Real estate agent Angela Hightower was in early. She was usually an afternoon customer who also came in once a week with her book club. "How is Clara?"

"She's well." Maggie took out her pen and paper. "What kind of pie?"

"I'll have a slice of the eggnog, and give me a whole mince to go, please." Angela's shoulder-length dark-blond hair was half hidden under a midnight-blue beret that matched her wool dress under her chic raincoat. "I happened to notice that her name came up in the dating service a friend of mine uses. Think it's a typo?"

Maggie felt Angela's sharp eyes watching for any sign that would give her away. She wrote down Angela's order and put her pen back in the pocket of her jeans.

"I don't know. I don't use dating services. Are you looking for someone?"

Angela blushed. Everyone knew she was on her fourth marriage to a man half her age. "Like I said, a *friend* of mine uses the service."

Maggie shrugged, wondering how bad an idea it had been to register her aunt with Durham Singles. She turned to go and get Angela's pie when the front door swung open and Donald Wickerson stumbled into the pie shop.

He held out a bloody hand to Maggie, as if reaching for support to steady himself. There was blood on his brown leather coat too. "Clara! Clara!" he gasped.

Maggie had barely started shouting for help when he collapsed on the dark-blue tile.

Four

Maggie dropped to her knees beside Donald, panic setting in. His eyes were closed and his breathing was labored. His face was very white.

Maggie urgently scanned the group of inquisitive faces around her, each wanting to know what was going on. "Someone call 911! I don't know what's wrong with him, but he needs help!"

Professor Simpson called for help on his cell. Then he continued to eat pie and sip his coffee without the slightest sign of awareness that anything unusual had happened.

Someone wadded up a sweater and pushed it under Donald's head.

"I think he's been shot." A young college student gave his assessment. "I had a year of premed before I switched to business management. You want me to take a look at him?"

"No." Maggie could already hear sirens coming their way. "Help is on the way. They'll know what to do." She went to look for her aunt. The kitchen was empty, and the back door was open. "Aunt Clara?" She could see her aunt's tiny footprints in the snow, but there was still no sign of her. Maggie thought she was probably outside in the alley with the cat.

"Maggie?" Angela came to the back door. "There's a man dying in here. What on earth are you doing?"

"Looking for Aunt Clara. She's been out here feeding some stray cat."

She went back inside with Angela. She was right, Maggie decided. One of the shop owners should be there when the police came.

She wished Aunt Clara would come back. This might be the only time she'd have to say good-bye to Donald.

"Isn't that *Clara's* boyfriend?" Angela murmured as they were walking through the door from the kitchen to the dining area.

Maggie didn't answer. Angela was a gossip. She didn't want to start any rumors. If Donald had been shot, it would be hard enough on Aunt Clara.

She took a deep breath, knelt on the floor, and looked at Donald again. If it was possible, he was even paler than before. She couldn't tell if he was still breathing. When would help get there?

Aunt Clara finally came out of the kitchen to see what was going on. She pushed through the crowd surrounding Donald and gasped. "Maggie, what happened?"

Maggie got to her feet and put her arm around her aunt. "I don't know yet. He came in asking for you and collapsed. I think he was injured somehow."

"Maybe not *asking* for her exactly," Professor Simpson observed. "It was more like gasping her name—perhaps in surprise and bewilderment. There were some strong emotions in him."

"Is that blood on his coat?" Aunt Clara's face blanched.

"I think so." Maggie lowered her voice. "This is what I was trying to warn you about. The man is, or *was*, mixed up in some very bad things. Where were you a few minutes ago?"

"I was just outside in the alley, looking for the cat," Aunt Clara sputtered as she carefully knelt down on the floor beside Donald and held his hand. "You told me that he killed older women for their money." She shot a sharp look at Maggie. "It looks to me as though someone might have tried to kill *him*." Tears began to well in her eyes. "I'd say you and Ryan were off the mark."

Before Maggie could respond, paramedics pushed through the front door, followed by a police officer.

"Where's the victim?" the lead paramedic asked.

"Move aside please." The officer made room for the medical personnel. "Where's the owner? Did anyone see what happened?"

"I'm Maggie Grady, one of the owners. I saw Mr. Wickerson come in." She described, in detail, what had happened as the lead paramedic examined Donald.

"We'll probably need you to write that down, ma'am." The officer was polite but distant. "Was he a friend of yours?"

Maggie wished the officer would evict all of their customers from the pie shop, even if that meant losing some business. She didn't want to discuss her aunt's boyfriend in front of everyone they knew.

"He and I have been dating for a few weeks." Aunt Clara wasn't shy at all about it. Large tears rolled down her cheeks, and her lips quivered. "He's such a wonderful man. I can't imagine who would want to hurt him."

"Unless it was someone who knew one of those six women *he* allegedly killed." Professor Simpson's loud lecture voice overpowered the rest of the sound in the pie shop.

The police officer craned his neck, trying to see who'd spoken. "All right. Everyone, I need names, phone numbers you can be reached at, and addresses. Give your statement to my partner here, and then exit the shop."

"That's just what it says right here in the *Weekly*." Professor Simpson held up his copy of the newspaper. Donald's face was on the front page.

Ryan had done exactly what Detective Frank Waters had told him not to. He'd used Donald's real name and a picture of him with a story about the suspicious deaths of his six wives.

"Okay." The officer took off his hat and ran his hand through his thinning brown hair. "I'm calling for a homicide detective, and the ME should be on his way. Everyone take a seat, and we'll talk to you one at a time."

"I didn't see anything," one of the pie shop's regular customers complained as he nervously eyed Donald lying on the floor. "I can't see any reason for me to be late for work because this man died."

"He's not dead," Angela declared. "They're still working on him, for goodness' sake."

"Once I get your name, address, and phone number, sir, you can go." The officer sounded irritable. "I'll need to do a short test for GSR too."

Professor Simpson stayed. So did Angela. The student who'd once been premed stayed too, along with a jogger who came in every morning. They all claimed to have seen Donald stumble into the shop.

"I'm sorry, ma'am," the lead paramedic said to

Aunt Clara, who still held Donald's hand in hers. "I know this is hard for you, but this man is dead. You'll have to move aside so the medical examiner can get in and examine the body."

"The *body*?" Aunt Clara's green eyes were angry and filled with tears. Her voice trembled. "Where is your respect, young man?"

The lead paramedic hung his head. "You're right. I apologize, ma'am. Could I help you to a chair before the medical examiner gets here to examine your friend?"

Aunt Clara nodded and sniffled. She laid Donald's hand on his chest, and the young man helped her to her feet. "I can't believe he's dead." She rested her hand on his arm as she walked to the nearest chair and sat down.

Maggie joined her there after she thanked the paramedic for his help. "Oh, Aunt Clara . . . I'm so sorry . . . Are you okay? Can I get you something?"

"I'm as good as I can be with my boyfriend lying dead on the floor in front of me." Her aunt dabbed at her eyes with one of her old handkerchiefs. She never brought any of her good hankies to the shop. "How is this possible? What happened? Why is there blood on him, Maggie?"

"I'm not sure. Someone will tell us when they know what happened to him."

Aunt Clara inclined her head closer to her niece's. "He came here looking for me. I failed him.

He was so good to me. I couldn't help him." Maggie saw Ryan standing outside the pie shop, camera in hand. He must have heard about what had happened. Apparently the police weren't letting him in until the ME arrived and did his job.

"I don't know. I–I think he wanted to be with you. Maybe he knew he was dying. We'll know when the police clear this up."

Aunt Clara couldn't get over seeing Donald that way. She used her hankie to cover her eyes. "It's like some terrible nightmare."

Ryan waved to Maggie and held up his cell phone. Her phone started ringing.

"I guess we'll find out if Ryan knows anything."

"What's going on in there, Maggie?" Ryan asked when she answered.

So much for Ryan knowing anything about it. "Donald Wickerson is dead."

"That's crazy! What happened? *When* did it happen?"

"I don't think he had a chance to read your article about him, if that's what you're worried about." Maggie filled him in on the details and watched through the window as his eyes widened with surprise as the information sank in.

"It was probably someone from his past. Probably a relative of one of the women he killed."

"Maybe." Maggie looked up to see Frank Waters enter the pie shop. "I have to go. Talk to you later."

Frank Waters was a tall, thin man—a little hard-faced but a good cop.

At least Maggie thought so. She saw his gaze drift around the pie shop until it found hers. He beckoned to her and walked into the kitchen.

"Frank wants to talk to us." Maggie took her aunt's hand. "Are you up for it? If not, I'll tell him he has to talk to you later."

Aunt Clara squared her slender shoulders and pushed herself to the fullest height of her slight stature. "I'm as ready as I can be. Poor Donald. We have to help Frank find his killer. That's all we can do for him now."

The police officers let them join Frank in the kitchen, where he was perched on the stool Ryan often occupied.

"You two know it's Christmastime, right? I haven't done a lick of shopping for my wife or my kids. I should be out doing that right now. It's my day off."

"Of course we know it's Christmas," Maggie said. "It's not like we *want* you to be here investigating this, whatever it is. Donald came in here, covered in blood, and fell over. It had nothing to do with us."

"It most certainly *is* our fault, Maggie. Donald came here looking for help. We let him down. Well, *I* let him down. I should have been here, not outside. I just wanted to help that poor cat."

Maggie sighed heavily. Frank looked at them both like they were crazy.

"So you weren't here when Mr. Wickerson came in?" Frank asked Clara.

"No." Clara's gaze lingered in the distance. "I was trying to find where that darn cat hides. I think she may not be alone."

"I know Mr. Wickerson was dating you, Clara—courtesy of Maggie's boyfriend." Frank's voice was kind but inquisitive. "How long has that relationship been going on?"

Aunt Clara tapped her chin with a flour-covered finger. "Let me see. It was earlier in the fall, after Maggie met Ryan and I went out with Ryan's father. Garrett was too vocal for me. I can only take politics in small doses."

Frank rolled his eyes. "You know I can only afford one new car on my salary. My wife drives it. I have a Toyota that had seen better days a hundred thousand miles ago. I would *really* like to make captain. If I can figure out what happened to Mr. Wickerson, that would be good. Sometime in the next six months or so would be even better."

"Aunt Clara has only been dating Donald a couple of months," Maggie clarified. "They met at the library. Donald said he loved mince pie. They spent some time together. That's all we know."

Frank rocked a little back and forth on the stool. His brown hair needed a cut, and his usual cheap suit had something that looked like ketchup on one lapel.

"In other words, neither of you knows anything about why or how Mr. Wickerson ended up dead."

"Yes. That's right." Aunt Clara held her head up as she started crying again. "He was a very nice man. I can't imagine why anyone would want to hurt him. I never believed those stories about him."

"But you know about the six wives?"

"Yes," Clara admitted. "Maggie told me about them just last night because Ryan was concerned."

"Why was he concerned?" Frank seemed determined to drag it all out into the open.

"They were afraid Donald might try to kill me." Clara started crying again. "It would be ironic if it wasn't so sad."

"Well, we don't know anything for sure yet." Frank shrugged as he got up from the stool. "Time will tell. Thanks for telling me what you know. I'll give you a call if we need anything else from you. Does either of you know if Mr. Wickerson had any family?"

"You should probably ask Ryan," Maggie suggested. "He knows all about him."

Aunt Clara impulsively hugged him. "Thank you so much, Detective Waters. You've been a good friend to us. Would you like some pumpkin pie? I have one that's cool."

"That's okay, Clara." He smiled and changed his mind. "Maybe I could take it to go?"

Maggie found a box and gave him the whole pie.

It couldn't hurt. Aunt Clara had a theory that pie made everything better. Maybe she was right.

A police officer came to the kitchen door. "Detective Waters? The assistant medical examiner wants to talk to you."

"Excuse me, ladies. Thanks for the pie."

Maggie and Aunt Clara followed him. All the customers were gone, but the police and EMS people still filled the shop. There was a young man sitting on the floor beside Donald's body, which was now covered by a green sheet.

"What's the news?" Frank asked him.

"It looks like a nine millimeter, close up. I found powder burns on his coat. Whoever shot him was looking right in his face as he did it. This wasn't an accident. I'm afraid this is murder."

Five

Frank told Maggie and Aunt Clara that the crime scene team would have to make a thorough sweep of the pie shop. “Nothing extensive. We know he wasn’t killed here. You should be able to reopen tomorrow.”

Aunt Clara stamped her foot. “Outrageous. Why aren’t you out on the street looking for whoever killed Donald?”

“We’re doing what needs to be done,” Frank explained. “There could be some trace evidence from his clothes or shoes. There could be something he dropped when he fell. The medical examiner will go over everything carefully. That's how we solve crimes. I'm sorry for your loss, Clara, and your inconvenience."

Ryan came in as the medical examiner's team was leaving. He was in such a hurry to get to Maggie that he didn't notice Frank until the detective grabbed him by his dark wool jacket.

"Didn't I have a conversation with you about Donald Wickerson?" Frank was in Ryan's surprised face. "Didn't I tell you to let the system work? But you couldn't let your theories go."

Ryan was defensive. "I told the story the way I thought it should be told. You can't tell me what to print. This couldn't go on. I was protecting Clara, and everyone else, by alerting the public—something *you* weren't willing to do."

"I know you didn't pull the trigger," Frank argued, "but your story could've been the catalyst for Wickerson's murder. Did you think of that? What time did the paper begin spreading the word this morning? If someone from his past knew he was here in Durham, it might've been enough to set them off."

Ryan didn't look remorseful. "The first papers are on the street at four a.m. I did what I thought was best. I realize a man is dead, but he was a killer himself. Sometimes those things end badly."

Frank let go of his jacket. "I can't do anything to you, but stay out of my way on this."

"Sure." Ryan watched him leave, his bright blue eyes wary. He turned to Maggie as soon as they were alone and hugged her. "Are you two okay? I'm so sorry, Aunt Clara. I really only did this to protect you. Maggie didn't have the heart to tell you the truth about Donald. I knew I had to do something."

"I know you meant well," Aunt Clara said. "I think you and Maggie were way off track about him."

"I'm afraid I'm going to have to ask you all to leave," one of the crime scene techs said. "We'll give you a call when you can come back."

Ryan glanced at his watch. "Let's go down to the sub shop by the office. They're having two-for-one today. We can talk there."

Ryan drove them to Betty's Subs in his late-model Honda. Maggie had been thinking about buying a car with her severance, but she couldn't convince Aunt Clara to stop walking to the pie shop. It seemed pointless to have a car and not use it. They were still in negotiations.

Betty English called out a cheery hello as they entered her sandwich shop. It was cleverly decorated to look like the inside of a submarine to go with the name of her place, Betty's Subs. She'd had students draw and paint pictures of cartoon character Betty Boop all over the walls. It was a very popular place for Duke students and teachers.

Maggie and Aunt Clara had never eaten there

before they'd met Ryan. He ate there all the time—it was cheap and close to the newspaper office.

Now they were regulars. Betty gave them a special deal when they came. Aunt Clara reciprocated by giving Betty specials on pies when she visited them.

"Hey!" Betty, a large, energetic woman with curly dark hair, called them over. "I heard what happened at Pie in the Sky. That had to be scary. Was he trying to rob you? Did you shoot him, or was it a customer that shot him?"

Maggie clarified, reminded of the old axiom about how rumors get started. "No one in the pie shop shot him. It happened somewhere else. He wasn't there to rob us. He was Aunt Clara's boyfriend. We're not sure why he came there."

Betty hugged Aunt Clara in her strong arms. "Gee, I'm so sorry. Was that the big Marlboro-looking man who came in here with you? He was chunky hot for an old dude."

"Thank you." Aunt Clara got through the bear hug. "It was terrible."

"Sandwiches for all three of you, on the house," Betty declared. "What can I get for you?"

Maggie didn't want to take advantage of Betty's generosity, but her aunt said it would be rude not to accept her offer. Each of them ordered the cheapest sandwich on the menu, with a drink.

Aunt Clara sat down at one of the small tables to wait while Betty's son, Bobby, made the sandwiches.

"I'm sorry you had to go through that." Ryan rubbed Maggie's shoulder and then put his arm around her. "And I feel terrible for Aunt Clara too."

"Thanks. It was really horrible. I hate to say it that way." Maggie glanced at her aunt. "I really think he thought we could help him. Maybe if he'd stumbled in a few minutes sooner. I don't know."

"Since he was shot at such close range, he probably didn't have much of a chance."

"How do you know that?"

"I have my sources."

"You were standing outside the shop the whole time. What sources?"

Ryan filled his glass with sweet tea and plenty of ice. "I gave one of the ME techs ten bucks and promised not to use his name."

She laughed and filled her glass, and Aunt Clara's too. "I get it. I'm thinking of sources like people in trench coats meeting in alleys. Your sources are everywhere, even in broad daylight."

"That's right. A good newspaper reporter has sources everywhere." Ryan's bright eyes were troubled. "I also spoke with Professor Simpson on his way out of the shop. He said he didn't think Wickerson was calling for your aunt when he went in and said her name."

"I know—he said something weird like that inside too. I don't know what he's talking about. It must be his years of stage drama."

"What about Angela Hightower?" His gaze was intense on her face. "She said your aunt was missing when Wickerson came in."

"What does that mean?" Maggie was beginning to get angry about Ryan's questions, even though she knew he was only repeating what he'd heard people tell the police. "Aunt Clara was outside in the alley. So what?"

"So nothing—I hope."

"You have a suspicious mind, Ryan."

"*Psst!*" Betty waved them closer. "I didn't want to say anything in front of Clara, but I saw the old Marlboro dude here yesterday with another, younger chick. They were having lunch and he *paid*."

"Did you know her?" Ryan asked.

"She comes in once in a while. She probably lives or works around here. They were kind of chummy. He was feeding her ham, and they shared a drink."

"He was cheating on Aunt Clara?" Maggie couldn't believe it. "Really? How many women could a man his age handle?"

"Don't think of his age," Ryan advised. "Some people have better stamina."

Betty agreed. "My first husband—he had some stamina. He was married to me, and we had Bobby and Betsy in the first two years. Come to find out, he was out there with two other women. One of them was pregnant. Can you believe it?"

"That's some stamina," Maggie agreed.

"Anyway," Betty confided, "I know Clara is upset, but this was probably for the best. She didn't need to be with some two-timing dude who was taking advantage of her."

Maggie took the drinks to the table and went back for her sandwich. She thought about what Betty had said.

That seemed to completely contradict what Ryan had said of Donald—that he set his sights on one woman at a time, building up her trust. She wondered if Donald was courting a better prospect than Aunt Clara because he realized she wasn't as vulnerable as he'd thought. Maybe he'd already given up on her.

"I'm going to powder my nose." Aunt Clara had stopped eating after a few bites of her chicken sandwich. "I'm afraid I'm not hungry right now. I hope Betty won't take offense."

"We'll get it to go." Maggie tried to be upbeat. "Maybe it will seems better for dinner."

As soon as Aunt Clara was gone, Maggie tackled the subject of Donald's philandering, her tone muted.

"You think Donald was worried that he couldn't get anything from her?"

Ryan shrugged. "It's possible. Maybe he was trolling for his usual lonely widow. You wanted to convince him that Clara wasn't alone. Maybe he took the hint."

"That might mean that Donald's killer doesn't

have to be someone from his past," she theorized. "It could be someone trying to protect their mother, grandmother, et cetera, right here in Durham."

"We could look into it." He took another bite of his cheese-and-jalapeño sandwich, chewed, and swallowed it. "If that's the case, it *could* be a reader of the *Weekly*. I've been running those articles about him, without using his name, for a while. Maybe this morning was the last straw. What I wrote may have had an unexpected impact."

He seemed almost buoyant about it.

"Don't be so happy about it." She stared at him. "Maybe Donald's death is *your* fault, like Frank said."

"My fault? I was trying to save someone from getting killed. That's my *responsibility*, not my fault."

She sucked the last of her drink from her straw. "Whichever it was, you were plain enough in the paper today that your readers knew what Donald looked like. He, or she, could've been stalking him."

"Yes." Ryan wiped his mouth with a napkin. "I suppose that's true. The papers had been out on the street for hours at that point."

Maggie nodded at him when she saw Aunt Clara approaching. "I'm not saying anything about this to her."

"She's gonna see it sometime."

"I'll deal with it then."

Maggie and Ryan were done eating. Maggie asked for a to-go box for Aunt Clara's sandwich, and told Betty how much they had enjoyed their lunch.

"You're very welcome." Betty wiped her hands on a clean towel. "Would you like me to give you a call if that other woman shows up again?"

"That would be great!" Ryan immediately took her up on her offer.

"She might not come back again without Donald. But if I see her, I'll call you."

Ryan scribbled down his cell phone number on a napkin. "Thanks."

"Will do." Betty put the note in her pocket.

Aunt Clara walked out of the sub shop with Maggie. "I hope they're finished with the pie shop. Making some crust right now would do me a world of good."

"They said they'd call. I haven't heard anything. Maybe Ryan could drop us off at the house. We could always make crust there and freeze it for tomorrow."

"Freeze it? Bite your tongue, Maggie Grady! Frozen crust never tastes the same. I thought I taught you better than that."

"Sorry. I was only thinking you'd have something to do."

"I have to get back to the office," Ryan interrupted. "Do you want me to take you home?"

"Yes, please." Aunt Clara glared at Maggie. "It looks like someone needs further instruction on the fine art of pie making."

Ryan smiled at Maggie. "You got it. I'm sure Maggie would be a much better pie maker if she made a few pies for dinner tonight. I'll bring Chinese."

Maggie gave Ryan a dirty look, but her aunt was pleased with the idea.

They stepped out of the sub shop and abruptly stopped in their tracks.

Right in front of them was a large man, tall and heavyset. He wore an expensive black suit with a black fedora. He held his gold-headed cane with one gloved hand and a bouquet of white and red tulips in the other.

"Clara! So good to see you. I heard you're looking for a special man in your life. I think it may be me."

Six

Maggie couldn't believe it. Albert Mann was on the Durham Singles website? She'd never even thought of him being married, or otherwise.

The man was a nuisance, as far as she was concerned. He'd been in and out of their business since she'd come home.

Mann Development, Albert's company, had been badgering Aunt Clara to sell the land the pie shop was on since before Maggie had come home. He'd been devious and underhanded about it, but had offered her a large amount of money. He wanted to build a medical office building on the spot.

Aunt Clara wasn't interested in selling for any amount of money. She wanted to run the pie shop.

"Albert, I know you mean well." Aunt Clara neatly stepped around him. "Now is not a good time. I just lost Donald. I'm not looking for a new beau yet."

He looked puzzled. "I had no idea you were already dating someone. It was a little flirtatious of you to already have one boyfriend and look for another. Are you a bad girl, Clara, my dear?"

"I don't know what you're talking about. I'm going home." Aunt Clara glared at Ryan. "You said you were taking us, didn't you?"

Ryan had also been paralyzed by the sight of the real estate developer standing there with flowers. "Oh. Sure. Sorry." He rushed to open the passenger-side door on his Honda.

"Thank you." Aunt Clara held herself very primly as she seated herself in the car, eyes straight forward. Ryan closed the door.

"Well, Maggie. This must be some of *your* shenanigans." Albert Mann rocked back on his heels and glared at her. "Clearly she wasn't expecting the offer of a date."

"You're not supposed to show up," she hissed. "You're supposed to respond with an email. Have you ever done this before?"

He ignored the question. "Who is Clara talking about anyway? Who is this Donald character?"

"Donald Wickerson. Aunt Clara was very close to him. He died suddenly today." Maggie hurried to the back door of the car as Ryan got in the driver's seat and started the engine. "She's distraught."

"You're not talking about that man in the *Weekly*, are you? The man who takes advantage of widows?" Albert shook his flowers at her. "And you have the nerve to set *me* up as a villain. I thought you'd take better care of your aunt."

Maggie closed her car door without a reply. She still couldn't wrap her mind around all that had happened.

Of all the men in Durham her aunt's profile could have attracted, why had it attracted Albert Mann?

He probably thought he could find a way to take advantage of her aunt. What was wrong with everyone? She'd thought it might be different with the older Silver Foxes dating group.

It was hard to imagine him looking for his "true" love. On the other hand, she knew he had to be a member of the dating service to have seen Aunt Clara's profile.

This wasn't what Maggie had had in mind at all.

"What was going on back there?" Ryan spared a glance at her in the rearview mirror.

"I don't know," she lied. "You know him. He'll try anything."

"I can't believe even *he* would be so callous," Aunt Clara said. "Donald isn't even in his grave, and there's Albert trying to court me. What times we live in."

Maggie kept her opinion to herself. She planned to rush home and look at the Durham Singles site again. She wouldn't have done this to Aunt Clara if she'd known the types of men she'd attract to her poor aunt—not to mention what would happen to Donald. She might have to remove her profile.

When they reached the house, Ryan helped Aunt Clara from the car. He went inside with them.

"I'm going up to my room for a while, Maggie." Aunt Clara was still sniffling a little.

Ryan waited until her aunt was gone before he turned to Maggie at the bottom of the stairs. "Okay. Spill it. I can see the guilt all over your face."

There was no sign of Aunt Clara. Still, Maggie took him into the parlor and whispered, "I didn't mean for this to happen. I thought about the idea of signing her up with a dating service. I thought someone else could take her mind off of Donald. I didn't know Donald was going to die, or that Albert Mann would want to date her."

Ryan laughed a little and put his arms around her. "I can't believe you did that! I mean, it's kind of funny. That was your way of getting rid of Donald? Haven't you heard all the horror stories about online dating?"

Maggie hugged him. “It’s not funny. And talk about horror stories—you’ve been telling me for the last month about Donald killing the women he hooked up with. How does it get worse than that? Even Albert only wants her property.”

“Sorry.” Ryan kissed her cheek. “At least your heart was in the right place.”

“Why don’t I feel better about it then?”

“Cheer up. Nothing happened. I don’t think your aunt will go from Donald to Albert anytime soon.”

“Thanks.” She kissed him. “That helps.”

“I’ll say.” He kissed her again. “I understand what you’re saying. You don’t want Clara to be alone. I think it’s nice that you thought of it.”

“Thanks. Even though I ruined it.”

“Not ‘ruined’ necessarily. Maybe something good will come of it.” He glanced at his watch. “I have to run. There are a lot of people to question about Donald’s death.”

“It won’t do you any good until next week. The paper just came out.”

“You know me.” He kissed her quickly on the lips. “I need information as quickly as possible to get the jump on the daily guys. I’ll see you later.”

Maggie sighed when he left. He was lucky she liked him so much. Sometimes it seemed like everything was another story to him.

She went upstairs to talk to Aunt Clara. Her aunt was asleep, one slender hand tucked under her chin. She looked so tiny lying there on the large bed she and Uncle Fred had shared for so many years.

Aunt Clara was fragile and yet had an iron will that had kept her going through so many years of being alone. She'd lost almost everyone in her family, including her sister, Delia, Maggie's mother. Maggie was her only living relative.

Maggie didn't wake her. She crept back downstairs to look for their copy of the *Durham Weekly*. Usually her aunt got it from the doorstep and read it before they left for the pie shop on Wednesday. Not surprising, she found the newspaper on the table in the parlor, where Aunt Clara must have read it before waking her that morning at four thirty.

What had she thought of the strong case Ryan had made against Donald? Had she still been convinced that he was innocent?

If Ryan's words had changed her mind at all, Maggie hadn't been able to tell it on their walk to Pie in the Sky. Aunt Clara didn't change her mind very easily, though. Maggie was grateful for that. Her aunt had always believed in her, and no newspaper articles had changed that.

She sat on the velvet sofa in the living room and kicked off her shoes before she opened the newspaper and read what Ryan had said about Donald Wickerson.

He'd only been alluding to a man who'd recently moved to Durham in his previous columns. He hadn't mentioned his name, although he *had* mentioned the names of the women the police suspected Donald of killing.

Ryan had abandoned all pretense of shielding the man he'd been talking about in this week's paper. There was almost a frantic quality to his words—he sounded desperate to convince anyone who would listen that Donald was a killer. Not only did he give Donald's name, he had several pictures of him that looked like photos Ryan had taken recently as he followed him around Durham.

Aunt Clara wasn't mentioned, and she wasn't in any of the pictures, thank goodness. Maggie wondered if Donald had any family left and, if so, what they thought of Ryan's article.

There was no doubt that Donald's death had thrown a monkey wrench into Ryan's case against him. Instead, Donald was the victim.

There were also the usual articles about new laws passed by the city council and stories about parking problems downtown. Ryan faithfully covered many events that happened in the community. Sometimes she wondered how he had time for her at all, but she'd never had cause to complain since they'd met.

Maggie got up and wandered into the kitchen. She wasn't sure about Aunt Clara's ideas on pie making being a stress reliever, but with everything going on, she was willing to give it a try.

Besides, her aunt had mentioned again this

morning that Maggie's piecrust was a little dry. She'd advocated some slower practice time since their mornings at the shop were so hectic.

Maggie took out flour and the big mixing bowl that Aunt Clara always used. She put those and the other items she'd need to work on her piecrust in the refrigerator. That was Aunt Clara's number-one rule for flaky crust: everything had to be cold.

That meant she'd need to wait for a while so things could chill. She knew what she needed to do while they were chilling. Aunt Clara didn't need any more unwelcome suitors right now. Maybe she'd try again later when things calmed down.

Maggie sat down at the antique desk her aunt hadn't let her touch when she was a child. Now her laptop and all of their financial records were kept there.

Things had changed since she'd grown up with her aunt and uncle acting as her parents, and yet many more things had stayed the same.

She'd wanted to completely spruce up the house when she received her severance. Aunt Clara wouldn't hear of it.

She let her do some small things—repairs and replacements of minor items. Maggie knew many items in the house were sacred to her aunt. They had belonged to the family for many generations.

Her aunt had grown up in this house too, with Maggie's mother. Delia had moved out when she'd married Maggie's father, John. She'd left Clara and Fred to take care of the family heirlooms. That was exactly what Aunt Clara had done, and meant to continue doing.

Maggie had sprung for new towels and sheets. She'd done some work in her old bedroom, painting the walls and moving some of her childhood treasures into the attic. The bathrooms had needed some plumbing work and some repairs on the ceramic tile.

She went to the Durham Singles site and put in the password she'd created for her aunt. And there was Albert Mann. Her eyes widened. Maggie thought *she'd* told a few white lies about Aunt Clara, but Albert's whole profile was a lie—except the part about him being a wealthy man. Fifty? *Hardly.* Handsome? Maggie shuddered. Understanding and sympathetic? Not that she'd noticed.

There was no point in continuing to dissect Albert Mann's profile on the site. He had a nice picture of himself. She wouldn't have recognized him. According to the date he'd joined, Albert had been there for almost a year. So much for thinking that he wasn't looking for his true love!

Maggie was about to remove her aunt's profile when she suddenly noticed another familiar face on the site. Donald Wickerson was looking for a partner too.

Or at least he had been.

She took a screenshot of the listing and emailed

it to Ryan. If Donald had been actively seeking out other women, maybe Ryan was right about him dropping his potentially deadly intentions with Aunt Clara.

He'd joined a little over a month before. He hadn't needed Durham Singles to cozy up to her aunt; seeing her at the library a few times was enough.

She looked at Donald's profile. He had a very good picture of himself. He was chopping wood, his plaid flannel shirtsleeves rolled up. "Man of action," part of his bio read.

He listed no family. Of course, with his background, it was probably smart not to. He listed his home as Atlanta. His interests included reading, riding horses, and swimming. Obviously a chick magnet.

Maggie heard a scratching sound at the back door. It wasn't like knocking. Besides, someone would have to get into the fenced backyard to knock on the door. Everyone came to the front.

Grabbing a poker from the fireplace, she advanced toward the kitchen, not turning on a light to let anyone know she was awake. If someone was trying to break in, he or she would get a big surprise.

She tiptoed to the door and waited. The scratching sound started again, louder this time. She raised the poker, ready to attack as her heart began to pound loudly in her chest. No one was coming through that door without getting his or her head banged.

Seven

The scratching stopped again. Maggie waited patiently for someone to try to get inside. Nothing happened.

She stood there waiting for what felt like twenty minutes. The scratching finally stopped. Nothing else happened.

Yawning, she put down the poker. She wished the back door had a peephole like the front door. There was no way to see outside. She couldn't stand there all night waiting to find out if someone was trying to break in. Besides, who would hang around waiting to see if they could get in?

Finally, she couldn't stand it anymore. She picked up the poker again and held it before her like a sword. Carefully, she opened the back door an inch at a time. There was nothing there. She switched on the outside light. *Nothing but darkness.*

Laughing at herself and her silly fears, she started to close the back door when something small darted past her and into the kitchen.

It was that scrawny alley cat that Aunt Clara had been feeding.

"Hey! Wait a minute. Did you follow us from the pie shop?"

It couldn't have followed them that night—they hadn't walked home. That meant the cat had probably followed them home before and her aunt had also been feeding it at home.

Now there was a cat running rampant through the house. It was going to be difficult to find something that small with so many nooks and crannies for it to hide.

Arming herself with a flashlight and a pillowcase to catch the animal, she decided to start on the ground floor. She pulled out a piece of hot dog, thinking the hungry cat would go for it. She could throw the pillowcase over the cat and that would be that.

An hour later, she was on the second floor. She

had looked everywhere on the floor below with no sign of the cat. Believing strongly in the hot dog's ability to attract the animal, she poked around through every dark spot. The cat seemed to have disappeared.

The door to the attic was closed. The cat couldn't have gone in there. It was the same with the basement door. She could hear the old furnace wheezing and coughing down there, but she knew the area had to be cat-free.

Maggie hated to disturb Aunt Clara, so she'd left her bedroom for last. The cat had to be in there.

"Here, kitty-kitty," she whispered into the darkness.

Her aunt had heavy blinds up on her windows so the light couldn't come in on the mornings she wanted to sleep late. Maggie remembered when Uncle Fred had put them up.

She'd been a teenager, about fifteen or so. The neighbors next door had a bad habit of throwing late-night parties with plenty of lights and noise. The noise and lights were her aunt and uncle's reason for putting up the blinds. They'd never come down, though she guessed the parties had stopped many years before.

"Where are you, stupid cat?" Maggie searched impatiently.

A light suddenly came on—it was the lamp with the rosebud shade beside Aunt Clara's bed. The flowered shade threw pink shadows across the room.

Her aunt was sitting up, blinking like a sleepy owl. "What in the world is going on?"

"I'm sorry," Maggie apologized. "I was looking for . . . that cat! Has it been in here the whole time?"

The multicolored cat was sleeping in the middle of Aunt Clara's bed. It lifted its head and stared at Maggie as though daring her to try to kick it out now.

Aunt Clara focused on the cat. "Oh my goodness! How did she get in?"

"You've been feeding her here too, haven't you?"

"Well, we aren't at the pie shop on the weekends. It made sense to have her follow us home so I could feed her here. Did you let her inside?"

"No. I opened the door and she ran in."

"I forgot to feed her with everything that happened." Aunt Clara stroked the cat's fur. "Would you mind? I'm keeping the cat food in the little pantry by the door. Don't overfeed her. She only eats about half a cup. The rest will go to waste."

Maggie couldn't believe all of this was going on, and she'd never even noticed. Her aunt must have bought cat food when she'd gone out on her own. It certainly wasn't part of their normal shopping list.

"Why didn't you tell me you'd decided to adopt a cat?"

Aunt Clara smiled. "You seemed so against it at the pie shop."

"You've been feeding her a lot longer than that."

"True. I guess she's my secret friend. She could be your friend too. She could stay in the house and walk with us to the shop during the week. What do you think we should call her?"

Maggie rolled her eyes as she moved away from the bed with her flashlight, pillowcase, and hot dog. "You could always call her Kitty. I'm going to bed. I love you, Aunt Clara."

"I don't know. Kitty doesn't seem to suit her. It reminds me too much of that floozy on *Gunsmoke*. Who did she think she was fooling?"

"Whatever sounds right. Good night."

Maggie fed the cat after discarding the hot dog. She went to her room wondering why Aunt Clara hadn't wanted to tell her about the cat.

Maybe because she thought she'd make a fuss over it, as she had. She decided then that any cat of Aunt Clara's was a friend of hers. Yawning, she got ready for bed and switched off the lights in the bathroom and bedroom. She checked the alarm to make sure it was set for 5:00 a.m. She sat down on the bed and started to lie back.

"Yeow!" She and the cat shrieked at the same time. "What are you doing in here?"

Maggie expected the cat to jump down and run away. Instead, the brassy female jumped into her lap.

"Don't think you can win me over with a little purring."

She stroked her hand across the cat's fur. Not only was it rough and scratchy, she could feel every bone in her body.

"You're not in good shape, are you? I guess you need someone to feed you. It may as well be Aunt Clara. You can stay inside for tonight. Tomorrow, you have to go outside."

The small cat purred a little louder and bumped her head into Maggie's hand, as though she understood. Maggie urged her to get off of the bed before she went to sleep.

But when the alarm went off at five, the cat was sleeping on the pillow next to her head.

"My stars!" Aunt Clara walked into Maggie's room with a flashlight. "I've been looking all over the house for the cat. Here she is on your bed."

"I didn't invite her, believe me." Maggie sat up as Aunt Clara turned on the overhead light.

"Poor thing." Her aunt picked up the cat, cradling her in her arms. "I'll take her to my room for a while. Maybe we should call her Winky. She has a way of blinking her eyes as though she's winking."

"That's fine." Maggie yawned. "As long as I don't have to yell outside, 'Hey, Winky.' That sounds bad."

"Well, we can't keep a cat with no name. We'll have to think of something."

Maggie waited until her aunt was gone before she forced herself out of bed. She hadn't slept well. She couldn't blame it on the cat.

She'd had slow-motion nightmares about Donald stumbling into Pie in the Sky and falling down dead over and over again. In one horrible version, it was Aunt Clara who died.

Getting up, showering, and dressing made a huge difference. Maggie felt more like her normal self. The radio announcer was calling for more snow that day.

A group of schoolchildren from the elementary school a few blocks over was coming in to make snowflake pictures and drink free hot cocoa at Pie in the Sky. Ryan had promised to take pictures for the paper.

"We're running late, so I made you a slice of toast." Aunt Clara yawned and pushed a piece of peanut butter toast toward Maggie. "There's juice. I might have you make me a cup of coffee from that fancy coffeemaker today too!"

Maggie ate her toast while she put on her coat. The cat was waiting at the front door for them to leave. "Do you really think she'll go back and forth with us?"

"She has been." Aunt Clara put on her purple coat and wound a pink-and-purple scarf around her throat. "I think she likes commuting."

"Or she likes to eat pie scraps." *Why didn't I notice?*

"I like her going back and forth. Now that you

know, she can walk *with* us instead of skulking through the yards on the way."

Maggie didn't really expect it to happen, but the cat walked at their feet down the wet sidewalk all the way to Pie in the Sky. It was amazing for someone who'd never had a cat before. She didn't know a cat would do something like that.

Uncle Fred had bought her a puppy when she was very young. It was a cocker spaniel with golden hair. Maggie had really loved that dog. She'd called him Buttons.

Buttons had died when Maggie was fifteen. He was old and sick by then and had passed away in his sleep one night. Her heart had been broken, and she'd never considered having a pet again.

The cat was different. It was Aunt Clara's cat, for one thing. She wouldn't get so attached to it. She opened the pie shop door and turned on the lights. "I was hoping it wouldn't be this bad." Aunt Clara stood in the middle of the shop and shook her head. "I can't believe Donald is really dead. I thought he might be my second chance at love, you know? That's what I get for reading all those silly romances."

The chairs were spread everywhere, in no certain order. There were still dirty footprints and blood all over the blue tile floor in front.

Maggie hugged her. "I know. I'm sorry this happened. I wish I could change it for you."

Aunt Clara smiled. "I know you do, dear. I appreciate that."

"You go in back and start on the pies. I'll take care of this. What's the pie of the day?"

"I haven't even given it a thought. I suppose we'll make it Pumpkin Pizzazz, just so it will be easier." Aunt Clara sighed and took off her coat as she went into the kitchen.

Maggie followed her, mimicking her actions. They put their coats on the rack in the kitchen at the same time. She ran hot water, bleach, and soap into the rolling metal bucket.

She could tell her aunt's heart wasn't in making pies today, but maybe getting to work would be good anyway.

By 6:00 a.m., the floor was clean and the chairs were rearranged. Maggie made an espresso for herself while she watched the coffee perk in the big urn. Aunt Clara had changed her mind about the "fancy" coffee and had a cup from the urn.

The pie shop was busy as usual first thing in the morning. It was a little busier with people asking about what had happened. There were more strangers than normal. Some people even came in and wanted to take photos. A lot of them asked questions and stood around talking about Donald's death.

Maggie didn't have the time or inclination for that. It seemed to her that the less said about yesterday and Donald's death, the better. Aunt Clara said she felt the same too, but she stood at the service window between the kitchen and the dining area each time she heard the subject mentioned.

Mr. Gino and his handsome young nephew, Tony, brought the supplies they'd missed on their last visit. Mr. Gino gave Aunt Clara a hug and a new mug with his business name on it. He expressed his sympathies and said he'd see her later in the week.

"Don't worry, Clara. This will go away. Business will even be better for a while, yes?"

Mr. Gino reminded Maggie of Mario in the video game. Tony was a large, solidly built man with curly dark hair and the longest eyelashes she'd ever seen. He always wore a tank top, even in the winter.

Probably to show off those muscles, she thought, watching him move a box in the kitchen. He winked at her when he saw her staring. Maggie looked away.

Saul Weissman from the Spin and Go Laundromat next door stopped in for plain coffee and asked about Donald's death. He was a short, gray-haired man with heavy black glasses. He bought two whole pies to go and said he hoped Aunt Clara would be okay.

"It's all over the news, you know," he told Maggie. "Maybe it will be good for business. People like a little notoriety."

By the time he left, the pie shop was full. Maggie hadn't had time to go into the kitchen and help Aunt Clara make pies. They were already far behind in their orders for the day—too many nosy customers.

She was glad to see Ryan. She'd taught him to run the cash register and wait tables. She took full advantage of his willingness to help.

"I have some new information." Ryan rang up an Elegant Eggnog pie and coffee. "Thanks for the tip about the Durham Singles website last night."

"We'll have to wait to talk about it. I'm sorry. Aunt Clara is swamped in the kitchen. I have to help her."

"Sure." Ryan smiled and got the next customer in line. "I don't know how to work the coffee gadget yet. If someone wants a latte, I'll have to call you."

"Okay. Thanks."

Maggie ducked into the kitchen. Aunt Clara was moving slowly through the tasks of pie making. This would've been a good time to have some frozen crust on hand. Maggie put on a white apron and started making crust.

"Are you okay?" she asked her aunt.

"I suppose so. This is one time I could've stayed in bed all day." Aunt Clara smiled at her. "It's probably just as well I had to come here. No one likes a mopey old person."

"It's okay to mope a little," Maggie assured her. "You've suffered a loss. It's going to take some time to recover."

There was a loud knocking on the kitchen door.

Maggie went to answer, hoping it wasn't Mr. Gino again. Instead, it was a local TV newsperson who wanted to interview her and Aunt Clara.

Despite the possible publicity the interview could bring, Maggie turned her down. "I'm sorry. This isn't a good time for us. Maybe later."

"Can you answer if you think your aunt was being targeted by Donald Wickerson?" The pushy reporter shoved a microphone toward her.

"We're not talking about this today. Thanks." Maggie closed the door in her face. It seemed to be the only way to get rid of her.

"I feel like such an old fool." Aunt Clara was mixing more filling for the pumpkin pies. "Do you *really* think Donald wanted to be with me so he could steal my house?"

Maggie hugged her aunt. "We don't know that. Even if it was true for other women—that doesn't mean he didn't love you."

"Do you really believe that?" Aunt Clara's green eyes searched her niece's face.

"I really do." Maggie wasn't sure what to believe, but undermining her aunt's confidence wasn't going to help anything. Donald was dead. Everything else was speculation. And right now, what her aunt needed was love and support.

Aunt Clara kissed her cheek. "Thank you, honey. You're a very good person—not a spectacular liar, but I love you."

"I'm a really good liar," Maggie argued as she put another crust in a pan.

"It might be because I know you so well. You always do this little twitchy thing with your mouth."

"What?"

The two women stood side by side making piecrust and filling. Maggie made extra crust so her aunt could take a break if the shop stayed busy all day. Clara made tons of pumpkin filling.

"You know, your Uncle Fred didn't like pumpkin pie." Clara concentrated on what she was doing while she talked. "It's why I started making mince. We had to have some kind of pie to serve at this time of year."

"I didn't know that." Maggie put two more crusts into pans. "I remember he liked key lime in the summer. He used to sneak in here when you weren't looking and snatch some."

Aunt Clara stopped working. "Really? I never knew. Surprising how you think you know someone so well and then learn something new about them."

"I know what you mean. Take you, for instance."

"Me?" Clara stared up at her. "What have you learned new about me?"

"You're willing to give people a second chance, no matter what. And that you love snow."

"That's true. I guess you can learn something new every day."

Ryan walked into the kitchen. "We're clear out here for a few minutes, Maggie. Can you talk?"

Aunt Clara shooed them out of the kitchen. "I'll be fine. You two discuss what you need to."

Maggie and Ryan sat down at one of the small tables. Snow was falling a little heavier, hitting the plate-glass windows and making a splattering sound.

"I kind of hacked the Durham Singles site and came up with five other women who Donald was either interested in or actively dating. Any of those women could be a suspect." Ryan ate a bite of Delia's Deep-Dish Cherry pie, named for Maggie's mother.

"Five other women? Are you serious? It's a good thing he died before I killed him for leading her on that way!"

"As you pointed out, I was very clear about Donald in the newspaper. One of these women may have read the paper and had the same reaction you did. Anger and jealousy are powerful emotions. Most of the murders are caused by these emotions. The paper had been out for hours. Walking up and shooting him may not have been a premeditated plan. It could've been a spur-of-the-moment kind of thing."

"You better hope Frank doesn't see it that way. He could charge you with conspiracy or something if he thinks you were the catalyst after he asked you not to print that stuff."

"I'm not worried about Frank. I have a constitutional right to print the news. Police from three states, including this one, have investigated Donald. Frank wanted to turn a blind eye and wait to see what happened. That's not my problem."

Maggie wasn't sure about that. Frank had been angry at the shop yesterday.

"Who were the five women Donald was dating?"

Ryan took out his cell phone. "Anna Morgan. Sylvia Edwards. Angela Hightower. Lenora Rhyne. Debbie Blackwelder. Any of them ring a bell?"

Her brows elevated at the list of women. "Definitely Angela. Also, Lenora Rhyne. She's a friend of Aunt Clara's. I think they went to school together."

"I'm going to take this list of names to Frank as a peace offering." Ryan shrugged. "Maybe he'll get over our disagreement. And one of these women could be the killer."

Eight

After Ryan had left to use his list of possible suspects to placate Frank, Maggie gave all the tables and chairs a quick clean. There were a few pie spills, and customers always spilled coffee on the floor. She'd just finished mopping when Lenora and her daughter came in.

Lenora had been crying. Her brown eyes were red-rimmed with tears. She was shaking and occasionally let out a low moan.

"Take it easy, Mama." Alice Majors, Lenora's

daughter, helped her to a chair. "You said you wanted to do this. I told you it was a bad idea."

Lenora was a heavyset older woman with long gray hair that spilled down her back. Her Shalimar perfume was so strong that it almost overpowered the aroma of baking pies. "It's so hard," she sobbed. "Donald and I were so much in love."

"*Shh.* I know. I'm so sorry." Alice was a younger version of her mother. Her hair was long and dark, a swath of bangs cut across her forehead. Her brown eyes were keen on her mother's face. Alice was a large woman too, but tall enough to still make it look good.

Maggie wasn't as surprised as she might have been if Ryan hadn't just shared the information about Lenora being on Durham Singles. She knew her aunt and Lenora were competitive with each other. Aunt Clara was always coming home from their meetings with stories about the other woman's one-upmanship. She may have started dating Donald because she knew Clara was.

Maggie had listened to stories of Lenora volunteering for jobs at the library because she knew Clara wanted them, but that was only lately. She could remember as a child that the two women were constantly finding ways to annoy each other.

At the end of the day, though, they still remained friends.

Still, it seemed strange to have her come here today. Was this another attempt at beating Aunt Clara out at something—in this case grief?

"Can I help you with something?" Maggie didn't want to interrupt their moment, but she didn't want to think what would happen if Aunt Clara saw her rival in the pie shop, crying for Donald.

"I wanted to see the spot where he died." Lenora bit hard on her lip to try to stem the tears. "I wish I could've been here for him. I wish I'd been here to share his last moments."

Alice looked up at Maggie. "You're Clara's niece, right? It's nice to meet you. Your aunt talks about you all the time."

Maggie didn't know Aunt Clara had regular visits with Lenora and Alice. She knew they met occasionally at the library. Clara and Lenora's friendship just wasn't something she understood. She didn't know why they wanted to spend time together when all they did was snipe at each other. Well, it was their friendship. She didn't have to understand.

"Nice to meet you," she replied. "I didn't know your mother was dating Donald Wickerson."

Alice nodded. "Imagine her surprise when she read the *Durham Weekly* and found out that Donald might have been a serial killer. We'd barely assimilated that information when we heard about his death—and that he'd been dating Clara too."

"I can imagine that was very traumatic," Maggie empathized. "I'm so sorry. Can I get you something—coffee, water?"

"Some water would be nice." Lenora's voice was weak and trembling.

"It's very quiet out here." Aunt Clara peered through the service window between the kitchen and the dining room. Her eyes widened when she saw Lenora. "What's going on?"

Maggie had hoped to avoid this. "It seems your friend Lenora was also dating Donald. I'm sorry."

"What?" Aunt Clara scurried out of the kitchen, wiping her hands on her apron. "Lenora, were you trying to steal Donald from me?"

"Me trying to steal him from *you*?" Lenora managed a pathetic laugh. "That's rich. He was probably dating me first."

"That's what you said about Fred forty years ago." Aunt Clara put her hands on her hips as she approached her friend and rival. "I was dating Fred *and* Donald first. Must you always covet my leavings?"

"What are you talking about, Clara Lowder?" Lenora pushed herself to her feet and glowered down at her. "At least I have a daughter who is really mine, not one dropped off at my door that belonged to someone else."

"Maggie is just like a daughter to me."

"*Just like* isn't the same thing. Did you push her

out of your body after days of painful, near-death labor?"

"Is it always like this?" Maggie whispered to Alice.

"Always. They actually got kicked out of the library a few months ago." Alice shrugged. "I'll take some coffee and a big piece of Amazing Apple pie with a slice of cheddar, if you have it."

"Sure. I'll get it for you." Maggie hoped the disagreement would be over before the snowflake-making schoolchildren got there. After the commotion yesterday, two old women on the floor pulling each other's hair out was not going to be good for Pie in the Sky's reputation.

"You've always been a greedy woman, Lenora," Aunt Clara told her. "I think you should leave now."

"I will. I only came to pay my last respects to Donald. I felt like I needed to visit the place where he spent his final moments." Lenora looked at Alice. Maggie was about to put pie and coffee in front of her. "We're going now."

"I'm not going until I eat the pie, Mama." Alice put a bite of apple pie in her mouth and smiled. "Divine!"

"*Well!*" Lenora sat down hard on her chair again.

Maggie thought it might be better if they left right away too, but she knew Aunt Clara was close to Lenora, despite everything. "Maybe you'd like something now too," she suggested. "Aunt Clara has to go back into the kitchen and make more pies. The morning is only starting. We'll still see a lot of customers today."

Aunt Clara took the hint as Professor Simpson and two firefighters from the local station came in the front door. She marched into the kitchen like a pint-sized majorette, shoulders back and head held high.

"No dead bodies so far," Professor Simpson macabrely joked as he sat down with his newspaper. "I think you should try to keep the riffraff out of the place, Maggie. I'll have coffee, and a slice of that apple pie with a little cinnamon on top. Thank you."

The two firemen wanted coffee and slices of Fantastic Fig pie to eat there, with an Evie's Elegant Eggnog pie to go.

Maggie kept her eye on Lenora and her daughter as she dashed around the dining area, taking orders and delivering food. She hoped that the disagreement was over between Aunt Clara and her friend. She'd never seen the two women together before—and hoped it wouldn't happen again soon.

Alice seemed okay. They'd only just met, but Maggie liked her. At least she seemed normal.

"I guess we'll be going now." Alice approached the cash register and took out her wallet.

"Don't worry about it." Maggie waved away her money. "It's on the house. I think we've all been through enough with what's happened. How is your consignment store doing?"

"Fair." Alice put away her wallet and swiped her longish bangs from her eyes. "It will pick up. Getting started isn't easy. You were lucky to walk into something established like this."

"I know." Maggie patted the top of the cash register with her hand. "I'm glad it was still here when I came back."

"Let's do lunch sometime." Alice smiled. "It was nice meeting you."

As Alice was walking out the door, Aunt Clara called out, "Is that man-stealer gone yet?" She didn't even look through the window between the kitchen and the dining room.

"Yes. They just left." Maggie put up a new order for a slice of pumpkin pie. "You know, she's as hurt as you are by all of this. Donald played her false too."

"*Bah!*" Her aunt didn't want to hear it.

They were busy again for another ninety minutes before the crowd slacked off. Maggie cleaned up, put on a fresh pot of coffee for the after-lunch crowd, and went back in the kitchen to help Aunt Clara.

"Ryan is bringing us lunch," Maggie told her. "I hope pizza sounds good."

"That sounds fine. I'm not especially hungry. It's been a hard morning." Aunt Clara put six pies in the oven. “I’m starting to feel better. Any word from Ryan about Donald’s killer?”

Maggie told her about the women on the dating service site, trying to find a way to explain without making her aunt feel worse.

“So he was more than two-timing me?” Aunt Clara shook her head in devastation, but then her expression changed to disgust as she cleaned off the counter. “Maybe the police shouldn’t even bother looking for his killer. The world may be a better place without him.”

As soon as the words were out of her mouth, she started crying again.

“I’m sorry.” Maggie put her arms around her. It broke her heart to see her aunt hurting like this. “Maybe he was afraid you were going to reject him. Or maybe he put his profile up on the site before he knew you. As for Lenora, we only have her word that she was even dating him, right? You know how jealous she is of you.”

Maggie didn’t really believe any of that, but she kept her theories to herself. She felt bad playing on the two women’s rivalry to make her aunt feel better, but she hated seeing Clara cry.

“Thank you for being there, Maggie. I guess we all make mistakes.”

They made ten more Marvelous Mince pies. Maggie was careful not to overwork the crust. She noticed that the ingredients, as well as the bowl and mixing implements, weren't as cold while she was making the last five crusts. Maybe that was the problem. Her aunt had always insisted that keeping everything cold was a big part of fabulous crust.

She asked her aunt about it.

Clara considered the problem. "Maybe we should only do five at a time. We could re-chill everything for a few minutes. That might help."

"I'll do that next time."

"I'll try it too. You know, I'm not perfect. We've been working in such volume since you came back. We may have to try some different ways of doing things. I can learn something new too."

"I don't know." Maggie laughed. "I like you the way you are."

Clara's pretty face blushed, and tears gathered in her eyes. "Thank you, dear. I like the way you are too."

"Who's hungry?" Ryan called out from the dining room. "I've got pizza that smells so good, I thought I'd have to eat it by myself on the way over here."

Maggie poured sweet tea for herself and her aunt. Ryan laid out the pizza box and then got himself a soda.

"What did Frank think about the dating service idea?" Maggie asked as they sat down to eat.

Ryan shrugged. "I couldn't really tell. He was so busy reading me the riot act over my piece in the paper that he didn't say much of anything else."

"You *did* go against his wishes." Aunt Clara took a bite of pizza. Ryan and Maggie stared at her. "I'm old, not deaf. I can hear the two of you plotting things when I'm upstairs at the house. You might want to keep that in mind next time you're getting a little frisky in the parlor."

"Okay." Ryan laughed and took a sip of soda.

It was Maggie's turn to blush. She changed the subject to Lenora's visit that morning. "She was really upset about Donald's death. She said she read your article and then found out about Aunt Clara dating Donald. That's why she and her daughter came today."

"They say the killer always finds a way to revisit the scene of the crime," Ryan reminded her.

"Oh, Lenora is annoying, but she wouldn't hurt a fly." Aunt Clara shot down that idea. "What about the other women on the list?"

"I'm planning on visiting them tomorrow night since I can't get them on the phone." Ryan helped himself to another slice of pizza. "I was hoping you could come with me, Maggie."

"Sure. That would be great. Aunt Clara has her bingo tomorrow night."

"Don't worry about me anyway. I can always find something to do." Aunt Clara smiled at them. "Good pizza. I can't eat any more, but thanks for bringing it, Ryan."

A bus driver stopped in for pie and coffee. Aunt Clara told Maggie to finish her lunch with Ryan and she'd take care of it.

"What about the actual scene of the crime?" Maggie asked him when she was gone. "Do they know where Donald was shot yet?"

"Frank briefly told me that the shooting happened on the far end of the strip shops, next to the X-Press It place, almost in the alley. There was blood over there that matched Donald's, and a blood trail that came here on the sidewalk."

"That's about five hundred feet away from Pie in the Sky."

"Something like that. Frank doesn't have any suspects. He's still looking for the gun."

"Has he contacted the families of the murdered women Donald was married to yet?"

"I don't know. Maybe you should ask him. I think it will be a while before Frank and I have a civil conversation again."

Ryan had to leave to attend a city council meeting about proposed new bus lines. "I'll see you later," he said. "You're going to talk with Angela, right? I figure since you know her, she's more likely to give you a decent response."

Maggie nodded as he kissed her. "She's coming in for the book club this afternoon. I'll ask her about it then. I'm sure she'll have an interesting excuse.

I'm not telling Aunt Clara about Angela and Donald being together too. I don't want a repeat of what happened with Lenora this morning."

"I won't say a word." He grinned. "But my money would be on Clara in a grudge match between them."

Maggie shook her head as she took the pizza box to the kitchen. There was a large piece of crust with some sauce and cheese on it. She opened the back door and looked for the cat.

"Kitty-kitty?" She didn't see her in the alley. "I have food for you that isn't pie."

The cat came out slowly from behind the large trashcan next to the shop. She and Aunt Clara used it for recycling since the city didn't provide receptacles for it.

Maggie put the pizza on the stoop, and stepped back. The cat pounced on it and dragged it away.

"Are you feeding that creature?" Saul from the laundromat next door grumbled. "Bad habit. It won't go away."

She didn't say anything in return and closed the back door. Hadn't she said almost the same thing when she'd first seen Aunt Clara with the cat?

That was before she'd realized how thin the poor thing was. No animal should have to live that way. She'd be safe now with them. No more nights on the street.

Maggie ignored Saul's warning and asked Aunt

Clara what she thought about keeping the scrawny cat at the house.

"I think that's a wonderful idea! We can get a bed for her and take care of her. But we have to give her a name."

"What about Queen?" Maggie washed her hands.

"That's terrible." Aunt Clara tapped her chin as she thought. "What about Starlight?"

Maggie saw the school class starting to come in to make snowflakes and drink hot chocolate. They'd have to talk about a name for the cat later.

Maggie took care of their orders. She loved to watch Aunt Clara with the little kids. She made snowflakes too, and hung all the children's snowflakes on the big window in front of the shop.

She would've made a wonderful mother, Maggie thought with a smile.

She kicked herself mentally. What was she thinking? Aunt Clara *was* a wonderful mother, and Uncle Fred was a great father. Maybe it wasn't the same as Lenora and her daughter, but it was as good as any other mother-daughter relationship—better than some. *Much* better than what she'd seen between Lenora and Alice.

The book club ladies started coming in a few minutes after the schoolkids left. Maggie was finishing the cleanup of cocoa and tiny white pieces of paper.

"The book club is here," Maggie told her aunt.

She wasn't sure what she was going to say to Angela. It wasn't a crime for her to be listed on a dating service, even if she was married. It was certainly none of Maggie's business if Angela was looking for her next Mr. Right.

The book club met at Pie in the Sky every week, and liked to share their opinions on what they read with one another, as well as with Maggie, Aunt Clara, and anyone else in the pie shop at the time.

Angela was clearly the leader of the group. Maggie knew the type—always the leader of any group.

Angela owned her own real estate brokerage in town and dressed in classy, brightly colored suits with lots of chunky jewelry. She was good with makeup.

Between that and her shoulder-length dark-blond hair, it was hard to say exactly how old she was. Maggie guessed at somewhere between forty-five and fifty-five.

"Hello, Maggie." Angela was already moving a few of the small tables together for her group. They always sat in the corner away from the big windows at the front of the shop.

"Hi, Angela." Maggie took out her order pad. "What can I get for you?"

"Definitely coffee." Angela wrapped her arms around her chest and shivered. "It's cold out there. I'd like a latte. An agent from my office was raving about your Viennese Cinnamon. I'd like to try that."

"Sounds like a good choice." Maggie smiled at her and tried again to think of some way to introduce Donald into the conversation.

"Terrible thing about that man being killed here yesterday." Angela shook her head. "Are you and Aunt Clara never going to get a break, or what?"

Nine

Actually, he wasn't killed here. That's the good news." Maggie realized Angela had opened the door for the conversation by bringing up the subject. "Still, it's hard for Aunt Clara. You know they met on the Durham Singles site."

It was a little white lie. Maggie needed to push open that door a little more.

"I didn't know that." Angela rubbed her long, slender hands together. "It's difficult to imagine a woman Clara's age wanting to be listed at a place like that."

"Everyone gets lonely." Maggie took out the milk and coffee she needed for Angela's latte. "I looked at the site—Aunt Clara needed my help with the computer. There were hundreds of people listed there—younger and older."

Angela stood close beside Maggie as the coffee was brewing. "You saw my name, didn't you?"

"I did." Maggie added a touch of cinnamon. "I was a little surprised to see you there. None of my business."

"We're all friends here, right?" Angela smiled in a predatory way. "I'm married, but the life has gone out of that relationship. I started thinking that maybe I was reaching down too far, too young. So I began looking in the Silver Foxes. I saw Donald there."

"Did you two date?"

"Of course not! Clara is my friend. As soon as I knew who he was, I backed off." Angela smoothed her hair back from her attractive face. Her bracelets clanked together on her arm. "I was glad I didn't date him after I saw Ryan's story in the *Durham Weekly*. I think Donald might have gotten what he deserved."

"Maybe so." Maggie steamed the milk, not convinced that Angela would back off of *anything* without a fight. "It was terrible."

Angela put her hand on Maggie's shoulder. Her strong, musky perfume permeated Maggie's senses even over the aromatic smell of the coffee. The combination made her sneeze.

"Bless you." Angela gave the usual response in a cheerful tone. "I'm glad Clara escaped him. He was obviously a horrible man."

"Obviously." Maggie finished the cup of coffee and put it on the counter. "I'm wondering who did the deed, you know? There are a lot of people to choose from. Was it someone related to one of the women the police think he killed, or was it a scorned lover?"

"That's a good question. I'm sure Ryan and the police will be looking into that answer." Angela stepped away and pointed to a piece of pie in the refrigerated case. "I'll have the eggnog pie today, Maggie. It looks great!"

Maggie didn't feel like she'd learned much from Angela. She wasn't sure what else to ask her. Ryan had a knack for picking up on what people were saying that she couldn't duplicate. Maybe that was why he was the reporter.

By that time, Jean, the super-thin nursing instructor from Duke, was there for the meeting. She always wore green scrubs and liked to complain about how bad her students were. Jean wanted a plain coffee and a piece of Pumpkin Pizzazz.

"Hiya, Maggie!" Barb, who was a Duke counselor, wasn't wearing her usual frown that day. "I won twenty-five dollars in the lottery this morning. Can you believe it? I'm taking myself out to dinner tonight. I've never won anything before in my life!"

"Congratulations," Maggie said. "Have a coffee on the house to celebrate!"

The three women had been friends since childhood. They were quickly joined by Liz and Sissy, who were new to the group.

Liz had straight black hair that she wore short and dramatic. She liked heavy black eye makeup to complement her look. Maggie knew she was the theater director for the Children's Theater in Durham. Her speech was very clear, full of enunciation.

Sissy was a married woman with sandy-colored hair and freckles. She had three children she liked to brag about. Her husband was from a wealthy family. She sympathized with the women in the group by frequently reminding them that she'd never worked. Needless to say, she wasn't very popular.

After taking their orders and coming back with the food and drinks, Maggie was surprised to see that their book of choice for that week was a young-adult vampire novel.

"That's an unusual book for you to read." Maggie smiled as she put down the slices of pie from her tray.

"It's my doing," Liz said. "I've always had a thing for the supernatural. When I lived in Paris, I dated a *real* vampire."

"Really?" Maggie put their tickets down on the table too. "Was he in one of Anne Rice's books?"

Liz giggled. "No. *Real* vampires never come out and tell people about themselves. I knew only because I was his lover. It was sad when we broke up. He was a hundred and fifty years old, but he looked like he was twenty. And he was an *awesome* lover."

Angela grimaced. "That's a little *too* old. I'm thinking late fifties, maybe sixty, with some money."

"Sounds good." Barb picked up her coffee cup and sipped. "Put me down for one of those too." Maggie left the women alone at their table to discuss their book. There were two students studying together at another table. It usually took them an hour to drink a cup of coffee and start on their pie.

She went into the back to see if her aunt needed help. Aunt Clara was starting to take a whole tray of pies out of the oven.

"Let me give you a hand with that." Maggie put on oven gloves and took the tray of five mincemeat pies from her. "They smell wonderful, even though I don't like mincemeat."

"The crust is enough to tease the nose," Aunt Clara said. "That's what my grandmother always said. She didn't think pies needed filling to be good."

"I suppose that could be true if you really *love* crust." Maggie put the pies on the cooling racks beside the big oven. "I like the filling, except the mincemeat. Even with your secret lemon peel addition, it makes me shudder."

"Everyone has their favorite."

"I was thinking that we might consider selling ice cream when the weather gets warm again." Maggie laid the oven mitts on the counter. "Lots of people ask if they can have ice cream with their pie. It might be worth it. We'd have to have a separate, smaller freezer to get it in bulk."

"I'm sure Mr. Gino would be glad to give us a price on that."

"I'm sure he would." Maggie wasn't sure they were getting the best prices from Mr. Gino, but her aunt had been dealing with him for years. She liked him and trusted him.

"Let's think about it," Aunt Clara said. "Our more immediate problem is what to name the cat."

"I have to think about refilling some coffee cups." Maggie grabbed the coffeepot.

Angela wanted another latte. Maggie made sure everyone was full of pie and whatever she was drinking, and then made the next latte for Angela. Because the lattes took a little time, she tried to make sure everything was running smoothly before she turned her back on the other customers to make them.

A tall, robust man in a nice gray suit strode into the coffee shop while she was making the latte. Maggie glanced back as he almost pushed the door into the wall. He apologized while he was waiting for her to finish Angela's coffee.

"I'm Heath Jernigan." He put his hands into

his coat pockets. He was one of the few not wearing a heavy coat that day. "I'm here to see Clara Lowder."

Maggie immediately eyed him with suspicion. "What did you want to see her about?"

"I saw her profile at Durham Singles and then read about her terrible misfortune in the newspaper."

"Misfortune?"

He nodded vigorously. "Her loss, if you will. I'm here to give her a shoulder to lean on and a firm hand on the reins."

Does Durham Singles only sign up crazy men?

"I'm sorry, Mr. Jernigan. My aunt is very busy right now."

Aunt Clara heard her name and rushed out of the kitchen in her apron, flour on her cheeks. "What's going on?"

"You must be the woman I'm looking for." Jernigan quickly took her hand and kissed her fingers. "You don't know me yet, but when you do, you'll be pleased as punch about it."

"Who are you?" Aunt Clara retrieved her hand and wiped it off on her apron.

He quickly introduced himself again. "I'm the man of your dreams."

"Don't be foolish." She avoided letting him take her hand again. "You don't even *know* me. I think you should leave now."

It took several more attempts to get Jernigan to leave the pie shop. Maggie finally threatened to call the police.

When he was outside the front door, Aunt Clara turned to Maggie. "What in the world is going on? First Albert—and now this man. Has everyone lost their minds?"

Maggie watched her aunt go back in the kitchen. Obviously it had been a mistake putting her name on the Durham Singles site. She'd meant well, but things weren't working out as she'd hoped.

Even worse, she'd forgotten to remove Clara's profile last night when she started chasing the cat. Now there could be more crazy men on their way to court her aunt. Weren't they supposed to call or something first? Maggie had never used a dating service, but she'd thought it would be more confidential than this.

Angela sidled up to her. "You forgot to mention to Clara that you put her on the dating site, didn't you?"

Nice to have it happen with an audience. "She knew. She wasn't expecting so much attention," Maggie explained. "More pie?"

Angela smiled and sat back down with her friends. Maggie was sure she knew exactly what had happened.

Frank Waters came in a little while later. He asked for a cup of coffee and a slice of mincemeat pie. "I'd like a little conversation too, if you have the time, Maggie."

The book club ladies were getting ready to go. One of the students had left. The pie shop was almost empty. She sat down with him at a table near the window.

"Anything in particular you want to talk about?" She wiped a coffee stain from the tabletop after she had his order ready.

"I think that would be obvious since I'm a homicide detective and a man you knew died in here yesterday."

Frank could be a little brusque. Maggie knew he was good-hearted behind that serious countenance and flat, no-nonsense style. Still, she was always careful with her words when she was around him.

"I don't know what else I can tell you about what happened. I answered all the questions yesterday."

"Humor me." Frank dug into his pie. "Let's pretend we don't have all the facts about Mr. Wickerson's death—including who killed him—which we don't."

"I'm not sure I understand what you're looking for."

"Someone knew Mr. Wickerson spent plenty of time here. He or she waited until he was almost here before coming out to shoot him up close and personal. The killer ditched the gun at the back of your shop and went on his or her merry way. Mr. Wickerson stumbled into the pie shop and died. Does that sound like the *whole* story to you, Maggie?"

"You found the gun."

"I found the gun," he confirmed. "It wasn't too hard. The killer had wedged it behind one of your trashcans in back. It's plastic. I've seen a few of these before, but it's unusual."

"That's good news, right?"

"It all depends on what you call 'good.'"

"Okay." Maggie glanced around the empty pie shop. "What's bad about it? You can use it to trace the killer, yes?"

"Probably not. No fingerprints."

"Oh."

"Normally, we'd question your aunt about this since she and Mr. Wickerson were having a relationship." Frank slurped some coffee. "I know your aunt. I don't think she'd hurt a fly."

"Not to mention that she was here working the whole time."

"See, that's the hard part about this. Your aunt was here, but Mrs. Hightower told us that Clara *wasn't* in the kitchen when Donald came in. Odd, huh? Where was she?"

"She's been feeding a stray cat we're adopting." *He can't possibly be serious about Aunt Clara killing Donald!*

"From my boss's point of view, she could've slipped out the back door and killed her boyfriend, hidden the gun, and then slipped back in like nothing happened. How long was it between times that you saw her?"

Maggie's eyes widened. "You're joking, right? I don't know how long it was. I wasn't keeping track. You know she'd never do such a thing."

He shrugged. "I know that. My boss doesn't know her as well as I do. He has this crazy theory that your aunt read Ryan's story in the paper that morning and wanted revenge on Donald. And since no one is stepping up to take responsibility . . ."

"That's the craziest thing I've ever heard." Maggie leaned closer to him. "You *know* that didn't happen. Can't you convince Captain Mitchell?"

"Not until we've checked out everything. Did you know she put up a dating profile for herself on some website? That looks bad too, Maggie. Like she was already planning for the future without him."

Dating profile? Oh no! "I put her up on that dating site. She wouldn't know how to do that."

He shrugged. "I don't like it either, Maggie, but the captain is right. Clara looks guilty for killing her boyfriend. If it was anyone else, I'd be going after her like this pie!"

"So what can I do?" She felt sick at the idea that anyone would think Aunt Clara had killed Donald. It was insane.

"The captain thinks Clara had motive and opportunity. She's on that singles' place with those other women your boyfriend thinks could be suspects. Telling the captain that someone else knew *exactly* when to kill Donald—the moment when your aunt was missing from the kitchen—sounds like I'm reaching."

"I don't know what else to say. What can we do to protect her?"

"One thing happened in your favor. A rookie officer at the scene checked everyone's hands for gunshot residue. Clara's hands were clean."

Maggie remembered the officer putting the sticky substance on their hands and keeping the results. "But Captain Mitchell still thinks she could be guilty?"

Frank shrugged. "She could've washed her hands or been wearing gloves. We need another suspect."

Maggie didn't like where this was going. "Please don't talk to Aunt Clara. She's still in shock over what happened. This could push her over the edge." Maggie knew an accusation like this could ruin the rest of her aunt's life.

"I just want some answers. Ryan is playing hard to get right now. I know I chewed him out, and I'd do it again in a similar circumstance. He's lucky I don't arrest him. I know newspapers have the right to print what they want, but he was trying to circumvent an ongoing police investigation with that piece."

Maggie's heart was beating wildly. Her eyes were burning with unshed tears that she quickly wiped away. She couldn't show Frank how upset and scared this little conversation had made her.

"All right. You want me to ask Ryan about his information." She gleaned what she could understand from his words.

"Now you're talking. I know our boy has been investigating Mr. Wickerson for a while. I spoke with people from the families of his late wives. Unless one of them hired a hit man, they didn't do it. None of them were near Durham at the time of the shooting."

"There are so many of them," Maggie retorted. "Maybe they got together and hired a hit man."

Frank ate his last forkful of pie. "You know, I'd like to believe that. These people have suffered trying to find justice for their loved ones. But I can't buy that theory—unless they hired some third cousin who has a nine millimeter he was dying to try out. The hit was amateurish. No pro kills like this."

Maggie had no answer for that. While Ryan was feuding with Frank, she'd have to act as the go-between and encourage Frank to look in another direction.

"What do you want to know from Ryan?"

"I want to know the names he's gathered during his investigation. I want his facts and figures. Does anyone here in Durham have ties to Mr. Wickerson? He can save me some time."

"I'll talk to him." Maggie frowned. "You know how juvenile this is, right? You and Ryan should sit down and resolve your differences."

"I'd be willing to do that if your boyfriend was willing. I didn't shoot him for messing up everything with his stupid story. I thought that was pretty generous. What is it about these media people anyway?"

"I don't know. You aren't serious about Aunt Clara, right? That was just a cruel way to get my attention, wasn't it?"

Frank slid his chair back and got to his feet. "I wish I wasn't serious. You're a smart girl, Maggie. Pump Ryan for that information and then dump him. You could do better. Maybe *you* should try that singles' site. My sister found her new boyfriend online."

"You've got to be kidding me!"

"Oh! Frank!" Aunt Clara noticed him in the dining room and waved through the opening between the two rooms. "Nice to see you."

Ten

Even though Maggie thought Frank was mostly pushing her buttons with his talk about her aunt being a suspect in Donald's death, she still worried about it the rest of the day.

They closed up Pie in the Sky early as the winter weather was getting worse. There was little point in being open when everyone was at home, waiting for the cold rain to go away.

Aunt Clara encouraged the tortoiseshell cat to follow them home. The cat was still too skittish to allow them to pick her up. Instead, they used some leftovers to keep the animal moving along the icy sidewalk.

"Maybe we should call her Crusty," Maggie suggested as the cat followed them into the house with no problem. "You know, like piecrust."

"That's even worse than Miss Kitty. We have to keep thinking. What about Esmeralda? I had a cousin with that name when I was growing up."

Maggie shook her head. "Too long. What happened to her?"

Aunt Clara closed and locked the back door after they were inside. "The cat? She's right here."

"I'm talking about Cousin Esmeralda. I don't remember ever meeting anyone with that name in the family."

"Oh no." Aunt Clara hung her jacket on a rack by the door. "She died, tragically, before you were born."

Maggie's coat joined hers on the wall. The cat circled their feet, purring and rubbing against them. "How did she die?"

"She entered a hot-dog-eating contest and choked to death. It was such a pity. She was so young. Well on her way to being a champion eater too."

Maggie hid her smile. She suspected that few of her aunt's stories were actually true, but she enjoyed them. "What about calling the cat Fantine? The young woman in *Les Misérables*?"

Aunt Clara thought about it. They'd gone through

a box of tissues while watching the movie a month before.

"I suppose it would suit her, wouldn't it? We could call her Fanny for short. That way maybe she won't meet that poor woman's fate."

"It seems to me that she's already met that fate, and now we're saving her." Maggie hugged her aunt. "We're cat rescuers."

Aunt Clara fed Fanny while Maggie rummaged in the refrigerator for dinner. She found and removed the pie-making implements she'd left in the freezer the previous night, before she'd started chasing the cat.

Even though Maggie had learned to make pies since she'd come home, she still wasn't much of a cook. She was better with microwave and frozen dinners than anything else. It had occurred to her that she could probably learn to make food from scratch, if she wanted to. If she could make piecrust, she could do anything.

Her phone rang. It was Ryan offering to bring dinner if he could eat with them. That made Maggie's quest for food easier. Aunt Clara was thrilled that he was bringing fried rice from her favorite Chinese restaurant.

While they waited for him, Clara watched Maggie make piecrust. "I think you're putting a little too much *oomph* into it, dear. It doesn't take hands of steel. You need a light touch so the crust doesn't get tough. Also, I think you're adding a little too much flour for the rolling process. It can be tough if it's too dry."

Aunt Clara demonstrated, her supple hands gently rolling the dough into the right size.

Maggie tried another piecrust, using her aunt's motions. "You're right. I'm definitely using too much *oomph*."

Aunt Clara laughed. "Don't think of it as crust. Think of it as silk. Push it around and it will flow."

Maggie completed a piecrust with a little less *oomph* and put it into a pan. "I hope we have something to go in it. I'd hate to have to throw the crust away."

Aunt Clara grinned. "Not a problem. There's always something we can use for filling."

Maggie's aunt wouldn't freeze piecrust to use at the shop, but she would freeze fruit and other fillings. She pulled out some leftover peach filling. "This should do it."

Of course, that meant a lattice for the top. Maggie had hoped for crumb topping. They were out of brown sugar.

"Remember, gentle hands." Aunt Clara let Fanny outside again. "It's so cold out there, I can't think why she'd want to go out at all."

"We don't have a litter box," Maggie reminded her. "Maybe she's just being considerate. I'm sure she'll be fine."

The pie was baking in the oven when Ryan arrived. The aroma of the peaches, sugar, and crust filled the house.

"What a mess out there tonight. It makes me glad that I don't own a daily newspaper. This way, all I have to do is mention the rotten weather in the next paper. Otherwise, I'd have to cover every accident and stranded driver on the interstate."

He left his shoes and jacket in the front hall and followed Maggie back to the kitchen, after a quick cuddle in the hall.

"What smells so good?" He sniffed, his arms around her. "I suppose it must be pie."

"How did you ever guess?"

He sniffed her and kissed her neck. "I don't know. It could be you!"

"I'm glad you're here safely, Ryan." Aunt Clara came downstairs and joined them. "It can be treacherous out there once the sun goes down and everything freezes. Maggie said you have fried rice for dinner."

Ryan produced two large containers of fried rice. "They were closing down when I was there, so they gave me extra rice and a bag of fortune cookies. We might not want to eat them if there's pie—but we could have some fun reading the fortunes."

They divided some of the rice out on plates and put the rest into the refrigerator. Maggie took the peach pie out to cool. Aunt Clara went to answer the scratching sounds at the back door.

"Oh my stars!" She took a step back.

"What's wrong?" Maggie went over to see what was happening.

"Looks like you rescued a cat *and* some kittens." Ryan smiled as he opened a fortune cookie. "This fortune fits the situation: 'There is always more than you expect.'"

"Fantine has six babies." Maggie stepped aside for the small furry family to enter the house.

"We're grandparents now." Aunt Clara laughed, and clapped her hands. "It happened so quickly too."

"Actually, I think it happened about six weeks ago," Ryan quipped. "They're walking around with their eyes open. They have teeth too."

"I don't know how we'll come up with names for all of them." Aunt Clara studied them. There were three tortoiseshell cats, like Fanny, and three black-and-white kittens. "I can't tell if they're male or female."

"We can worry about that later, I guess. The rice is getting cold." Maggie took a pitcher of sweet tea out of the refrigerator and put it on the table. "Let's eat."

When they sat down to eat, the kittens kept tripping over their feet. Aunt Clara laughed at them and gave them bits of rice, which they gobbled greedily.

Dinner was delicious. Ryan kept them laughing with his stories about the city council meeting he'd attended that day. The kittens commanded center stage for a while, trying to pounce on Fanny and ending up rolling away.

Aunt Clara excused herself, and Maggie wasted no time telling Ryan about her conversations with Angela and Frank.

"I can't believe he'd use you to get to me." Ryan kept his voice low, understanding that Maggie didn't want Clara to hear what Frank had said. "The man has no conscience."

"The two of you need to make up and share information," Maggie urged. "He might need you to help catch whoever killed Donald, especially with Captain Mitchell thinking it could be Aunt Clara."

"So you didn't get any kind of vibe from Angela, huh? You think she really didn't date Donald out of respect for your aunt?"

"I don't know. I don't think knowing my aunt would stop Angela from taking something if she really wanted it. Maybe when she actually met him, he was too old for her. She's lived with men much younger than her for a long time."

Maggie also explained that Angela was clear of gunshot residue at the scene too, like she and Aunt Clara were.

He shrugged. "I'm sorry I added to your aunt's problem with the police. I wanted the captain to see that checking out the other women who had dated Donald could help him."

"To get back at Frank because he gave you a hard time about writing that piece for the paper, right?"

"I suppose." He ran his hand around the back of his neck. "I really only wanted to help. I didn't get the feeling that Captain Mitchell was that impressed with my idea. I still plan to go and talk to those women on the list."

"But first you're going to talk to Frank, right? Maybe over the phone would be best. He mentioned something about shooting you. The phone or email could work until he's not so angry."

"I like Frank," Ryan admitted. "He's a good guy. But he can't tell me what I can and can't write."

"I'm sure that's not what he's saying." Maggie hoped this disagreement would go away quickly. "He's frustrated that he can't do more on the case. And I don't think he wants to see Aunt Clara involved in this any more than we do. That's why he gave me the heads-up."

"I'm sure you're right." He kissed her as Aunt Clara walked back into the kitchen.

"Need me to go back the way I came?" She laughed.

Ryan's phone rang. He took the call but didn't seem too happy about it. "My father is stranded at the country club. He refuses to drive if there is any snow or ice on the road. I have to go get him."

"Be sure to tell him hello for me." Clara began to clear the table. "Be careful on the streets."

Maggie walked Ryan to the front door. He wrapped his arms around her, and they exchanged a few heated kisses.

"I'll talk to you later." He twined his hand with hers. "Don't worry about me and Frank. Something will come up to make everyone forget that your aunt was ever even mentioned. Whoever killed Donald won't stay hidden for long."

"Thanks. I don't want Aunt Clara to get a hint of this. She'd be devastated if she thought Frank had considered her a suspect at all."

"It's going to work out, Maggie." He kissed her again. "I'll make sure of it."

After watching him slip and slide on the sidewalk to the street, she closed and locked the door. When she went back to the kitchen, Aunt Clara was putting down extra rugs and towels as beds for the kittens and Fanny.

"I don't know if we can take care of seven cats." Maggie voiced her doubts.

"We'd never have to worry about mice again." Aunt Clara patted one of the blankets and made cooing noises at Fanny. The cat ambled slowly toward her and finally sank down, purring.

"She looks exhausted," Maggie said.

"You would be too if you had six children to keep up with. I'm sure that's why she's so thin too. She's a good mother. She went out to get her babies once she heard it was going to be the coldest night of the year. She knew they'd be safe here."

Once the cats were settled in, Maggie and Aunt Clara cleaned up the kitchen. The cold wind whistled through the eaves in the old house.

Maggie shivered, hearing it. "I hope the furnace can make it through until spring. I wouldn't want to find a repairman on a night like this."

"Me either." Aunt Clara wiped down the kitchen sink. "You know, I was really surprised today when Frank suggested that I might have killed Donald. What did Ryan think when you told him?"

Maggie stopped covering the rest of the peach pie in a plastic container. "You heard that? Why didn't you say something?"

"Why didn't *you* say something?"

"I was afraid it would hurt your feelings. I was hoping you didn't hear it."

Aunt Clara laughed. "I'm not deaf, dear. I can hear quite well. I think we've discussed this before. I have a decent memory too."

"Of course you do." Maggie put the rest of the pie in the refrigerator as her aunt turned off the kitchen light. "I'm sorry you heard that. Believe me, Frank wasn't serious. He was only trying to get my attention so I'd talk to Ryan."

"I think he *was* serious. It seems like Donald's death has put him in an uncomfortable position,"

Aunt Clara continued as they went upstairs together. "I can understand why he's questioning everything. It's his job. I want to know what happened to Donald too. I know it wasn't me, but I suppose you never know what someone is likely to do."

"I'm sorry I didn't say anything to you about it," Maggie said. "I guess I always think you're more fragile than you really are."

Her aunt laughed. "I've never thought of myself as *fragile*. I'd rather know the truth straight up anytime. I don't run away from my problems, Maggie—never have, never will."

As they parted to go to their separate rooms, Maggie smiled and said good night. "I won't ever think you're fragile again."

"Good night, dear. Your piecrust tonight was excellent. Just remember at the shop, don't push so hard, and not so much flour on the rolling pin."

Maggie went to her room and put on her warm flannel nightgown. She lay in bed listening to the wind for a long time, wondering how it was possible that the chain of events could have led Frank to question whether or not Aunt Clara was guilty of murder.

There was no doubt that she and Ryan had to find some answers to clear her aunt's name. Soon.

Eleven

The next morning dawned bright and clear. By 10:00 a.m., the streets were wet but clear of snow and ice. The trees dripped heavily on the sidewalks and houses, soaking everything. The sky was blue, and the warm sun beat down, bringing the temperatures up into the fifties.

The pie shop was busy that day, with many people wanting to get out and enjoy the fine weather. Between that and the Christmas shoppers, Aunt Clara and Maggie were busy right up until closing time. They sold a record number of pies and congratulated each other as they locked up the shop that evening.

Maggie and Aunt Clara got home, ate something quickly, and changed clothes so they were ready to go when Ryan arrived. He was dropping Aunt Clara off at the library before he and Maggie went to talk with the other women on Donald's dating list.

Ryan held Aunt Clara's arm as she walked down the stairs. Maggie followed, locking the door behind them.

"Do you think Fanny and the kittens will be all right alone in the house?" Aunt Clara paused to consider.

Maggie smiled. "We can't be here with them all the time. I'm sure they'll be fine."

"Seven cats," Ryan mused. "That's a lot of cats."

A tall man with a red cap and matching scarf walked down the sidewalk from the neighbor's house next door. He reached them as Ryan was helping Aunt Clara into his car.

"Maggie! It's you, isn't it? After all these years."

Ryan looked at her, and she shrugged. It was hard to say if she knew the man or not. He was bundled up so much that his face was barely visible.

"David. David Walker. Remember me from school?" He unwrapped his scarf and took off his hat. "Sorry. I'm up from Florida visiting, and it's *freezing*."

"David!" Maggie remembered her childhood friend well. They'd gotten in many scrapes together when they were growing up. The fence still swung loose between their two yards, a victim of their escapades.

Maggie and David hugged briefly, and laughed as he replaced his hat and scarf. She wasn't sure how he'd recognized her—she wouldn't have known him on the street. He was as tall and thin as she remembered, but his face was thinner, and his dark hair had gone salt-and-pepper.

Ryan closed the passenger door and coughed, almost discreetly.

"Oh. Sorry. Ryan Summerour, this is David Walker. We grew up together. It's been a long time since we've seen each other."

David reached his gloved hand to Ryan.

"Sorry to interrupt," David said. "My mother said you were back, Maggie. Maybe we can have dinner sometime before I go back home. It would give us a chance to catch up."

"I'd like that." She smiled at him, and Ryan started the car. "I have a few things to do, but I'll be back later. It's wonderful to see you, David."

"You too, Maggie!"

Maggie got in the back of the warm car and waved to David as they pulled away from the curb.

"He's looking well," Aunt Clara added. "I think his mother said that he's a successful electrical engineer in Miami. Good field to be in. He owns his own home *and* a sailboat."

"I can't believe he knew it was me." Maggie smiled out the window, recalling all the good times she and David had together when they were young. "I'm sure I look a lot different now too."

"I saw your yearbook picture. I would've recognized you," Ryan said. "Besides, who else would be coming out of your house with your aunt?"

"I suppose that's true." She caught his eye in the rearview mirror. "It was still a big surprise. I never expected to see him again."

Aunt Clara laughed. "I'm sure his mother gave David a heads-up too. She probably called and told him you were home again. You know that boy always worshipped you. He was devastated when you went to New York."

"I wouldn't say 'worshipped.'" Maggie felt her face get warm. "We had some fun together, but we were only kids."

Ryan dropped Aunt Clara off at the library, taking an extra minute to make sure she got into the squat building safely. He came back out to the car—Maggie was in the front seat.

"So David worshipped you, huh?" He grinned, but his blue eyes were serious. "How did you feel about him?"

"I felt about him like any fourteen-year-old feels about her friends. If you're asking if we were romantic—"

"That's what I was asking."

"We weren't. I never let myself get romantically involved with anyone in high school, or even college. I knew I was leaving, going to the life I'd always dreamed about, and they were probably going to stay here."

Ryan squeezed her hand. "You don't have to live in Miami or New York to be successful."

"I know." She kissed him. "Look at *you*."

Ryan began driving to the address he had for Anna Morgan, the first woman from the dating service on his list. Maggie regaled him with her and David's childish exploits to reach the moon and backpack to the Arctic.

"I'll bet David didn't feel as platonic about you. Fourteen-year-old boys tend to take their first love very seriously. Why didn't he go with you to New York?" Ryan asked in his reporter's voice

"I was very ambitious," she confessed. "David wasn't. Once we got into high school, that was the end of our friendship. I pushed him away. I never thought about him again, until I came back last year."

"Good." He grinned, obviously relieved. "You must've been hell on wheels back then."

"I was very driven and focused." She touched his hand. "Things are good now, though. I want different things. I'm glad to be back home."

Maggie knew she was a much different person than she had been when she first got out of school. All she'd been able to think about then was getting away from Durham as quickly as she could. But things were different now. She was happier and less intense. She knew what life was like on the fast track, and it no longer interested her.

Ryan jumped back into the possible leads in Donald's death. "I haven't been able to find much about any of the other people Donald dated. There is plenty about Angela, of course. Debbie Blackwelder owns a hair salon, so she's out there too."

Maggie was glad to move away from the subject of who she'd been. It was kind of fun seeing the jealousy in Ryan's eyes, but she didn't want to encourage it. She liked their relationship. It was uncomplicated, and they had a good time together.

"Nothing on Anna Morgan except her address, huh?" she asked.

"Well, there are always a few other things, if you're willing to look for them. I know what school she graduated from, and that she runs a day-care near the university. She's got good credit, and her husband is an economics professor at Duke."

Maggie raised her dark brows. "Another married woman looking for a good time?"

"Only one of the women on Donald's page has never married—Debbie Blackwelder. Lenora and your aunt are the only widows. I'll bet Donald wasn't interested in the married women."

"So you think he was shopping for the best bargain?"

"That's exactly what I think. No one tells the truth about themselves on the Internet. Donald sure didn't. He'd have to go out with a woman to be sure she was what he was looking for." Ryan parked the car in front of a large Tudor-style home. "Maybe Anna Morgan got angry when Donald rejected her. She could've seen that he was dating other women and snapped."

"I don't know if that makes sense. Why aren't we talking to Debbie Blackwelder first? She has her own business, part of Donald's MO, right?"

"You watch too much TV," he scolded as he opened his car door. "We have to stick to the plan."

Maggie shrugged. "I think the plan has a fatal flaw. It's too cold to go running all over Durham today." But she got out of the car and followed him up the sidewalk to the house anyway.

Ryan rang the doorbell. An attractive woman, probably in her late fifties, answered. He introduced himself and showed her his credentials. "I'm here to talk to you about your relationship with Donald Wickerson."

She twisted the pearls around her neck. "You mean the man from the dating service? I already talked to the police after his terrible death. I only went out with him once. I don't want my husband involved. It was a one-time fling."

Ryan pushed back in a calm, practical way. "Was it his idea not to see him again, or yours?"

"Mine. He wasn't my type." She looked back over her shoulder. "He was older, you know? From his picture at the dating site, I couldn't tell. That's not what I wanted."

Ryan thanked her, and he and Maggie left.

"That's almost exactly what Angela said," Maggie told him. "That's what happens when you lie *too* much on your profile."

"Is there a right amount to lie?"

"Maybe. I made Aunt Clara a little younger, but not so much."

They talked about Donald's death and Ryan's problem with the larger newspaper that had been printing the *Durham Weekly*. The larger newspaper had decided to shut down its printing operation in the city and send its printing operation to Raleigh. It was going to cost Ryan almost double what he'd been paying to have the *Weekly* printed.

"I think I'm going to have to hire a full-time salesperson to bring in more advertising to pay for the extra cost. I'm hit-or-miss on selling ads. I get too caught up in the story and forget to ask for the ads."

"Maybe that's for the best," Maggie said. "A full-time salesperson could take some of the responsibilities for the paper away from you."

"It should work that way." He'd stopped at a red light and turned to her. "Are you feeling left out? I know I'm scattered sometimes. I don't mean to be."

"*Sometimes?*" She laughed. "I'm just teasing. You're very passionate about your work. I love that about you."

He kissed her quickly, and the light changed to green. "You have a hunch or something about Debbie Blackwelder? Is that why you think we should see her?"

"I don't know. Except for *not* being a widow, she seems to fall into the same category as Aunt Clara and Lenora, that's all. He was looking for a well-to-do lonely lady with a successful business, and very little family."

"What about Lenora?"

"Aunt Clara swears Lenora wouldn't hurt anyone, although she fits the profile too. She and her daughter are just scraping by at the consignment store right now, but Aunt Clara says Lenora's husband left her a lot of money."

"Wouldn't having a daughter take Lenora off the list? Wouldn't she keep her mother from taking the big jump with Donald like you did with your aunt?"

"I don't know." Maggie considered that. "It's possible. She and Alice seem very close."

They arrived at the Dapper Dandy Salon about ten minutes later. There was a huge picture of a mustache and a bowler hat on the sign. Two men were walking into the small shop on the corner.

"I don't know if Debbie wanted to date Donald, or if he was coming here for manscaping." Maggie watched the men coming in from the discreet parking lot. They were all very well dressed.

"Manscaping? What does that even mean?"

"You know, trim everything up a little, or shave it off."

He frowned and shook his head before he got out of the car. "Never mind. Let's check it out."

Ryan introduced himself to Debbie. She was with a customer and said she would talk to him in a few minutes.

Maggie watched as Debbie shaved the portly gentleman's face, head, and chest. She smiled when she saw Ryan wince.

Debbie was medium height, with wild blond hair and extreme eyelashes that made her look as though she were wearing spiders on her eyes. She was a little portly herself, with a bountiful bosom that she showed off with a bright red tank top.

"She's really young for Donald," Ryan observed. "Marrying her would break away from his routine completely."

"Not necessarily. Even younger women can find someone like Donald attractive."

"You two." Debbie called them over after finishing with her client. She smiled seductively at the two men waiting for her. "Hang in there, boys. I'll be out in a minute."

She took Maggie and Ryan behind a beaded curtain. A desk and computer were in the tiny office along with a few chairs.

Debbie lit a small cigar and blew the pungent smoke into the air. "What can I do for you?"

"I'm looking for information about Donald Wickerson," Ryan said. "I believe you dated him?"

"Not 'date,' sweetie. He was a customer. A man like him is a rare find. Having him around was like old scotch."

"So you *wanted* to date him?" Ryan coughed a little as she exhaled smoke again.

"Not my type." Debbie's eyes lost focus. "He was interesting, though."

"Did you ever see him with another woman?" Ryan scribbled in his notepad.

"A woman dropped him off here once. He said his car was in the shop."

"Can you describe her?"

"She was an older lady. Long, gorgeous gray hair. Nice clothes. Conservative—not my style."

"Did he mention anything about her while he was here?" Maggie thought about Lenora.

"Nope." Debbie grinned, showing a tattoo of a rose on her front tooth. "They don't talk about other women when they're with *me*."

Ryan thanked her and got up. She stopped him by putting her hand on his chest.

"I should be going," he said.

"I could really do something *special* with you, baby," Debbie purred. "Ditch the girl. Stay a while."

He thanked her, and extricated himself with a smile and quick wink.

"She was lying," Maggie muttered when they got outside. "You said she was on his dating profile when you hacked it. Either she wanted to date him, or she wanted to know who he was dating."

"Whatever. She may have given us our first lead."

"What lead? The description of the woman who dropped him off sounded like Lenora. We already know Donald was seeing her. How does that help us find his killer?"

Before he could answer, Frank's brown Toyota chugged into the parking lot.

"This doesn't look good," Maggie said.

Twelve

"Ryan Summerour," Frank hailed him as he slammed his car door closed. "I hope you're here for a shave, and not because you're following *my* leads in the Wickerson case."

"Sorry, Frank. They aren't *your* leads. The names were on the Internet. That's public domain." Ryan glared at his friend as though they were prizefighters getting into the ring.

Maggie knew Ryan was lying about how he got the information, but she kept quiet.

"If you've got information I need for this case, you'd better hand it over."

"My rights as a reporter are protected by the Constitution. I don't have to hand anything over."

The two men were almost standing nose to nose in the parking lot.

Maggie inserted herself between them. "Can't we go somewhere for coffee and work this out? I know I could use a big cup. How about it, Ryan? Frank?"

Each man took a step back. Maggie took a deep breath.

"Suppose we could help you with a new lead?" she said quickly.

"What did you have in mind?" Frank still glared at Ryan, but was interested.

She told Frank about the woman who'd been meeting Donald at the sub shop before he was killed. "You could go over with us and question the owner." Maggie offered him the opportunity as an olive branch. "You could always come back here and question Debbie."

"Although Debbie didn't have much to say," Ryan added.

"Did you interview my subject?" Frank demanded.

"Never mind that right now," Maggie urged them. "Let's go to the sub shop."

Frank agreed—but Maggie and Ryan had to ride

in his car. Maggie didn't care. She climbed in the front seat beside Frank. Ryan grudgingly sat in back.

"So what *didn't* Debbie say?" Frank started the car and pulled into traffic.

"She wasn't dating Donald," Ryan replied. "She said he wasn't her type."

"But you said she was tagged at Donald's spot on the singles' site. That meant they were interested in each other," Maggie reminded them both.

"Debbie also said she saw a woman drop Donald off here when his car was in the shop," Ryan added.

"This man had his own little harem going on, didn't he?" Frank chuckled. "I don't know how he did it. I can barely handle one woman—my wife."

"Maybe that's why he's dead," Maggie suggested.

"I don't understand why he changed his pattern," Ryan said from the backseat. "In his other relationships, he seemed to just waltz into town and pick out the right widow. They got married. She died. Why was he having such a hard time finding the right woman here?"

Frank shrugged. "Maybe you were right about Maggie upsetting his plans. Let's think about it. He might've had his eye on Clara for a lot longer than we realize. When Maggie came into the picture, he'd spent so much time on her that it was hard for him to switch gears. It gets harder when you get older, you know."

Ryan considered the idea. “You could be right.”

“Aunt Clara mentioned him being at the library dozens of times before she actually brought him home,” Maggie explained. “Maybe he wasn’t sure how to restart, and that’s why he joined Durham Singles.”

“I think he was already at Durham Singles when he met Clara,” Ryan disagreed. “He was trolling until he found the right one.”

“Which brought him to two other women who were ripe for the picking.” Frank turned into the parking lot at the sub shop. “From what I can tell, that meant Lenora Rhyne and Debbie Blackwelder.”

“And maybe whoever was meeting him here before he died.” Maggie got out of the car and hurried inside the sub shop.

Betty was happy to see her. “She hasn’t been back for lunch, the mystery woman.” She pointed to the spot at the front window.

Frank introduced himself and then took out his rumpled notebook and pen. Ryan made notes on his cell phone.

“Describe her.” Frank shot a look of annoyance at Ryan, but let him stay.

“Long hair. Very pretty. Nice figure. I can’t really understand why she’d want to be involved with a man that much older. She could get anyone she wanted, I’d think.” Betty patted Ryan’s cheek. “Even you, baby face.”

Ryan's face turned red as he glanced at Maggie. "Did you see what kind of car she was driving?"

Betty shrugged. "I noticed her in here yesterday. I would have called Maggie, but when I looked up again, she was leaving. I tried to get her to take a bag of free chips. She wasn't interested."

Frank put his notebook away. "Maggie says you saw the same woman with Wickerson when he was dating Clara."

"That's right." Betty nodded. "They were here a few times."

"I guess that's about it." Frank took out his card and gave it to her. "Call this number next time you see her. This is an active homicide investigation. The police need to be kept informed."

Maggie suggested they stay to eat. Frank agreed. She had to talk Ryan into it. Finally, they all ordered their sandwiches and sat down at a table.

The conversation revolved around Frank believing that Ryan had information about Donald's dead wives that he wasn't sharing. Ryan assured him that he didn't have anything that wasn't available on the Internet.

"Maybe you could still pass some of it my way and save me some time," Frank gruffly requested.

"You'll share it with every other media source. I'm not doing their work for them."

"Maybe Frank would agree to look at what you have but not share it." Maggie tried to mend the fences between them. "If you find something helpful, Frank, you could give Ryan a little advance notice for the paper."

"I suppose." Ryan's head was stiff on his shoulders.

"Yeah. We could work something out," Frank agreed.

"Good. Since the *Weekly*'s office is right next door, you guys could go over there and share information. Does that work?"

Both men halfheartedly agreed that Maggie's idea could work. They finished eating and walked next door.

The building that housed the *Durham Weekly* was older but well kept. Ryan's father and mother had started the paper together forty years before, at about the same time Aunt Clara and Uncle Fred had opened the pie shop.

Ryan had taken over the paper from his father, who'd had a heart attack after his wife's passing and could no longer run the business.

The inside of the offices looked sparse and unused—not surprising since Ryan was the only employee of the paper. There were several desks with old typewriters on them. The phones were older too, some still with rotary dials. A fine layer of dust covered everything.

What surprised Maggie the most was the strong smell of printer's ink, even though the paper was printed in Raleigh. Ryan had explained by holding a fresh paper up to her nose. The strong odor had made her jerk her head back. She'd also seen his hands, black with ink stains, after handling the newspapers.

Even through the layer of dust and a few cobwebs, it was easy to see that this had once been a thriving newspaper. Now Ryan eked out a living with it by working as reporter, editor, salesman, carrier, and janitor.

Maggie sometimes wondered how long it would last for him. She supposed she could wonder that about Pie in the Sky too. At least for now, though, both businesses were still up and running.

Ryan was showing Frank all the information he'd collected on Donald's checkered past when Ryan's father, Garrett, stopped in.

He smiled when he saw Maggie. "It's good to see you again. How is Clara doing?"

Garrett was a lot like Donald in many ways. Both men were tall, broad-shouldered—handsome in the way older men can be. Garrett didn't have the tan or the polished finish that Donald had. He had worked all of his life and was proud of it. He could be a little stiff and standoffish.

Garrett had spent some quality time with Aunt Clara a few months ago, but their budding romance was short-lived. Maggie could tell Garrett still liked her aunt. Aunt Clara liked him too, but not in a romantic way.

"She's great. The pie shop is busy, and we're both excited about our first Christmas together in years."

"Good. I wish the two of you would have dinner with me and Ryan one evening to celebrate the holiday. Should I send her an invitation?"

"No. That's okay. I'll ask her. I'm sure she'd love to come. Did you have a date in mind?"

Garrett pointed at his son. "Ryan will come up with a day and time. I try not to get in the way of his work. He has a busy schedule, you know."

"Are you promising my life away, Dad?" Ryan asked him.

Frank, who'd known Garrett for years, came over to shake his hand. "Good to see you. I'm getting some information from your son about the man who was killed near the pie shop."

"I'm sure he has plenty to say on the subject." It was easy to see Garrett's pride in his son when he spoke.

"It helps that he's been taking the subject of Wickerson murdering his past wives more seriously than the police." Frank grinned at his old friend. "How's the golf course treating you? It must be nice to be a man of leisure."

"You know me—I'd rather be working," Garrett quipped. "Ryan constantly threatens to throw me out when I come for a visit."

"You can stop by the police department whenever you like," Frank said. "I'm always looking for someone to buy me lunch."

"Will do." Garrett shook his hand again. "Son, I need to have a word in private with you. Excuse us, Maggie."

As the father and son disappeared into the office Ryan used—the only spot without dust and cobwebs—Maggie and Frank sat down in the old waiting area at the front of the building.

Pinned to the walls were yellowing newspaper articles that told forty years of Durham's history. Trophies and plaques, dating back to before Maggie was born, congratulated the newspaper on its work.

"These pieces are how I remember the *Weekly*." Frank pointed to the newsprint. "Garrett was everywhere. I remember coming here on a class field trip when I was a kid. There were at least fifty people working at those desks. I don't know what happened."

Maggie shrugged. "Internet news, blogging, and social media. Things change."

Frank nodded and sat forward in his chair, putting his hands together before him. "I'm afraid Ryan is trying to compensate for that loss. He's going to work himself into an early grave."

"Wasn't Garrett the same way?"

"I suppose he was. I'd just made detective when Garrett retired. Maybe as a uniform cop, I never noticed as much."

"It can't be easy competing with all of that other media, and having to hold on to information for a week before it's published," Maggie said.

"I know you're right."

"Did he have the information you were looking for?"

"He did. And he emailed it to me while we were sitting there. Ryan's as good as his dad ever was. He's a risk taker, though. He could've wiped himself out with that story about Wickerson. Keep an eye on him, Maggie."

The two of them stood up as Ryan and Garrett approached them.

"Is everything all right?" Maggie asked when she saw Ryan's pale face.

"We've had some bad news," he explained.

"Ryan, you don't have to share the information with the rest of Durham," his father cautioned.

"I might as well. Everyone will know soon enough." Ryan turned to Maggie. "We're going to have to sell this building. I don't know where the *Weekly* will go from here."

"How did that happen?" Deep frown lines formed between Frank's eyebrows.

"Taxes," Garrett sighed. "It's either the building or the house. This place is too big anyway. Ryan is going to have to downsize like everyone else. He really only needs one room anyway."

"I'm sorry, Ryan," Frank said. "If I can do anything to help, let me know."

Ryan shook his hand. "Thanks. I hope that information works out. I'd like to know if Donald was guilty of killing those other women."

"I have to go." Garrett glanced at his watch. "I'm sorry for the bad news, son. We'll work it out. The paper will survive!"

Frank went outside with Garrett. Maggie watched Ryan lock the door to the building after Garrett was gone. She knew he was upset about losing the building. Conversation was nonexistent on the way back from the newspaper office. Frank parked his car at the salon and then went inside to interview Debbie.

"I'm so sorry about the building, Ryan." Maggie got into his Honda. "I'm sure you can find someplace else to set up. I'll be glad to help you look for a spot."

Ryan's hands rested on the steering wheel. He stared out the windshield but didn't start the car.

"I don't know how I can afford to pay rent," he said bluntly. "With these printing changes and the price of everything else skyrocketing, I wasn't sure I could make it in the old building."

"You should have some money from the sale of the building, right?"

"I suppose so. I don't know what that will go for, especially in this economy. Let's face it, the *Weekly* office isn't exactly prime real estate." He smiled at her and squeezed her hand. "But you're right. I'll figure something out. I might have to move the office to a table in the pie shop. All it really takes is me, a camera, and a laptop. I could eat pie and put the paper together at the same time."

Maggie hugged him and kissed his cheek.

"I guess we should go."

"Who's next on the list of suspects?"

"Sylvia Edwards." He started the car. "There's a connection here somewhere. We just have to find it."

Thirteen

Sylvia Edwards was out of town and had been, according to her maid, since before Donald had died. She was definitely off the suspect list.

"I think we should stick with what we know we have," Maggie suggested. "Lenora is well off, her husband is dead, and she owns a successful business."

"But she's your aunt's friend."

"They're very competitive. She might've started seeing Donald just to spite Aunt Clara. Then when she realized what Donald really had in mind, she killed him."

"That's weak," Ryan said. "I like Debbie Blackwelder better. She's younger, but otherwise she fits Donald's profile."

"I don't know."

"Let's go pick up Aunt Clara and go home. I need another cup of coffee, and we need to check on Fanny and the kittens."

Aunt Clara had been waiting outside the library when they pulled up. She marched out to the car and got inside before Ryan could get out and offer to assist her.

"That Lenora!" Aunt Clara fumed. "She had enough nerve to offer to make pies for the library fundraiser. That's the biggest event of the year for the library. I always make pies for it. She *knows* that."

Maggie glanced significantly at Ryan. "You can still make pies. You know they'll be better than hers."

"Too many pies," Aunt Clara complained. "I'm out of the running this year."

"What about something different?" Maggie suggested as Ryan pulled out of the parking lot. "I'm sure Lenora was offering sweet pies, dessert pies. What about savory pies? I was looking at some recipes for those the other day. I thought they might be something new to bring people in at lunch."

Pie in the Sky was always busy until lunchtime. Not many people wanted to eat pumpkin or apple pie for a meal. Their customers wandered off to other restaurants to eat lunch. Some came back later in the afternoon. Those midday hours were still costly for electricity, and other operating costs. Maggie had been researching some ways to fill that downtime.

"Okay." Aunt Clara grinned maliciously. "You had me at getting even with Lenora for stealing my thunder with the library fund-raiser. What did you have in mind?"

Maggie and her aunt talked about pies on the way home. Both women agreed that starting small, maybe a chicken potpie, could work.

"No point in confusing everyone," Aunt Clara said. "We can offer our regular pie menu and add one kind of savory pie to see how it goes—after the fund-raiser, of course. I don't want to give Lenora any hint of what we're planning."

"Sounds good to me," Ryan said. "I'm hungry already again. Hot potpie would really hit the spot."

"I probably have all the ingredients we'll need for a chicken potpie." Aunt Clara smiled as she thought. "Now we have a test subject. Let's go home and try it out."

But when they reached the house, there was a noticeable problem—no heat.

"That darn old furnace." Maggie grabbed a flashlight and went down into the basement. Ryan followed her.

"You said it was having trouble," he reminded her. "It's going to be hard to get someone to come out on a Saturday."

"I already had someone look at it. He said there wasn't much he could do. Aunt Clara doesn't remember when it was put in. Mr. Hernandez says it looks like it was built during the Civil War."

"That doesn't sound good."

"Maybe we can at least get it up and running until Monday." Maggie picked up a large pipe wrench that she remembered Uncle Fred using on the plumbing when she was a kid. She gave the big, dark furnace a few whacks with it and stood back.

"Is that your plan?" Ryan asked with a laugh. "I don't think it's working."

"You're right." Maggie gazed forlornly at the furnace. "I should've gone ahead and had it replaced. It's so expensive. I put all that money into the pie shop. I hated to spend the money from our savings."

"Why don't you give Mr. Hernandez a call? Maybe he'll make an emergency visit. It's nice out now, but it's supposed to be cold again tonight."

Maggie agreed and tried to reach Mr. Hernandez. His voice mail said he was out of town for the weekend.

"I guess you and your aunt will have to come and stay with me and Dad until you can get it fixed." Ryan walked upstairs in front of her.

Aunt Clara was already bringing in tree branches she'd found on the ground outside.

"We can use these in the fireplace until we get

the furnace fixed." She dropped a bundle on the floor.

"That won't last very long." Maggie eyed the branches with dismay. "I suppose we could run the dryer or something."

"Yes!" Aunt Clara agreed. "And the oven. I'm sure there are some hair dryers too. We could hold them to warm our hands."

"I don't think that will work," Ryan interrupted. "We have that big old house that's mostly empty. The furnace works, and so does the oven in the kitchen for your pie making. You can stay with us until your furnace is fixed. Go upstairs. Get some of your stuff together and we'll go."

Maggie was worried about causing more hard feelings between her aunt and Ryan's father. She hadn't planned to accept that invitation to dinner that Garrett had issued. They just didn't get along.

"We'll be fine, Ryan," Maggie said. "Right, Aunt Clara?"

"Have you ever lived in a house heated by an oven and a dryer?" her aunt asked with raised brows.

"No."

"I have." Aunt Clara started upstairs. "Let's get our things and take him up on his offer."

Maggie shrugged. "Okay."

"That's better," Ryan said. "You need any help?"

"We don't have any way of transporting Fanny

and her kittens," Aunt Clara called down the stairs. "What are we going to do with them?"

They ended up putting Fanny and her kittens into a cardboard box that Ryan placed in the backseat of the car as they were getting ready to leave. Maggie and Aunt Clara each put a bag into the trunk.

"I guess that's it." Aunt Clara looked up at the house as Maggie locked up. "I already miss it."

"We'll be fine." Maggie hugged her. "We're lucky to have someone who will take us in."

"Indeed we are." Aunt Clara smiled. "We won't let Lenora, or a broken furnace, keep us down."

Maggie had only been to Ryan's home once. She was uncomfortable there with its stiff formality. They preferred to meet at Aunt Clara's house.

Ryan's home was a large, two-story stone house that resembled a small castle in many ways. The grounds were well kept, surrounded by a tall stone fence that separated the property from the road. It was an impressive home, one that made it easy to believe that the *Durham Weekly* had once been a prosperous endeavor.

"My goodness!" Aunt Clara's eyes widened as they drove through the front gate with a lion on each stone pillar.

"It's a lot more than we need." Ryan pulled smoothly up the blacktop drive. There were carefully trimmed Bradford pear trees that faithfully followed along the sides of the winding drive. "We'd probably be better off selling this monstrosity and keeping the *Weekly*'s building. We could always live there."

"Don't be ridiculous," Aunt Clara chastised. "This is your family legacy, as much as the newspaper. Do you decorate for Christmas?"

Ryan laughed. "Dad and I don't do much of anything for Christmas, or any other holiday. We haven't had a Christmas tree since my mother died."

"What a shame." Aunt Clara's eyes roamed everywhere on the estate. "Someday you'll fill this place with children. That will make it come back to life."

Ryan parked the car near the front door and popped the trunk open. "Feel free to explore, or decorate if you like. I'll show you the guest rooms and the kitchen."

As he grabbed their bags and walked into the house, Aunt Clara pulled at Maggie's sleeve. "Imagine what you could do with this place."

"We don't have plans for anything like that right now." Maggie blushed a little, hoping Ryan hadn't heard her aunt. "I'll bet they have a great kitchen. Let's take a look."

The inside of the house was clean and comfortable, very masculine. No extras like vases or bric-a-brac. Everything was in good shape, but there was a utilitarian air about it.

"Almost like a hunting lodge," Aunt Clara muttered. "These men could use a few flowers and some Christmas lights. A rug or two wouldn't hurt either."

"You know you could marry Garrett, and all of this would be yours," Maggie teased her.

"That ship has sailed, dear."

"What do you think?" Ryan asked as he stood before the wide staircase. "Looks like a museum, right?"

"It's stunning!" Aunt Clara admired the woodwork and the large chandelier above her. "Maybe you could move your office here. There seems to be plenty of room."

Ryan considered her suggestion. "That could actually work! In the meantime, let me show you to the bedrooms." He picked up the box with Fanny and the kittens meowing inside and took it upstairs.

They settled the cats into Aunt Clara's bedroom and dropped off her bag. Maggie's room was next door. She was pleased to see that she didn't have to share the large bathroom with anyone.

Once Aunt Clara and Maggie were settled, Ryan took them down to the kitchen.

"Wow!" Maggie looked around at the kitchen, which was the size of the entire downstairs at her aunt's house. "You and Garrett don't cook at all, and you have this magnificent kitchen fit for a chef."

"My mom loved parties." He smoothed his hand along the light-colored marble countertop. "She spent hours in here getting ready for them. I don't know if she ever made the same food twice."

"I could live right here," Aunt Clara declared in

the center of the kitchen. "Double ovens! I love this place."

Garrett strode into the kitchen as they were looking around. "This is a surprise. Hello, Clara, Maggie."

Ryan explained about the furnace at Clara's house and his invitation for the ladies to stay there with them.

His father looked completely delighted. "That's exactly what this old place needs—a woman's touch. A little home cooking wouldn't hurt either. I hope there's enough food in the house. If not, we can send Ryan out for some."

"Maggie and I are going to make chicken potpie for the library Christmas fund-raiser," Aunt Clara explained. "I hope you and Ryan like potpie."

Garrett bent slightly, lifted her hand, and kissed it. "Dear lady, we would enjoy *anything* you care to make. I think we should have pie pans here somewhere."

Garrett and Aunt Clara started rummaging around in the cabinets and drawers. There were indeed several pie pans, dozens of mixing bowls, and anything else they'd need to make pie.

"There's no flour." Maggie unzipped the cooler where they'd packed the chicken and vegetables they'd planned to use for the potpie. She hadn't thought to bring flour. It seemed like something every kitchen would have.

"I'll get some," Ryan volunteered.

"From here it would be as close to go back to the house," Maggie said. "Let's drive back there and get our flour."

"And vegetable shortening." Aunt Clara was looking through the cabinets. "And tea and sugar. I like my potpies washed down with plenty of sweet tea, don't you, Garrett?"

"That sounds wonderful," he enthused. "Are you sure you don't want us to purchase those things?"

"We have plenty at the house," Maggie said. "We might as well bring them here."

She put her coat back on and got ready to leave again. Maggie didn't want to take money from Garrett, especially not now. They might have a big house, but she wasn't sure if they were in any better financial position than she and Aunt Clara.

She knew real estate could be deceiving. Someone might own a big, impressive house and be teetering on the brink of bankruptcy.

"I hope you don't think you have to cook for us," Ryan said as they were walking out the door. "We get along okay by ourselves. I don't want to put you and your aunt out."

"You're letting us stay with you. I think we could whip up a couple of potpies." Maggie laughed. "Aunt Clara could anyway. Outside of the normal pies we make, that's all I know besides microwave food."

"We have a whole freezer of microwave dinners." Ryan started the car. "I think we'll survive."

They were back at Aunt Clara's house in no time. "I'll just be a minute," Maggie said. "You stay here and keep the car warm."

Ryan agreed, and Maggie let herself in the house. She was putting the flour, shortening, tea bags, and sugar into a shopping bag when she heard a noise in the basement.

She shook her head. *Probably the old furnace still making groaning noises.*

She added a few other necessities to take to Ryan's.

Then another clanking sound reverberated up from the basement, but louder this time. It was definitely *not* a furnace sound. This was more like a tool dropping on the concrete floor.

With everything that had been going on recently, Maggie was spooked. She picked up a fireplace poker with trembling hands, swallowed hard, and then opened the door that led to the basement. She knew better than to turn on a light and alert a possible thief. Instead, she started down the stairs with the poker raised in her right hand.

Fourteen

It briefly crossed her mind that she should've gone out and alerted Ryan. She could've even called him from the kitchen before going down into the dark basement to see what was going on. If something happened to her, he'd at least know where to look.

Did all of those horror movies you watched teach you nothing?

Apparently not.

She reached the ground floor and looked around. There was a light coming from the back of the furnace. She couldn't see anyone, but she kept hearing noises from that direction.

Why would anyone want to be in the basement behind the furnace?

For a minute, she thought it could be Mr. Hernandez. Maybe he got back in town early, heard her message, and decided to come over and work on the furnace. It seemed like a long shot, but he was a very nice man, and nothing else made sense.

With the threat of danger diminished, at least in her mind, Maggie called out, "Hello? Mr. Hernandez?"

There was no response. She realized her voice was barely above a whisper.

Strengthening her grip on the poker, she cleared her throat and tried again.

This time, the light moved from behind the furnace.

Please be Mr. Hernandez. Please be Mr. Hernandez.

"David?" Was that really David back there?

"Maggie? I thought you were staying with your friends."

"I am. I forgot a few things. How did you know?"

"Your aunt called my mother."

"What are you doing down here?"

"I thought I'd take a look at the furnace and see if there was anything I could do. I think this is the same furnace I used to work on with your Uncle Fred."

She was bewildered. “But I set the alarm. How did you get inside? I know Aunt Clara didn’t give you the alarm code without asking me.”

He pointed to the small window right above the foundation line. “I didn’t know you had an alarm. I came in the way I always did when we were kids, remember? I guess the alarm doesn’t cover that window. You should have that looked at.”

“I will.”

“Maggie?” Ryan called from upstairs. “Are you okay? Where are you?”

“I’m down here,” she called out. “I’ll be right up.”

Ryan was on the stairs before she could go back up. “What’s going on?” He peered at David’s face in the flashlight beam. “What’s *he* doing here?”

“Just trying to help out,” David’s voice sang out. “I’m afraid Maggie was right. The furnace is dead. Fred and I put it back together dozens of times when I was in high school. I guess it could only hold up for so long.”

“Thanks for trying anyway,” Maggie said. “Why don’t you come out this way? It must’ve been hard squeezing through that little window. You’re a lot bigger now than you were back then.”

David agreed. Ryan went back up the stairs, and Maggie followed him.

“What about the alarm?” Ryan whispered to her. “Did you forget to set it, or have you already given him the code?”

"I'll tell you later." She didn't want David to explain how he knew there was another way into the house. She closed the door again after David emerged from the dimly lit basement.

"I'm sorry if I scared you." David turned off his flashlight and smiled down at her. "I only wanted to help."

Maggie understood. He'd always been that way. His face was covered in soot. She wet a paper towel and rubbed the spot on his cheek. Then she realized what she was doing and handed it to him.

"Mr. Hernandez will be back on Monday. We'll be fine until then. Thanks for trying anyway."

David rubbed the paper towel on his face. "Of course you will, Maggie. You've always been good at taking care of yourself. I wanted to lend a hand if I could. That's all. I know replacing a furnace can be expensive. I'll see you later."

He shook hands with Ryan, which left soot on Ryan's hands. Maggie thanked him again and put down the fireplace poker.

"You take care now." David leaned in quickly and kissed Maggie's cheek. Ryan turned back from the paper towel rack in time to see his display of affection.

He waited until David was gone. "Something you want to tell me?"

"We've known each other a long time." She shrugged, though she was secretly as puzzled as he was by David's quick kiss. "It has nothing to do with me and you. He was always affectionate."

Ryan picked up the shopping bag full of pie-making supplies. "So if my ex-girlfriend stopped in at my house to repair a major appliance and kissed me, all the time making remarks about our past history, you'd be good with that?"

"It's not like that." She opened the front door and let him go through, carefully setting the alarm and locking the door again. "That was pre–high school, and he isn't my ex-boyfriend. I think you're reading too much into what he said."

Ryan waited while she opened the trunk of the car. "Maybe you should tell *him* that."

She smiled. "You're really cute when you're jealous."

"Right." He put the shopping bag in the trunk and slammed the lid closed.

They both got in the car, and Ryan started the engine. Maggie could see he was still upset, but she knew there was nothing for him to be upset about. How could there be, since she hadn't seen or thought about David for at least fifteen years?

When they stopped for a red light on the way back to Ryan's house, Maggie smiled and touched his cheek. "You're not really upset about David, are you?"

"I'll let you know if my old girlfriend is at my house working on a freezer or something." But he smiled a little when he said it.

"Does she live here in Durham?" She knew he was joking—or at least she thought he was.

"When she became a super-hot runway model, she started traveling a lot. She comes back every now and then to repair a major appliance."

Maggie laughed. "You're crazy. And I don't think that's fair. David is hardly a super-hot model."

"No. But he *is* an electrical engineer, which probably means he makes more money than me, and isn't trying to keep a business already on life support alive."

"That doesn't mean anything to me," she said. "I like that you're trying to keep your newspaper running. Your dedication has a romantic appeal."

He glanced at her. "Romantic, huh? What did your last boyfriend do for a living?"

"He worked at the bank. It was more convenient that way. That's what I was looking for at that time. Expedient and easy. No emotional entanglements."

Ryan pulled into his driveway and stopped the car at the door. "That doesn't seem like you, Maggie." He kissed her and apologized. "Don't worry. Unless I can find something terrible in David's background to have him locked up for, I'll ignore him from now on."

Maggie looked into his steady blue eyes. "You're not joking, are you?"

He laughed as he got out of the car.

No help at all.

Garrett was in the kitchen with Aunt Clara when they went back inside. They were both sitting at the kitchen table, having a cup of tea and reminiscing about the way Durham used to be when they were growing up.

Maggie smiled. She realized that a few days with Garrett might be good for her aunt's self-esteem after Donald's death, or at least a welcome distraction. She knew it had been hard on her, especially with news of her boyfriend plastered all over TV and thc newspapers.

She and Ryan unloaded the shopping bag they'd brought from the other house. Ryan drifted off, probably to look up David on the Internet.

Maggie told her aunt about finding David in the basement at their house. "He said he was working on the furnace. Did you call Mrs. Walker and ask her to have him look at it?"

"I didn't think of that! Did he fix it?"

"No." Aunt Clara's words made Maggie pause and think. Why had David lied to her?

Was he embarrassed at being caught down there trying to do a good deed? Men could be so odd with their emotions—like Ryan being jealous of David.

"I'm surprised he couldn't fix that old furnace." Aunt Clara put the flour and shortening into the freezer with the bowls and other pie-making utensils.

"Being an engineer and knowing the furnace the way he does, it should've been a snap."

Ryan made a groaning sound as he came back in on the tail of the conversation.

"What's wrong, son?" Garrett appraised his face with a concerned frown. "You didn't hurt yourself lifting those bags, did you?"

"No." Maggie sat down at the table. "He's jealous of David and couldn't find anything bad about him on Google."

Garrett's chest puffed out. "Ryan has no reason to be jealous of *anyone*."

Aunt Clara chuckled. "Even if David is a *highly* paid professional?"

"Thanks." Ryan smiled at her. "Whose side are you on anyway?"

"Why, Maggie's, of course. May the best man win."

"Ryan *is* the best man," Garrett countered. "Though I'm not really sure what we're talking about."

"I think we should work on that filling." Maggie tried to shift the conversation.

A cell phone rang. Maggie, Garrett, and Ryan checked their pockets.

It was for Ryan. He spoke for a moment and then excused himself, leaving the kitchen.

"Probably the mayor or someone from the city council. They all call to talk to him." Garrett was obviously proud of his son.

Maggie and Aunt Clara took out the chicken, stock, vegetables, and herbs for the potpie. Maggie finely chopped carrots, onions, and potatoes. Aunt Clara had Garrett chop a little bit of sage.

"I just love sage in chicken potpie, don't you?" Aunt Clara asked Maggie as she worked on the chicken.

"I couldn't begin to tell you when I ate chicken potpie last," Maggie replied. "I don't like the little freezer kind."

"This won't be a bit like that." Her aunt strode around the big kitchen like a captain on a ship, as though she had that much space every day. "I think we can start on that crust now. Let's make four of them for the top and bottom of two pies."

Ryan came back into the kitchen. "I guess bad news travels fast. That was Albert Mann offering to buy the *Weekly* building from us."

Garrett looked up from his tedious task. "How much? Was it a decent price?"

"I suppose that all depends on what you think is a decent price." Ryan named the figure, and his father grinned.

"That sounds decent to me. Did you accept?"

"Not without talking to you. Both of our names are on the deed."

"I'll be happy to give him a call, son." Garrett got up from the table, brushing sage from his hands.

"I'm not thrilled about selling to him, Dad. The man is a little on the shady side."

"Who isn't in real estate? And what do we care? We just need the money."

"I suppose that's true."

Aunt Clara couldn't believe it. "You know what he's like, Ryan. How can you sell to him?"

"It's not the same for us as it is for you," he explained. "You wanted to keep your property. We can't afford to. I know this is a good offer, and it means we wouldn't have to look around for a buyer."

"How do you think he knew?" Maggie put the vegetables into a bowl. "You just found out. Did you say something to someone else about it?"

"I didn't." Ryan looked at his father. "Did you?"

Garrett looked a little shamefaced. "I might've mentioned it to a few of my friends at the club. That's why a person has influential friends. Believe me, they can be very helpful when one is in a bind."

Ryan tossed his cell phone carelessly on the table. "Mystery solved! We can sell the building to Albert Mann. Let's hire someone to make a banner for the outside of the building: 'Another Conquest by Mann Development!' "

Maggie could see in Ryan's face that he was miserable at the idea of it. She wished there were some other way, but she certainly wasn't in any position to help him out.

Aunt Clara took the flour, shortening, and water out of the refrigerator. Maggie got the bowl. They mixed up piecrust dough for two pies and tops and then rolled them out on the marble countertop.

Garrett followed his son out of the kitchen, trying to calm him and restate his case about why the building had to be sold. Maggie could hear them arguing through the house.

Aunt Clara patiently picked up each crust and set it into a pie pan. "I know this is hard for Ryan. His father too, for that matter. That building has been theirs for a long time. It's not fair for them to lose it."

"I know," Maggie agreed. "I hope Ryan can continue the paper. I know he really loves it."

"Yes." Clara stirred the filling before she put some into each crust. "Didn't he say he'd always wanted to be a police officer? Maybe he should change professions."

"I don't think he wants to do that anymore." Maggie lowered her voice and glanced at the open doorway. "I've never seen anyone as dedicated to their job as Ryan. He'll keep the *Weekly* going, even if he has to do it out of the basement here."

"Will you put those top crusts on and seal the pies?" Aunt Clara cleaned the flour from her hands and went to open the oven.

Maggie found a cookie sheet and put it down on the rack before she put the pies in on top of it. She didn't want the potpies to leak in Ryan's oven, as they did sometimes at home and at the shop. She could tell no one ever used the oven here—it was spotless.

As they got the pies in and Aunt Clara had closed the oven door, Ryan strode into the kitchen. Maggie was glad they weren't still talking about him.

"I have someone to talk to about Donald," he said. "He owns Durham Singles. Want to come?"

Fifteen

Aunt Clara said she would wait for the pies. "Besides, I'm in the middle of a new book and I'd appreciate some quiet time to read."

Maggie went with Ryan, hoping to get him to open up about losing the *Weekly*'s building more than anything else. Maybe they could even brainstorm some answers about where he could move.

"Marco Ricci actually met with Donald." Ryan started the engine before Maggie got in the car. "I think he might be able to shed some light on what he was doing and who he was dating."

"I understand that." Maggie put on her seat belt as the car raced out of the drive. "I'm not sure what good that will do."

"That's the thing. You never know what's really going on until you talk to as many people around the subject as you can," he explained. "Sometimes people don't even realize what information they have. You ask the right questions and it comes out."

"Well, I hope he has some better ideas about who killed Donald."

"If he doesn't know who killed him, maybe he can help us understand *why* he was killed."

Maggie stared at the side of his face. "Is that our new take on this?"

"Like I said, we have to look at it from all different angles, just like Frank does. You notice they're following the same leads. Maybe Marco has some ideas we haven't thought of."

"About the office," Maggie started. "Maybe Angela has some ideas about affordable rental space."

Ryan frowned. "She's on our list for Donald's murder. I don't think I can talk to her about a business deal until all of this is over."

"Except that Frank said she had no gunshot residue on her hands."

"She could have washed it off. It's not that hard."

"She was at the pie shop the whole time. That's why she knew Aunt Clara wasn't there."

He glanced at her. “You’re not being very helpful.”

“You’re being obstinate. I think it’s because you don’t want to think about leaving the *Weekly* building.”

“It’s objective journalism,” he corrected. “How would it look if I rented a space from her and then had to report that she’s guilty of murder?”

“Bad, I guess.” She shrugged. “I know you’re upset about this, Ryan. Maybe it would help if we talk.”

He pulled the Honda into a parking place in front of a three-story brick office building in the business district of downtown Durham. “After we talk to Marco.”

“You know you’ll feel better if we talk about it.”

“We will.” He took off his seat belt. “Look, I know you’re concerned. I appreciate that, Maggie. But I have to come up with some answers for my story about Donald before I can deal with losing the building.”

“I know.” She touched his cheek. “I’m worried about you. That’s all.”

He turned his head and kissed her hand. “This isn’t just for me. I don’t want Frank to go any further investigating Clara either.”

Durham Singles Dating Service was on the top floor. They took the elevator up, and Ryan pointed to the small sign for the company.

“I thought it would be bigger,” Maggie said.

"All he needs is a computer," Ryan replied. "It's pure profit. Maybe I should make the *Weekly* an online-only paper. I could cut out a lot of my costs that way."

"But you'd lose readers like Aunt Clara. She won't go near a computer unless she has to. I think she likes the paper smell too, and holding it in her hands."

He opened the door with the name "Durham Singles" on it. "That's true."

"Can I help you?" A beautiful, exotic-looking woman was seated at a small desk in a tiny outer office. There were two metal folding chairs set in front of her.

"I'm looking for Marco." Ryan flashed his *Durham Weekly* press pass. "I'm Ryan Summerour."

The woman looked suitably impressed. "He's in his office. He's expecting you."

"Thanks." Ryan opened the door into the second minuscule office, holding it for Maggie to go in before him.

If Ryan was right, this was the heart of Durham Singles. There was a laptop and a big computer on a desk beside a workspace where Marco was sitting.

Marco Ricci was of strong Italian descent with a large Roman nose and deep-set dark eyes. His black hair was threaded with strands of silver.

"You must be with the paper." Marco stood and shook hands with Ryan.

"Yes." Ryan also gave him a business card and flashed his press pass again. "Ryan Summerour. The *Durham Weekly*."

"Of course. I think we run a regular ad in your paper." Marco sat down again. "What can I do for you?"

"I'm here to talk about Donald Wickerson. I spoke with you on the phone. You said you've met him."

"That's right. We host an occasional meet and greet for our clients. Mr. Wickerson was at our last event." Ryan took out his phone and started taking notes. "When was that?"

"The meet and greet was about a month ago. Mr. Wickerson said he was new to the area and was interested in meeting some other Silver Foxes."

"But you had a few women who were interested in him that weren't Silver Foxes, right?" Maggie felt as though she should say something. It wasn't her style to sit and watch.

Ryan glanced at her with a quizzical look in his eyes.

Marco nodded. "You know there's always someone looking for a person much older—and much younger. We don't ask our clients why they need who they need. Our job is to help them find that special person."

"Did you notice anyone in particular with Mr. Wickerson while he was at the meet and greet?"

Ryan said it quickly, as though he was afraid Maggie might ask before him.

"As a matter of fact, he hit it off with one of our other clients. We have hundreds of new clients of all ages every week, you know."

"And she was younger?" Ryan tapped the answers into his cell phone.

"Oh yes. *Much* younger. And very good-looking. *Sexy.*" Marco grinned. "Know what I mean?"

"What's her name?"

"I can't give you her name. I'm sorry." Marco ran his hand through his thick black hair. "We have a strict privacy policy. We're famous for it. Our clients depend on our integrity."

"You know the police are investigating Mr. Wickerson's death as a homicide." Ryan's voice was smooth, his manner calm, as though the information meant nothing to him. "I suppose they haven't contacted you yet. I haven't written anything about Wickerson being part of the dating service yet."

Marco looked a little shaken. "I haven't heard from the police. We *do* keep that ad in your paper, Summerour. That should mean something. Maybe you could leave us out of your story."

"I'll do that as much as possible," Ryan promised. "The police already know that the dating service is involved with what Wickerson was doing. I won't divulge you as a source, but I can't promise what the police will do."

"All right. Give me a minute." Marco began to search through his files.

• • •

It seems to me that Debbie was going out of her way to make sure she kept tabs on Donald."

"Odd, since she said she didn't want to date him." Ryan held the door to the street open for Maggie.

He'd shaken hands with Marco after he'd given him Debbie Blackwelder's name, and they'd left his office.

"That doesn't mean she killed him," Maggie pointed out. "She sort of admitted that she found him attractive. I don't think it's surprising that she would chase him a little."

"Why are women interested in someone so much older?"

"Why are men interested in women who are *so* much younger?"

"I don't know. I wouldn't even know what to say to a woman in her early twenties."

"I don't think it has anything to do with *conversation*."

Ryan scowled. "You mean younger women only want to have sex with really older men?"

Maggie laughed. "No, they want to talk to them too. I think it's the wisdom factor. They've been a lot of places and know a lot of things. There's a maturity level that isn't there in younger men."

They paused for a red light, and Ryan looked at her. "Are you saying I'm immature?"

"Not exactly," she teased. "But men like Donald, or your father, are fascinating."

"You better be joking. If you start dating my dad—"

She kissed his cheek lightly. "Why would I want to be with your father when I could be with you—and we could spend all of our time running around chasing stories for the newspaper?"

"Exactly." The light changed and he started the car forward. "Wait. What?"

"Never mind." She laughed. "So we like Debbie for Donald's murder. What can we do to prove it?"

"For starters, we can see if she owns a nine-millimeter pistol."

"Which she wouldn't have, if it was the one that killed Donald, because it was found behind Pie in the Sky."

"True, but if she can't account for it, that adds to her profile as Donald's killer. And in my experience, where there's one gun, there are at least two more. My dad has about thirty of them. It's like collecting anything else."

"Even if we find out she has thirty other nine-millimeter pistols, that won't mean the one that killed Donald was hers. Besides, with the numbers filed off the gun, how would we know if it was hers or not?"

"If you build up enough circumstantial evidence in a case, you can do something with it. It might not be enough to arrest her, but we could take it to Frank and he could look into more about Debbie than we can find on the Internet."

"Is that even possible? I thought you could find out as much as the police."

"Not without paying for it."

"What did you find out about David? Don't bother telling me you didn't look."

"I didn't have time to do more than a cursory search," he admitted. "He seems to be who he says he is. No surprises."

Maggie didn't tell him that her aunt said she hadn't asked David to check the furnace. After all, it was probably only male chest pounding. There was enough of that going on already between him and Ryan.

They got back to Ryan's house as Aunt Clara and Garrett were setting the table for dinner. In honor of the occasion, Garrett had gone down to his wine cellar and taken out a bottle of muscadine wine from one of the local vineyards in the area.

"I feel like I'm presenting my first pie." Aunt Clara giggled as she put on large oven mitts and started to take the chicken potpies out of the oven.

"Let me help you with that." Garrett was eager in his attempt to assist her—too eager. He thrust his hands into the oven and grasped the cookie sheet that held the potpies. He let out a loud yelp and quickly released it.

"Are you all right?" Aunt Clara dropped the big mitts and looked at his hand. "Oh, it's very red. It may blister. Let's get it into some ice water."

Maggie picked up the gloves and moved the potpies out of the oven.

Ryan filled a bowl with crushed ice from the freezer. Aunt Clara put water into it and guided Garrett to the table where he could ice his fingers.

"I'm perfectly fine, Clara," he said in a gruff voice. "No need to make a fuss."

He started to take his hand out of the bowl. She immediately pushed it back down and held her delicate hand over his.

"Now, don't be a hero," she admonished. "A burn can be very bad. You sit here and leave your hand in the bowl. By the time everything is ready for dinner, you'll be in good shape."

Garrett subsided. His fate was clear. He even smiled as Clara patted his hand.

"I'd really like to have some salad with this." Maggie peered into the refrigerator. "Anyone else want some? There's romaine, cucumber, and a few carrots."

"None for me." Aunt Clara and Garrett said the same thing at the same moment.

"Jinx!" she called out. Garrett smiled.

"I'll help you with that," Ryan said. "Any fresh veggies you see in here are mine. Dad won't touch them."

"Aunt Clara is the same way. Makes you wonder how they got to their ripe old ages when they don't eat vegetables."

"Who's a ripe old age?" Garrett roared out.

"I believe she was talking about someone else. Both of us are barely middle-aged." Aunt Clara smiled at him as she continued to hold his hand in the bowl of ice water.

Maggie grinned at Ryan. She couldn't have asked for a better opportunity to bring her aunt and Ryan's father closer together. She really believed they had a lot in common. She knew Garrett liked her aunt. It was a matter of convincing Aunt Clara that Garrett could talk about more than politics.

When the salad was ready, and the potpie had been sliced and put on white china plates, everyone sat down to eat. Aunt Clara skipped the wine and had sweet tea instead. Garrett gallantly toasted her help in saving his hand from a horrible burn. By that time, his hand had been removed from the ice water and Clara had expertly dried it.

"So did you two find anything interesting when you went out?" Aunt Clara asked.

"We found another piece of the Debbie Blackwelder puzzle." Ryan cut a piece of pie with his fork and put it in his mouth. "Wow! This is great."

Aunt Clara blushed prettily. "Thank you. Maggie, you did an excellent job on this filling."

"How many pies are you going to need for the library fund-raiser?" Maggie asked.

"Probably twenty."

Maggie almost choked. "Really? That's a lot of potpies."

"You said I should show up Lenora by making potpies. How many did you think I'd need? It's the biggest event of the year!" Aunt Clara struck an indignant pose.

"That's fine." Maggie thought about the number of pies they made every day for the pie shop. "If we bake them at Pie in the Sky, we can do it a lot faster."

"I'd love to test them on the lunch crowd." Aunt Clara ate another piece of potpie. "I'm sure they'd be a hit. We don't dare, though—not until *after* the event. We don't want Lenora to steal our idea and make potpies."

Garrett cleared his throat. Maggie noticed that he had a habit of doing that each time before he spoke. It was as though he was about to make a speech in front of an audience and had something important to say.

"I was thinking about this problem you've been having with the police, Clara."

She waved her hand. “I wouldn’t call it a problem, Garrett. Detective Waters is a little worried that I may have killed Donald after reading the truth about him in your paper.”

“I was thinking that you could use a good lawyer,” Garrett continued. “I know it’s nothing right now, but it might be better to be prepared for it to be something. Our lawyer is on retainer. I’d be happy to arrange a meeting with him for you.”

“I appreciate that,” Aunt Clara replied. “But I’m fine. You’re a good friend to offer.”

They ate in silence for a while. Maggie hoped Garrett would drop that idea since her aunt seemed opposed to it. His way of strong-arming situations was something Aunt Clara didn’t like about him.

“I didn’t know you still had a lawyer on retainer,” Ryan said to his father. “Is that for the paper?”

“Of course. Every professional newspaper needs a lawyer. What if someone decided to sue you over a story?” Garrett asked. “What would you do without a lawyer?”

“We have access to attorneys as members of the Press Association. We can cut that expense from the budget. What else are you still spending money on for the paper that I don’t know about?”

Garrett’s shaggy eyebrows rose in an imperious manner. “I think I know what’s best for the paper, son. Let’s not argue about this in front of the ladies.”

The doorbell rang before Ryan could say anything more. Maggie could see that dinner was over for him. He had plenty he wanted to discuss with his father.

Garrett went to answer the door and came back with Albert Mann at his side.

"I thought we might as well close the deal on the building while it's still hot." Albert smiled when he noticed Clara and Maggie there. "Good evening, ladies."

"What are *you* doing here?" Ryan got to his feet

"I'm here to sign the papers on the *Durham Weekly* building, of course." Albert held up his briefcase. "I have a fresh pen ready to sign."

"Not tonight," Ryan protested. "We're not making any deals yet."

Sixteen

"Garrett, I thought this was a done deal," Albert said in an irritated voice. "I don't have time to bicker about this."

"Good," Ryan said. "No bickering. Just leave."

"Son, this isn't something I want to do either. We have no choice." Garrett tried to make his case, but Ryan stopped him.

"I've barely had time to think about his offer—or consider alternatives. We can't sell the building yet. Not until I know that I've tried everything I can to save it."

"Unless you can figure out a way to come up with a lot of money very quickly," Garrett threatened, "we'll simply lose the building to the county without any profit at all."

Ryan's expression was taut and angry. "Then I guess we'll lose the building, Dad. I need more time to think about it."

"Gentlemen?" Albert got their attention with a slick smile. "This offer won't last on the property. I'm giving you a lot more than I would anyone else, even though I'm going to have to foot the bill for razing the building. Don't make me wait."

"Not tonight." Ryan's tone was ragged. "I'm on my way out. Let me walk you to the front door."

Ryan left the house with an anguished glance at his father. Maggie could hear Albert grumbling until they got outside and the heavy front door closed behind them. Both cars started up and drove away after a few minutes. She imagined Ryan had had plenty to say to Albert.

Maggie wished she'd gone with him.

Instead, she helped Garrett and her aunt clean the kitchen before they sat down to a rousing game of Scrabble. The night dragged along until it was finally time for bed. Maggie wasn't sure if she had ever been so happy to say good night and escape.

She tried calling Ryan's cell phone. He didn't answer. She left a voice mail. He didn't respond. She understood that he was angry, but felt sure sharing it with her would make it better. Wasn't that what relationships were for?

Maggie and her aunt fed and stroked Fanny and her kittens. They had all stayed in the box they'd brought for them. The kittens weren't old enough to be adventurous yet. Once they were, nothing would be safe.

"Don't worry," Aunt Clara said. "Ryan will be fine. Sometimes we have to do things we don't want to do. Garrett doesn't want to get rid of the office either. Imagine the memories that are there for him. I don't even like to *think* about giving up the pie shop."

"I hope you never have to," Maggie agreed. "I'm more upset about Ryan leaving the way he did. He won't return my calls either."

"We all need a little alone time, don't we?"

"I guess so. I didn't expect him to leave while we were staying here tonight. It's a little awkward."

Aunt Clara hugged her. "I don't think so. We have nice beds, and we had a good meal. That's all I need. So you really think we should go with the savory potpies for the library fund-raiser? We aren't known for that."

Maggie sat on her bed cross-legged. "I think it could be a good thing for us to be known for. The library fund-raiser is popular. It could be exactly what we need to introduce the new product line."

"I love your new vocabulary." Her aunt sat beside her. "You sound so professional."

"Thanks. I guess that's a good thing."

"Fred and I got by on our good pies, great location, and nice personalities. Times change. I think you need more now."

"I don't know. I think that's the most important part of what we do." Maggie warmed to her subject. "People are starving for more than just food. They want attention, and they want to feel like they're at home."

"That's what I think too!" Clara bounced on the bed a little. "You and I think so much alike. I think we always did. It's so wonderful having you back home. It's a joy to be with you."

Maggie hugged her with tears in her eyes. It had taken a long time to reach this place with her aunt, but it was worth every misstep.

They talked for a while longer, and then Maggie said good night. She lay down in the spare room but couldn't sleep. It was too much like being in a hotel. She was never comfortable in those places, no matter how expensive.

Around midnight, she heard the front door open downstairs and got up to see if it was Ryan. She peeked over the railing into the foyer and watched him close and lock the door behind him.

Despite her Santa flannels, she crept downstairs to talk to him, following him into the well-stocked library.

The library was off of the main hall downstairs. He jumped when she called his name. He'd been in the process of pouring himself a drink from a crystal decanter. He seemed to be lost in thought.

"Sorry. I didn't mean to startle you," she apologized.

"That's okay. Come on in. I'm going to light a fire and get pleasantly drunk."

Maggie folded her legs under her in a comfortable chair near the fireplace. It was a massive stone hearth that was appropriate for the castle-like design of the Summerour home. There were two large lions guarding it, seated on marble bases.

Ryan sat opposite her with a glass of scotch. Maggie had declined to drink with him.

"I guess it may be official and we're going to lose the office," he declared in a flat tone. "I talked to everyone I could think of while I was out—everyone I knew with money who might like to invest. Nothing. It sucks being poor."

"I wouldn't exactly call you *poor*." She glanced around the stately room. "Maybe you could get a second mortgage on this place. It must be worth a fortune."

"It probably is, but my job description—editor-in-chief of a losing proposition—doesn't make me a good candidate for a loan. Newspapers are closing left and right. The banks know that too."

"There must be something you can do. I know

you feel the same way about the office that Aunt Clara feels about Pie in the Sky."

He sipped his drink, eyes gleaming with the light from the fire. "I love the old place. I'm sure I could get along without it if I had to, but losing it makes me feel like another piece of the *Durham Weekly* is gone forever. I'm not ready for that yet. I don't understand how Dad can sell it to Albert."

Maggie went to him and slid her arms around his neck. "You aren't looking in the right direction. You're smart. You'll find a way."

He kissed her. "Thanks. I don't know if things always work out that way. I appreciate the thought."

"You've helped me with my problems. Let me help you with yours."

He grinned. "Have you got a few hundred thousand dollars you can spare? I can't tell you when I can pay it back."

"I may have something much better—a smart boyfriend who is a problem solver. Want me to loan him to you for a while?"

"Please. Send him over."

• • •

Maggie was up early the next morning. There was no sign of Ryan. She knew he'd gone to bed late. She'd finally left him alone in the library when she'd begun nodding off as he was telling her about his childhood memories of the paper.

It wasn't that she was bored with his stories about taking photos at fires and helping his mother write copy. She was exhausted. Getting up at 5:00 a.m. took a lot out of her. She needed to be in bed by ten to survive.

Garrett and Aunt Clara were up and making cinnamon rolls for breakfast when she came down. The two of them were whispering and giggling as they rolled out the dough and cut the rolls to put them into the oven.

Aunt Clara smiled when she saw Maggie. "There you are. I had a strange call from Margie Walker this morning. She said David fixed our furnace during the night. Maybe you could go over and check it out."

"Please, take my car." Garrett handed her the keys. "It would be wonderful if your furnace was repaired, even though I would hate to lose my two lovely houseguests."

"These won't be ready for about twenty minutes." Aunt Clara nodded toward the oven. "You could probably get there and be back in time for breakfast."

Maggie wasn't sure if her aunt was trying to get rid of her or if she was in a hurry to get back home. Either way was good for her. She hadn't slept well and would be glad to have her own bed back before Monday morning.

"I'll go take a look. Should I offer David money if the furnace is working? I'm not sure how to react to someone spending the night in our basement, working on the furnace."

"Of course you can't offer him money," Aunt Clara said. "Unless he needed the money, which we know he doesn't. Since we know that, it would be better to make dinner for him. That would be appropriate."

"Okay." Maggie knew Ryan would be thrilled with her making dinner for David.

But she knew she could deal with Ryan. David wasn't staying in Durham. Ryan would forget him after a while. It wasn't as much fun as she'd thought to begin with, seeing Ryan jealous. She was ready to be done with it.

Maggie put on her coat and gloves and went to check on the furnace.

It was hard to imagine that David, who she hadn't seen in years, would want to do this for them on what must be his vacation. She certainly appreciated it, but she wasn't sure she would do the same for him, even if she knew how.

He'd always been a very generous, good-hearted boy. Those traits seemed to have followed him into adulthood.

It was really nice having a car to drive, even though it was a larger, older vehicle. Walking was okay in a big city, but all the real shopping was miles away from where they lived.

Taxis were unreliable and expensive, something she'd never thought about when she'd lived in New

York. Taking a bus was fine unless you had your arms full of clothes, food, or other supplies. She wasn't crazy about that. Even if they didn't use a car every day, it would be nice to have one.

Of course, that would be a major expense—much bigger than the furnace she'd been trying to save money for. On the other hand, if David *had* repaired the furnace, that could leave her free to save for a car.

Filled with her plans for the future, Maggie pulled Garrett's car into a parking space in front of their house. Even though she hadn't called to tell David she was coming home, he was sitting on their porch waiting for her.

"How long have you been here?" she asked when she got out of the car.

It was cold. His face was red from sitting outside. She felt bad knowing he'd been there.

"Only a few hours. I think your furnace will be fine now. I went upstairs after I fixed it, and it turned right on."

They'd been children the last time she and David had spent time together. This adult David was a stranger to her. Aunt Clara had never mentioned him coming over and talking to her while Maggie had been in New York. She guessed that she had inspired this sudden interest.

"Come inside and get warm," she invited as she opened the front door.

"Thanks. I'd forgotten how cold it can get here!"

The house was toasty warm inside. The furnace was still a little wheezy but doing its job.

Maggie turned to David after putting down her handbag. It was true that she wouldn't have known him without the introduction. So much of that fifteen-year-old she remembered was gone. He was still taller than she was, and thin. She used to tease him about how much he ate without gaining any weight.

His eyes, serious and chocolate brown, were the same, even behind the wire-rimmed glasses. How many times did they sit close together, dreaming about distant planets and what their grown-up lives were going to be like?

"Thanks for doing this. I feel kind of awkward about it. Who spends all night working on someone else's furnace?"

"A furnace repair man?"

She laughed. "Seriously. What do I owe you?"

"Nothing. I did it for you—and Aunt Clara."

He had a very nice smile. Somewhere along the time they'd been apart, he'd gotten his teeth fixed. At one time, he'd had a gap between his two front teeth.

"I appreciate that, David. I don't want you to be out of pocket. It was nice enough for you to spend your vacation time taking care of it for me and Aunt Clara. I don't want you to pay for anything."

"Don't be silly. It wasn't that much. I think you

should comfortably be able to get a few more years from the furnace. I was glad to be able to help."

What else could she say? They stood awkwardly in the foyer together. She could at least make him breakfast.

"I don't cook much besides pies, but I can make coffee, and I think we have some cookies."

"Sounds great!" He rubbed his hands together. His eyes held hers. "I love eating cookies for breakfast."

They sat across from each other at the kitchen table, drinking coffee and eating chocolate chip cookies. They talked about all the memories they shared of growing up here.

"Remember that time when Margaret Winstead was waiting for me after school?" Maggie shook her head at the past. "She was big and mean! She wanted to kick me around the corner a few times."

He laughed. "Instead, she kicked *me*!"

"She did! We walked home and I put the steak in your mom's fridge on your eye."

"And then you went back and beat up Margaret Winstead. She never bothered us again!"

She started to refill his cup. He put his hand on hers.

"That's it for me, thanks. I'm not much of a coffee drinker anymore."

She smiled and filled her own cup instead. "I'm still hooked on the stuff. I lived on it in New York."

He studied her closely. "You did it, though. You made it to that big job you always wanted."

"I did," she agreed. "And I almost lost myself doing it."

"I never wanted to do anything more than skateboard around the block, and now look at me."

"How did you end up in Florida?"

He shrugged. "It was a good opportunity. But Mom and Dad aren't as young as they used to be. Dad had a heart attack last year."

"That's terrible. Are you moving back to Durham?"

"I'm thinking about it. Are you staying?"

"Definitely yes!"

He glanced at his watch. "I guess I should go. I promised Mom a trip to the mall. You're welcome to come along—Aunt Clara too."

"I guess we have to bring everything home today, but thank you." Maggie tried her aunt's suggestion about making dinner for him. "When are you going back to Florida? We'd love to have you over for dinner one night."

"That would be great, thanks. I'll be here for a while, so no rush." He got to his feet. "Thanks for the cookies, Maggie. It was fun getting caught up."

She walked him to the back door. "It was fun, David. Just let me know when is good for you. And come by the pie shop sometime. Any pie you want—on the house—for furnace repair."

"I'll do that." He bent close to her and kissed her cheek. "You're exactly the way I remember you, Maggie. I hope we can talk more later."

Maggie touched a hand to her cheek when he was gone. David had grown up very nicely.

Seventeen

Aunt Clara was thrilled that they were moving their belongings back into the house.

Ryan had gone out again before Maggie got back. He was still trying to figure out some way to save the *Weekly* office. Maggie struggled with the box of kittens. Fanny had jumped down on the stairs on the way in. She was circling Maggie's feet, weaving in and out between her footsteps. It was hard not to trip over her or step on her.

"Well, it was very sweet of David to get the furnace fixed, wasn't it?" Aunt Clara pushed the rest of their belongings into the foyer. “He was always a very sweet boy. I’ve missed seeing him.”

“We had a good talk too.” Maggie smiled at the thought of sharing her memories with him. “I think I missed him without even realizing it.”

Aunt Clara slammed the door shut. “You know, he *was* your friend. The two of you were inseparable for a while.”

There was a knock at the door. “May I come in?”

“Oh, Garrett!” Aunt Clara realized she’d slammed the door in his face and quickly opened it. “I’m so sorry. Are you all right?”

“I’m fine.” He wiggled his nose with his fingers. “I’ve always thought I needed to get my nose bobbed. Too long, you know.”

She giggled. “I think your nose is perfectly fine the way it is. Thank you for bringing in the pie-making equipment.” She took all of her kitchenware from him. “Would you like to come in and sit down?”

“I don’t mind if I do.”

“I’m going to make lunch,” Aunt Clara said. “Will you stay and eat with us, Garrett?”

“That would be wonderful.”

Maggie heard his reply from upstairs.

She sighed and tried calling Ryan again. Still no answer. She knew he was out there, relentlessly searching for some way to save the office. She supposed she’d have to give him some leeway in his hour of need. She wished there was something she could do to help.

Her conversation with David bothered her a little. Was it possible she still had feelings for him?

It seemed unlikely. It was only a moment, remembering the past they'd shared. Nothing more. That kiss in the doorway was only something two friends would share.

It was a lazy Sunday afternoon for Clara and Maggie. They went out with Garrett after lunch to get a litter box for Fanny and her kittens. They also purchased food bowls and a climbing perch for the cats to scratch on.

When they'd come back, Garrett said he was exhausted and soon fell asleep on the sofa in the parlor. His snores echoed through the house. Maggie hoped he'd be able to keep up with Aunt Clara if the two of them continued to be friends. She was as energetic as a twelve-year-old sometimes. After that, they played with the cats and came up with a purchase order list for Mr. Gino that included what they needed for the chicken potpies.

"Let's also ask him about your ice cream idea," Aunt Clara said. "It's a long way until next summer, but you know how that goes. One day it's Christmas, and the next it's the Fourth of July."

Maggie laughed. "I'm glad it doesn't *really* go by that fast."

Her aunt agreed but was still determined to get

a price quote on a freezer and ice cream for the hot weather. "I don't know why I didn't think of it myself. You realize you'll have to do most of the ice cream scooping, right?"

"I know. If it helps keep our customers happy, I can scoop with the best of them."

Garrett finally went home after dinner that night when he'd heard they were planning to go to an outdoor winter carnival. He hugged Clara awkwardly and said he'd like to see her again.

Aunt Clara didn't make any firm plans. She thanked him for letting them stay at his home and straightened his coat collar. Maggie hid behind the stairs while they were in the foyer, but there was no kiss.

When Garrett was gone, they bundled up and walked to the nearby park where the winter carnival was being held. There were puppet shows, a man-made ice-skating rink, and even an ice sculpture contest.

The tiny white lights in the trees looked beautiful as visitors strolled the paths. College students had used a snow-making machine to enhance the frozen ground, which was brown and bare. There were piles of wet snow everywhere.

Ryan was there taking pictures for the paper.

Maggie almost decided to pretend she hadn't seen him. He'd been ignoring her phone calls and texts all day. She knew he was working, or had been looking for funding so he could keep the office. Still, he could've taken a moment to get back with her. She knew he was in a bad place, but it still rankled being ignored.

"There you are." Aunt Clara skipped around two babies being pulled along the park paths in a cute sled. "Where have you been all day? Maggie has been worried sick about you."

Maggie was thankful for the darkness around them. She couldn't help but smile at Aunt Clara's aggressive questioning on her behalf. She wouldn't have asked those questions the same way. She felt bad for Ryan—even if she was also a little angry.

He slung his camera over his shoulder. "I'm sorry, Aunt Clara. You too, Maggie. I haven't been avoiding you. I think I may have come up with a good idea to save the office. I won't know for a few days if it's going to work. I'd rather not talk about it until then, if you don't mind. I'm a little superstitious. Dad said you moved back to your house. Is the furnace fixed?"

"Yes, it is." Aunt Clara smiled up at him. "David Walker from next door repaired it for us. He's such a *sweet* man. And now that he may be living in Durham again, we'll be seeing a lot of him."

"Oh?" Ryan's gaze went to Maggie's. "I guess that's what I get for being out of the loop. You didn't get married while I was gone today, did you?"

"No," Clara said. "But he did ask her to marry

him when they were fourteen. I can't recall what your answer was, Maggie."

Maggie was ready to move past her aunt trying to make Ryan jealous. "Nice night, huh?"

"That's exactly what I was thinking. I'm glad you came."

"I'm going to get some snow cream." Aunt Clara laughed. "I hope they have banana flavor. That was my favorite when I was a child."

Ryan took out his camera again and snapped a few pictures of people using chain saws to carve large blocks of ice into bears, horses, and dragons. "I'm sorry, Maggie."

She could barely hear him over the sound of the chain saws. The smell of gasoline was overpowering. "What?"

He took her hand, and they walked away from the sound and smell. "I'm sorry about being out of touch today and last night. I'm not usually that way, am I?"

"Not usually. A text once in a while would be nice. But I understand."

Ryan put his arms around her. "I know. I get caught up. I try not to let it happen."

"I know you do." She hugged him too. Her eyes narrowed on a familiar form a few yards away, watching them. "This is going to be weird."

"What?" He started to look around.

She held him tighter. “No. Don’t look back. Debbie Blackwelder is watching us.”

“She’s watching *us*?” It was all he could do not to look at her. “We must have rattled her cage.”

“So she’s going to stalk us? We’re nowhere near her salon. She must know we live around here.”

“Well, if she killed Donald and made it look like Clara did it, it’s a good bet she’s been to the pie shop. It would be easy to follow you from there.”

“Great. I wasn’t looking for that when I went with you.”

“Cheer up. Maybe she’s following *me*.”

“That makes me feel *so* much better. What do we do?”

“Ignore her—unless she makes a move. We know Frank talked to her. It’s not like we’re the only ones. Is she still there?”

“No. I don’t see her.” She let go of his arm. “It’s getting colder. I think I’m going to find Aunt Clara and head home.”

“I’ll call you later. Promise.” Ryan grinned and kissed her. “If I’m right, it’ll be a much different story later this week—at least about what we can do with the office. I can’t wait to show my dad that I can handle problems that come up with the newspaper. He can’t armchair quarterback the business anymore.”

They said good night. Maggie found Aunt Clara,

and they linked arms to walk home on the sidewalks that still had thin ice covering them.

"Did they have banana snow cream?" Maggie watched her eat the concoction.

"No. They had watermelon. It's delicious. Want to try some?" Aunt Clara held out a spoon of the frozen sweet.

"Thanks." Maggie tried it and licked her lips. "Good."

"Ladies." A man dressed like an elf, complete with green pointy-toed slippers, stopped them. In the dark—and in costume—it was hard to say how old he was or exactly what he looked like. "My name is Randy Bannister. A man back there at the carnival pointed you out to me. You must be Clara Lowder? I'm a member of Durham Singles."

Aunt Clara sighed and put her gloved hand on her forehead. "Not again."

"You're supposed to email," Maggie told him. "Do none of you understand that?"

He shrugged his elfish green shoulders. "The early bird gets the worm. Would you like to go out for coffee?"

They both put their heads down and walked as quickly as they could away from the elf. Maggie reminded herself that the first thing she had to do when she got home was to remove Aunt Clara from the Durham Singles list.

• • •

It was cold and clear on Monday morning when the two women made their trek from the house to the pie shop. Fanny went with them, despite their best efforts to persuade her to stay home with her kittens.

"She might tear up the house trying to get out if we don't bring her with us," Aunt Clara said. "She knows how long we'll be gone. She knows what her babies need."

Maggie wasn't quite as convinced that the cat knew what she was doing. She was probably already adapting to their schedule, and she wasn't thinking at all about her hungry babies.

It looked as though they were stuck with her for the morning, at least. She supposed she could always walk back after lunch with the cat. By that time, Fanny might be glad to stay home with her kittens.

The streets were so quiet at that time of the morning. It seemed hard to believe how much traffic would go through here over the next few hours as commuters made their way to school and work.

They were surprised to see Frank waiting outside the pie shop when they arrived.

Maggie looked at his solemn face in the multicolored glow of the Christmas lights on the window as Aunt Clara opened the front door. She knew it wasn't a good thing that he was there.

"We have to talk," he said. "I hope the coffee is strong this morning."

Aunt Clara laughed as she switched on the interior lights. "You're at Pie in the Sky, Frank, 'where the coffee is strong and the pie is sweet.' My late husband used to say that. We ran a series of jingles with it on the radio one year. It was very successful, but too expensive."

Maggie waited until Aunt Clara had walked into the kitchen. "What's wrong, Frank? Why are you here?"

He took off his gloves and the cap he wore that covered his ears. "I wouldn't do this if I didn't have to. You know I wouldn't. The idea that Clara killed anyone is ludicrous. If it was up to me, I wouldn't take her in for questioning."

"*Take her in for questioning?*" Maggie's voice trembled as it went up and down like a bad musical instrument. "No. That's not right. You know she'd never hurt anyone. I'm sure she has no idea how to use a gun. You said there was no gunshot residue on her hands."

Frank put his hand on hers. "You know I feel the same. The captain had to remind me that we have to look through all potential suspects. She'll be fine. We both know she didn't do anything wrong. It just *looks* bad right now. Every other suspect we've run down has ended up with an unbreakable alibi."

"I want to go with her."

"You can come too, although you'd be better off calling a lawyer for her—and *I* didn't tell you that."

Maggie thought about Garrett's offer of his lawyer to help her aunt. "I'll call someone. Let me tell her."

She went back to the kitchen, where her aunt was humming as she began new piecrusts. Maggie put her arm around her and tearfully told her what Frank had said.

Aunt Clara stared at her for a moment, as though she couldn't take it in. Then she said, "Rubbish! Frank thinks I killed Donald? What is the world coming to? The police can't find the killer, so they grab anyone they can and try to pin it on them. Lousy coppers!"

It was so different than the response Maggie had expected that she laughed out loud. "Please don't call them that while you're at the police station."

Frank came into the kitchen and looked inquiringly at both of them. "Is everything all right in here? Clara, I wouldn't do this if my job didn't depend on it. Do you need some time to freshen up or something?"

"Spare me." She wiped her hands on a towel and went to get her coat and scarf. "This better not take too long, Frank, or you'll have to send someone to come and help Maggie make pies."

Astonishment in his eyes, Frank glanced at Maggie, who shrugged.

"I'll make it as quick as I can," he said.

"Don't worry about me, Aunt Clara. I'll take care of the shop. I'm calling Garrett's lawyer too. Everything will be fine."

Clara muttered to herself as Frank held the door to the pie shop for her and then opened his car door. Maggie got on the phone right away, but Garrett's lawyer was unavailable.

Now what should I do?

Providence sent Ralph Heinz, a lawyer and longtime family friend, into the pie shop for an early coffee and a slice of pumpkin pie. He confessed, as he ordered, that he didn't tell his doctor that he stopped by the pie shop regularly.

"Can you help Aunt Clara?" Maggie described the circumstances to the plump, gray-haired man.

His eyes focused sharply behind his thick glasses. "I don't really do that *kind* of legal work anymore. The stress was unbearable. I'm mostly estates, wills, and money matters. There was a time when I first got out of law school that I thought about being a public defender, though. I could sit in on the questioning with Clara."

Maggie ran around the counter and hugged him. "She's already on her way there. Can you go now?"

He looked at his pie and coffee. "Save this for me. I'll be back later."

"Thanks, Mr. Heinz. Bring her home, please."

Eighteen

He promised to do his best and went back out the front door.

Maggie was pleased with being able to find a lawyer at the last minute. She couldn't do any more than that for her aunt.

The whole idea of Aunt Clara being a killer was crazy anyway. Captain Mitchell would realize it once he talked to her aunt.

Panic set in as she realized that there were no fresh pies. The slices remaining in the refrigerated case wouldn't last an hour with normal traffic.

She called Ryan. “I have an emergency.”

“I’m on it,” he replied. “I’ll be there in five minutes.”

An hour later, Maggie and Ryan had an efficient system worked out. She made the pies and filled the orders he gave her. He took the money and poured the drinks. Instead of delivering pie to the tables, he took names and called them out as orders were ready.

The cat, who’d run to the alley again, started scratching on the back door. Maggie took a moment to give her some food. Fanny ran inside the kitchen instead.

“I know I said I’d take you home this morning, but something has come up. You’re going to have to cooperate with the system like the rest of us. As soon as we have a break, I’ll work something out. In the meantime, sit right here or you’ll have to go back outside in the cold. I told you to stay home this morning.”

She laughed at herself for talking to the cat even as Ryan rang the order bell again. There was a knock at the back door. Maggie opened it, and the cat ran out.

Mr. Gino walked in. “Where’s Clara?” He fingered his thick mustache as he looked around.

“She had to run out and take care of some legal matters.” Maggie danced around the question and answer. She wasn't prepared to handle this today—she wasn't prepared for any of it!

"She called and said she had some things to talk about."

"You can talk to me, Mr. Gino. We were both going to discuss some things with you."

Mr. Gino shrugged, the movement nearly making his large mustache touch his shoulders. "All right. You're the new partner. What do you need?"

Maggie talked as she made and filled piecrusts. She pulled a tray of ten mincemeat pies from the oven. In between those tasks, she mixed up eggnog pie filling and set it in the refrigerator. Mr. Gino opened the refrigerator door for her and smiled.

"The bell stopped working. I think it's broken." Ryan stuck his head around the doorway. "Do you want me to yell out the orders or what?"

"Just put them in the service window. I'll get them."

Ryan greeted Mr. Gino with a nod of his head. "Okay. I need three slices of Pumpkin Pizzazz."

"How's the coffee urn doing?" Maggie asked. "Have you checked it recently? It may need more coffee."

"I only have two hands," Ryan retorted. "Both of them are covered in whipped cream and pie."

Mr. Gino snorted. "What's the big fuss? Let me take a look at it for you."

He ambled into the dining area, which was packed with Pie in the Sky patrons.

When Mr. Gino came back into the kitchen, the coffeemaker was working. "There. You should be set up for a while. I'll go over your list and get back with you on prices. Chicken potpies sound like a good idea to me. And Pie in the Sky would be the only spot around here to serve ice cream in the summer. Good idea!"

"Thanks, Mr. Gino." Maggie was grateful for his help and his feedback.

Ryan called out that he needed two slices of apple pie with cheddar. "And how do I use the espresso machine? I knew someone was going to want one."

"Tell them it's broken and the next one is on the house."

"Gotcha."

When the rush was over two hours later, Maggie and Ryan slumped into chairs, exhausted by their efforts.

"How do you do this every day?" he asked her.

"I just do it. How do you sit through all those boring city meetings without going to sleep?"

He smiled. "Who said I don't sleep through them? I record everything so I can listen to it later."

They both laughed at that. Maggie asked if he had any news about his new idea to save the *Weekly* office. He told her he was still banking on the idea he'd set in motion.

"We have to figure out who actually killed Donald." Maggie was finally able to express her fear and frustration. "I don't like that the police have run out of suspects to the point that they wanted to take Aunt Clara in for questioning."

"That's what we've been doing. I have some new information from the ME. I'm not sure how much good it will do us."

"Let's hear it."

He took out his cell phone and looked at his notes. "The ME's assistant found traces of hand lotion on Donald's face."

"Is that it? That doesn't sound like much."

"There was also lipstick on his lapel. The police aren't sure if that happened while he was killed or before. The shooter was very close, so it could go either way. They're trying to match the shade and possibly brand."

"I wish they'd find something more conclusive—like the killer's wallet in his pocket or something."

"There is one thing they found that bothers me. Flour."

"Flour?" She wrinkled her nose. "You mean like piecrust flour?"

"I'm afraid so. It was on the outside of his jacket. The ME's assistant told me some flour was also found on the gun."

"Like Aunt Clara ran out of the kitchen with flour on her hands, shot Donald before he could reach the pie shop, and ran back inside after hiding the gun behind the trashcan."

"Like that." He closed down the note program on his phone. "They're still looking at the body. I suggested that the flour on Donald could have come from the pie shop floor since he collapsed here. That doesn't work for the gun. That's probably why Captain Mitchell had Frank bring Aunt Clara in for questioning."

They both sighed as they considered what could happen.

But the next moment, the pie shop door opened and Aunt Clara bounded into the dining room. "What a couple of gloomy faces. Did one of you burn a piecrust or something?"

Maggie jumped up and went to hug her aunt. Ryan did the same. Ralph Heinz followed a few minutes later.

"Are you okay?" Maggie asked her aunt. "No one was mean to you or anything, were they?"

"Like Ralph would've let someone be mean to me." Her aunt smiled at her friend. "He was fierce in that interrogation room. No matter what Captain Mitchell asked, Ralph was quick on the draw."

"*Mitchell* interrogated you?" Ryan seemed surprised.

"There was a little dustup between Detective Waters and Captain Mitchell," Ralph explained. "The captain doesn't seem to think Waters is doing a good job on the case. He thinks he's biased because he knows Clara."

"But you're fine." Maggie smiled at her aunt. "That's what matters."

Two students, yawning and asking for coffee, came in and sat down with tablet computers. Maggie and Ryan waited on them before taking drinks and pie to the table where Aunt Clara and Ralph were sitting.

"I'm not going to lie to you all," Ralph said between bites of pumpkin pie and sips of coffee. "I haven't done this kind of law in a long time, but the police have a lot of circumstantial evidence against Clara. It would be hard to *convict* her, but that won't necessarily stop them from trying if they get the go-ahead from the DA. Can you imagine a jury thinking Clara killed this man?"

Maggie shuddered when she considered the implication. She didn't want this to go any further. "Is there something we can do to counter these accusations against her?"

Ralph considered her question. "You should hire a criminal attorney. Someone with experience would be better able to tell you how to proceed."

Aunt Clara finished her cup of coffee. "I'm going into the kitchen before the next rush. Thank you for being there, Ralph. I don't think we should give any of this another thought. I didn't kill Donald. The police will find the person who did."

Maggie thanked Ralph again too and went to join her aunt in the kitchen. "Maybe Garrett's lawyer can still take your case."

Aunt Clara was putting on her apron. "We're not hiring anyone to defend me. I'm not wasting our money that way."

"You're joking, right? You heard Ralph. They have a lot of evidence against you."

"*Circumstantial evidence*," her aunt corrected. "Let them figure it out. We'll be fine. What did Mr. Gino think about the chicken potpies and ice cream?"

Maggie had no choice but to avoid the subject of Donald's death. Her aunt refused to discuss it. They talked about potpies and ice cream instead.

Aunt Clara laughed as she started making more Amazing Apple pies. "I'm glad he liked the ideas. Mr. Gino has a good nose for what works in the restaurant business."

Maggie got the apples out of the refrigerator and started peeling. "I hope he's right about the potpies. It could turn our lunch crowd around, at least in the winter. I'm not sure about summer when it's hot outside."

Ryan joined them and said Ralph had to go to work. "My dad called too. He finally got in touch with his lawyer. They'll be over this afternoon."

Aunt Clara waved the information away with her slender hand. "Don't bother with that. I don't need a lawyer. I'm sure the chicken potpies will do me more good than a hundred lawyers."

Ryan started to argue. Maggie shook her head.

"Okay." He shrugged. "I'll tell my dad. But you can't hide your head on this, Aunt Clara. The police won't stop investigating until they have someone in custody."

"That's what I'm counting on," she replied. "Don't you have a newspaper to write or something?"

She thanked him for helping Maggie while she was gone and then began rushing around the kitchen, humming and making piecrust.

Maggie walked Ryan to the front door. "She won't budge on this."

"You'll have to try and change her mind. I don't like the way this is going."

"Me either. I'll talk to her again after lunch."

Maggie's cell phone rang. It was Betty from the sub shop.

"You know I told you about that younger woman that I saw here with Donald? Betsy, my daughter, took a picture of her. We've got her now!"

Nineteen

Maggie didn't want to leave Aunt Clara alone at the pie shop. Pie in the Sky wasn't busy at that moment, but it could get crowded quickly. She and Ryan had a hard time keeping up with it. Her aunt would be swamped.

Ryan volunteered to go alone. Maggie told him to remember to let her know what he found. "Take some pictures if you need to."

He kissed her cheek. "I won't forget."

"Unless you get a call on another story," she observed. "I want to know right away."

"I will. Promise."

Ryan left as three customers came in. They were professors from Duke who regularly came to argue politics and sports over coffee and pie. Maggie got them coffee and apple pie right out of the oven. They were in the middle of a debate on school policies, sparing her only a moment to place their orders.

"I doubt if they'll remember to leave a tip," Maggie told her aunt in the kitchen. "They didn't even look up at me."

"You know how they get sometimes." Aunt Clara dumped more flour onto the pie-making board. "You know, you could've gone with Ryan. I know it can get busy sometimes, but people make excuses for older people like me if we're a little slow getting to their tables."

"There was no reason for both of us to go anyway. Ryan can handle it. It might not be anything."

"What might not be anything, dear?"

The door chime sounded, and Maggie made a hasty retreat. She didn't want to tell Aunt Clara about Donald having lunch at the sub shop with someone else—not yet anyway.

Despite her promise to tell her aunt everything, she found herself unwilling to share this further evidence of Donald's perfidy.

A few students came in and tossed their books and jackets on the table. They ordered one piece of

Clara's Coconut Cream pie to share between them with one cup of coffee.

Maggie took their order, not surprised. Everyone knew the pie shop had no minimum order like some other eateries close to campus. Her aunt and uncle had decided years ago that they wanted to give students a break.

After everyone in the dining room was set up, Maggie went back to the kitchen and started peeling more apples. With the rush on apple pies today, they might be needed.

"What did Captain Mitchell say to you about Donald?"

Aunt Clara shrugged her delicate shoulders. "Oh, you know. Why did I kill Donald? Wouldn't it be better if I told the truth about it?"

"Seriously? What did *you* say?"

"I told him he was a rude and obnoxious young man to ask me such ridiculous questions. I've never fired a gun in my life. You know your uncle would never have allowed a gun in the house or in the pie shop. He always said that's what baseball bats were for."

Maggie smiled as she sliced apples. She couldn't imagine her aunt, or Uncle Fred, shooting a person or hitting someone with a bat.

"He asked me if I read about Donald in the paper that morning before we came to the pie shop."

"Did you?"

"Yes. I didn't believe it when you told me those things about him. I didn't believe it when I read Ryan's article either—although it was very well written. He has a wonderful way of getting to the heart of the matter, don't you think?"

Maggie agreed. "You must've thought *something* was unusual about Donald."

"I try not to judge people." Aunt Clara got ready to put more pies in the oven.

"Let me get that for you." Maggie lifted the tray of pies and put it in the oven.

Her aunt was staring at her, green eyes like her own, narrowed. "You aren't beginning to think I can't do this job, are you?"

"You never put in ten pies at a time in the old oven. I don't see any reason not to help you when I can. You do more than your share around here. I have to pull my weight too."

Her answer pleased Clara. She looked outside the kitchen door for Fanny. "I don't see her out here. I hope she's not lost. What would we do with all those kittens?"

"I don't think cats get lost." Maggie headed to the dining room as the door chimed again. "Maybe she went back to the house on her own."

Leaving her aunt to fret about the cat, Maggie went out front as David was sitting down at a table. His smile, when he saw her, was warm and welcoming.

"You decided to stop by! I'm glad you did." She smiled at him and put away her order book. "What can I get for you?"

"Pie in the Sky hasn't changed a bit." He glanced around the dining room. "Actually, it looks even better than I remember."

"We remodeled recently." She proudly pointed out the things she'd done. "I think the photos from Duke are nice, don't you?"

"I like the tie-in, although I don't see any pictures of us."

"And you won't either." She laughed. "I only use pictures I want other people to see!"

He laughed with her. "Do you have a minute that you could sit down?"

"I do—for an old friend who I believe invented space exploration in our backyard. Let me get you something first."

"Okay. I'll take some eggnog pie. That sounds good. And some sweet tea."

"Coming right up! You're gonna love the eggnog pie. It was one of our contest winners."

"I'm sure all of it is good." David watched her get the pie and tea. "Remember when we used to come up here after school and your uncle gave us money to go to the dime store down the block for candy?"

Maggie set his tea and pie down on the table. "I'm not sure I was ever *that* young."

"And he called us scamps. I know you remember." He took her hand in his as he spoke.

Maggie smiled and disengaged her hand from his as Ryan pushed open the front door and walked inside. He frowned when he saw them but said nothing. He walked back to the kitchen.

"Excuse me," she said to David. "I'll be right back."

Ryan was perched on the stool by the wall phone.

"Well? Who was she?"

"Never mind that," he growled. "What's with the next-door neighbor?"

"Nothing. He was just being friendly. Aren't you going to tell me what you found out?"

"Me too," Aunt Clara said. "You know I don't like being excluded."

Ryan nodded. "All right. Then I hear about the neighbor, right?"

Maggie agreed.

He took out his cell phone and showed her the image that Betty had transferred to him. "Remind you of anyone?"

"Debbie!" Maggie's eyes narrowed. "I wonder if the police have brought *her* in for questioning. She gets around."

Ryan changed the subject abruptly. "Your turn. Does he have feelings for you after all these years?"

"Isn't it more important that we talk about Debbie? I think we should call Frank and tell him what we know about her."

"Who is Debbie?" Aunt Clara was confused by the discussion.

Maggie broke down and explained why Ryan had gone to the sub shop.

"That's not possible," Aunt Clara denied. "Donald spent so much time with me. How would he have been able to see all those other women?"

"What's important now is that the police know she's a viable suspect," Maggie said.

"I know you're either lying to me about your neighbor, or you're at least keeping something from me." Ryan gazed into Maggie's eyes. "I can take whatever it is."

Hmmm. Maybe he is that good. Maggie ruminated about it for a moment before David poked his head through the doorway.

"Am I interrupting anything? I can come back later if now isn't good."

Aunt Clara laughed. "You were always the jokester, David."

"I hear you might be staying in Durham." Ryan put out his hand toward David. "Maggie said the two of you grew up together."

David shook his hand. "That's right. I'm living next door right now, just like when we were kids. Thank you for helping Maggie and Aunt Clara out until I could get their furnace repaired. I'm sure you're a good *friend*."

Ryan bristled at David's assessment of his relationship with Maggie.

"Oh, they're *way* more than friends," Clara added. "You should hear them downstairs in the parlor on Saturday night after they think I'm upstairs sleeping."

David looked a little angry. Ryan smiled triumphantly.

The steaming noises from the espresso machine penetrated the staring match being held by the two men in the kitchen, as a customer had ordered a mocha latte. Aunt Clara ignored both men as she got new piecrust ready and lined pie pans with it.

"She's a wonderful woman," David said to Ryan. "I hope you know how lucky you are."

"I do," Ryan said. "Thanks."

David smiled. "I guess I should get going. I'm interviewing for a job today. Durham has a much smaller pool of jobs for hydraulic engineers than Miami."

"I suppose so. Let me know if I can help." Ryan shook David's hand again.

Maggie boxed up David's pie and put his tea in a cup with a lid when he told her he had to leave. "Thanks for stopping in. Sorry things got busy."

"That's okay." David glanced at Ryan. "There will be other times. See you later, Maggie." He lightly kissed her cheek and was gone.

Ryan's gaze followed David to his car at the curb. "I don't think he only wants to be your friend."

"He's just being nice," she disagreed as she cleaned the table where David had been sitting. "Are you jealous?"

"No. Well, maybe. He's known you a lot longer."

She laughed and kissed him. "Don't worry. Your secret is safe with me."

"You may not have thought of him as a childhood sweetheart," he observed. "But I think he thought of *you* that way. I think he still does."

"No. Not at all. I told you, I didn't have time for that stuff once I was old enough to know what it was. David and I were adventure friends, you know? We made a spaceship out of some flowerpots in the garden. That kind of thing."

"Then he's changed his mind." Ryan glanced at the mocha she'd made for the other customer. "Can I have one of those too?"

• • •

Ryan had to leave after he drank his mocha. He had to take pictures at the Angel Tree festivities at the mall. Ninety children were receiving gifts from tags that shoppers had picked up for boys and girls under twelve. Maggie felt sure there would be many teary-eyed people at the affair.

After he was gone, she ordered lunch for her and Aunt Clara from Bombay Grill. Raji delivered it personally with an invitation for them to come in later and try their holiday treats.

"Ahalya and I are eager to have your feedback on our foods," he told them "We've taken your suggestion, Maggie, and repurposed some of our traditional foods that were never meant for Christmas. We hope you'll enjoy them."

Maggie said they would be there, but when Raji was gone and they were eating lunch, Aunt Clara wasn't sure.

"I don't understand why they want to make their food different."

"I guess they want to fit in."

"I suppose we should take a pie with us," Aunt Clara said. "My mother always told me and your mother never to go and eat at someone else's house without bringing food. What kind do you think we should take?"

They decided to take a mincemeat pie. Aunt Clara said she needed to bake a few more of those anyway. "And I think the raisins and spices will complement their food, don't you?"

Maggie agreed and started cleaning up the dining room after the morning rush as she always did. The sound of Aunt Clara working in the kitchen made her smile. She hoped her aunt was right about the police figuring out that she wasn't involved with Donald's death. It was frightening for Maggie to think about losing her aunt.

The blue tile floors were still wet when Lenora and Alice came into the shop again. Aunt Clara took one look when she heard the door chime and turned away to keep working.

"Hello," Lenora said. "I'd like some coffee, please. My daughter will have the same—black, no milk or sugar. She's trying to lose a few pounds. And no pie."

Alice's attractive face turned red, and Maggie saw her bite her lip.

"Everyone doesn't need to know our business, Mama." Alice smiled at Maggie.

"Don't worry about it." Maggie put her order pad back into her pocket. "People say that kind of thing all the time. I think it's the pie. It makes them feel guilty."

"Thank you," Alice said. "My mother is still a little out of sorts today about Donald's death."

"You would be too if the love of your life was suddenly snuffed out and the police had no idea what happened."

"We just came from speaking with the police," Alice explained. "They don't seem to have any viable suspects, although there was a reporter there who said your aunt had been questioned by the police. I can't believe they'd think she could be responsible."

Maggie's smile was a little less welcoming as she returned with their cups of coffee. "They're fishing right now. It's because it happened close to here, and Aunt Clara was dating him."

"Of course." Alice demurely accepted her coffee. "Thank you."

"Not that Donald cared anything for her," Lenora explained. "I told the police captain that too. If anyone had cause to kill Donald, it was me. I know he was crazy in love with me. He was using Clara to make me jealous."

Alice took a sip of her coffee. "Mama wanted them to question her, but they said they were following up other leads right now."

"Can you imagine?" Lenora asked in an outraged voice.

Maggie was wishing that the police *had* made Lenora their person of interest instead of Aunt Clara. She didn't say so and turned away to wipe down the refrigerator case.

The door to Pie in the Sky flew open, and Garrett jogged in. His hair was almost standing up on end, and his face was very red.

"Is Clara all right?" he demanded.

"She's fine," Maggie answered. "What's wrong?"

"I heard on the radio only a moment ago that the police had made an arrest in the Donald Wickerson case. They didn't say who it was. I assumed it was Clara."

Twenty

Aunt Clara came out of the kitchen in her flour-covered apron to hear the rest of the story, despite the fact that Lenora was still there.

"Clara," Lenora acknowledged her.

"Lenora." Clara's nod was curt.

"What radio station were you listening to?" Maggie asked.

"I don't know," Garrett conceded. "The one that's always on in the car. They have all those crazy commercials with Santa selling tires for Christmas."

Maggie had no idea what he was talking about.

She could tell from the looks on the other women's faces that they didn't either.

"Ryan will know." She took out her cell phone. Of course, he didn't answer. She left him a message. "I guess he'll get back to us as soon as he can."

"Did they say anything else about Donald's killer?" Lenora demanded.

"No." Garrett shook his head. "Well, I was coming here anyway to talk to Clara about using my attorney. I thought I should check in. They might've said something else and I missed it."

"We don't have a radio in here," Aunt Clara said. "Maybe we should go out and listen to yours. They play the news all the time, don't they?"

Maggie watched in fascination as the three women walked out to Garrett's car with him to listen to the news. The pie shop was empty. She finished cleaning the refrigerator case and wiped down everything else in the dining room.

Her cell phone rang— it was Ryan.

"I called my friend with the police since I knew Frank would have nothing for me," he said. "You won't believe who they arrested."

"Don't keep me hanging."

"Debbie Blackwelder. Can we pick 'em or what?"

"Why did they arrest her?"

"She has a gun permit for a nine millimeter, but says she can't find it. They're checking her lipstick against the type on his jacket. She's also the daughter of one of the women Donald is suspected of killing—her real name is Fran Belk. She also has a PI's license. She said she'd been trailing Donald for years, trying to prove he killed her mother."

Maggie was surprised to hear that. "Why didn't you know that when we went to see her?"

"Because she's been using a fake name since she came to Durham. The police say they think she was following him for at least the last year. They think she killed him because she finally found evidence against him."

Maggie sat down at a table, overwhelmed with relief that it was finally over. Her knees felt shaky, and a feeling of thankfulness rose up in her, making her want to cry.

"They still don't have all the details," Ryan said. "But this is more than they did with your aunt. They're pretty sure to have arrested her. Good news, huh? Where's Clara? We should tell her too. Are you okay?"

"I'm fine." Maggie pushed at a few tears that were at the corner of her eyes.

Garrett, Aunt Clara, Lenora, and Alice all hurried back inside the pie shop.

"We can't sit out there all day. It's freezing!" Aunt Clara said. "Lenora, quit making goo-goo eyes at Garrett! He's not interested in you."

"What are you talking about?" Lenora's eyes opened wide. "My dear Donald isn't even in the ground, and you're dating another man. No wonder he loved me better."

"I'm not dating anyone," Aunt Clara snarled back.

"Mama, please." Alice tried to stop what was coming.

"Donald barely knew you, if he knew you at all." Aunt Clara got nasty. "He sought me out at the library long before you got your claws into him."

"My claws?" Lenora came at Clara. "I'll show you my claws."

Alice and Maggie got between the two older ladies. Garrett sat down to watch with a look of consternation on his face.

"I'm so sorry about this," Alice said to Maggie. "I wouldn't have brought her if I'd known."

"That's all right." Maggie propelled her aunt toward the kitchen. "We have pies to make for the tree trimming tonight, right, Aunt Clara?"

Her aunt's reply was unintelligible.

In the kitchen, Maggie tried to calm her aunt. She could hear Alice doing the same in the dining room.

"The nerve of that woman! And after she tried to take away my pies from the library fund-raiser too. I don't know what's gotten into her."

"She's upset about Donald too. She was dating him. He was dating a lot of women, trying to find the best one, I guess."

Maggie told her aunt about Debbie Blackwelder's arrest. She had to explain how she knew who Debbie was in the first place.

"You've been keeping quite a lot from me," her aunt protested. "I can handle things, Maggie. You don't have to count on Ryan for everything."

Garrett walked into the kitchen with a grin on his face. "Those two are gone, Clara. I know you told me you weren't ready yet, but I'd be pleased if you thought of me as more than a friend."

Aunt Clara kissed his cheek. "You're a sweet man. I need to change my apron."

As she started back making pies, Garrett drifted from the kitchen in a pink fog that Maggie could actually see forming around him. Aunt Clara might not love him, but he certainly had strong feelings for her.

"I'll see you later, Maggie," he said as he was leaving. "Clara invited me to the dessert tasting at the Bombay Grill tonight. I'm looking forward to it."

A few new customers dropped in, ordering hot chocolate and Delia's Deep-Dish Cherry pie, as well as a whole Caramel Apple Without a Stick pie to go.

"Do you know if anyone around here is hiring?" one of the young women asked. "I have some restaurant experience."

"We're not hiring here. Sorry. You could try Biscuitland up the street."

"Thanks." The girl smiled and drank her hot chocolate.

Maggie helped Aunt Clara box up the twenty-two pies for the tree-lighting ceremony at the community center a few blocks away. They'd planned on attending, but Raji's invitation was more personal. The hundreds of people at the tree lighting wouldn't miss them—Raji and Ahalya would.

They choose different varieties of pies, except for the cream pies. They didn't travel well, and the community center hadn't asked for them in particular. It was a nice selection anyway. Ryan had promised to stop by and help Maggie deliver them.

When he showed up at about 4:00 p.m., he was almost bouncing with excitement.

"Are you that excited about the police picking up Debbie Blackwelder?" Maggie asked when she saw him.

"No. I got it, Maggie. I'm going to be able to save the office." His blue eyes gleamed, and there was a happy pink glow in his cheeks.

"That's wonderful!" She hugged him. "What happened? What did you do?"

"I was at the university regent's meeting last month, and they were talking about looking for a building that wouldn't cost a fortune to use for an outreach project with the small business students. They didn't want to build until they could try out the incubator and see what happens."

Maggie was confused. "Incubator? I don't get it."

He swung her around and kissed her. "I'm the

new landlord for the small business incubator! It will be a place that helps students and other members of the community who are trying to get small businesses up and running. They can use my fax machines, computers, and have micro office spaces. It's gonna be great, and I can write about it."

"That sounds awesome. Congratulations!"

"Sometimes it helps to know everything about everyone."

"I'm sure that's true. Albert Mann is going to be disappointed."

"I already called him *and* my father. Neither one of them were particularly happy about it. I don't care. This is for the best. I still have an office for the face of the *Durham Weekly*."

Maggie enjoyed his excitement. "Do you still have time to run all of these pies over to the community center?"

"I certainly do."

Since they'd entered the slow time for the pie shop, Maggie went with him to deliver the pies and collect the money. She felt sure Aunt Clara would be fine now that it was later in the day, almost closing time.

"What about Debbie Blackwelder?" Maggie asked as they drove away from the pie shop.

"I told Frank he needed to look at the families of the women who'd been killed." Ryan shook his head. "That's how he found her."

"The only thing I don't understand is why Debbie wanted to set up Aunt Clara. Even Frank admitted it had to be someone close to us for them to know just when to do it. And they even put flour on the gun!"

"I guess Debbie knew about your aunt dating Donald. Or she just wanted someone else to blame it on so she wouldn't get caught. We know she was watching us. We don't know for how long."

"I suppose that's possible. Has she confessed to killing him?"

"Not that I've heard. No matter what, the police should leave your aunt alone now. They can figure out the rest."

Maggie considered that, and she was glad that Aunt Clara was off the hook for Donald's death. It bothered her to think that Debbie had known enough about them and their routines to be able to make it look like her aunt had killed Donald. It felt odd to think that she'd been watching them.

The people at the community center were glad to see all the pies. They were unhappy that Clara and Maggie wouldn't be there that night but understood how many holiday parties overlapped. Maggie was thrilled to take their check. She loved big checks.

"We know Debbie was seeing Donald at the sub shop too. She had him down. All she had to do was wait for the right moment," Ryan said as they were leaving. He was obviously still mulling all of it over in his brain too.

"That's true," Maggie agreed. "I suppose Donald reaped what he sowed. I can understand why Debbie would want revenge after he'd killed her mother."

"Possibly the best endgame on this, besides her getting revenge, would be that the police might reopen the investigation into her mother's death." Ryan started the car. "That might be enough to make killing him worthwhile."

Still, the perfect timing and planning of Donald's death nagged at Maggie. She supposed she should put it behind her, but it was difficult.

Maybe she was just so relieved that it was over. Her mind couldn't seem to take it all in.

Debbie had killed Donald and wanted to make it look like Aunt Clara had done it. That made sense to Maggie. Of course she hadn't wanted to get caught. Learning that Donald was seeing Aunt Clara would have been easy enough.

She understood that it would be easy to put a little flour on Donald's lapel and stash the gun behind the trashcan at Pie in the Sky. But knowing exactly when Aunt Clara was messing around with the cat had to be difficult, as was picking that time to shoot Donald.

She didn't mention it again to Ryan. The police had their suspect in custody. Maggie knew she should be happy that Aunt Clara was free of any charges.

After the pie shop was cleaned and closed, Garrett and Ryan joined her and Aunt Clara for Christmas sweets at the Bombay Grill.

Aunt Clara was so happy. Maggie could tell she was relieved that her part in the investigation surrounding Donald's death was over. Her aunt had put on a brave front and acted as though it hadn't bothered her at all.

Maggie knew that wasn't true. Aunt Clara was very good at pretending things didn't bother her. She remembered that from getting in trouble a few times as a child. Her aunt had always acted as though it didn't matter—until she was ready to give her an earful.

"I'll take Clara home," Garrett said when they got outside. "You and Maggie go on. We can get along fine without you."

Maggie smiled as she got in Ryan's car. "They are so cute together. I wish something would work out between them, once Aunt Clara is over Donald."

"Did you take your aunt's profile down from Durham Singles?"

"Yes. I hope that's over. I'm not sure if Albert will give up so easily."

Ryan had a police scanner in his car. There was a

call for officers to join the Durham Fire Department at an address regarding a three-alarm fire.

The Honda stopped abruptly, cars honking their horns as Ryan pulled to the side of the street and made a U-turn despite the heavy traffic.

"That's the *Durham Weekly* office."

Twenty-one

When Maggie and Ryan reached the old newspaper building, the entire structure was in flames. The bright red and orange danced against the dark sky as firefighters shot water from their hoses to try to douse the flames.

"No. This isn't possible." Ryan ran his hands through his hair. "How did it happen?"

Maggie could see he wanted to go and ask questions. "See if you can find out. I'll wait here for you."

It was an old building. She watched in terrible fascination as the flat roof caved in. She could tell by the expressions on the firemen's faces that there was nothing they could do but keep the fire from spreading to the buildings next to it.

Police officers ranged up and down the sidewalk, keeping spectators from getting too close. About fifty people, some who appeared to be from competing media outlets, took hundreds of photos. Cars slowed in the street, their drivers and passengers gawking at what was happening.

It was a terrible blow to Ryan, especially after he'd been so happy to have found a way to save the place. Maggie hoped insurance wasn't something they'd skimped on. At least then Ryan could be compensated for the loss of the building. But nothing could compensate him for the loss of his newspaper's identity and the countless pieces of history that had been housed inside.

She saw a familiar figure in a parked car a few yards up from where she was waiting for Ryan. *Albert Mann.* Her mind went off into dozens of theories.

Could he be involved in the fire? No doubt it would get him the property he wanted. He would've torn down the old building anyway.

No. That wasn't a fair assumption. Even though Albert had been annoyingly persistent when he wanted the property Pie in the Sky was on, he hadn't resorted to anything like this. True, he'd played some dirty tricks on her and Aunt Clara. Those were more annoying than dangerous, though. This would be a whole new low for him.

Ryan came back to the car about an hour later. Maggie had called Aunt Clara and Garrett to let them know what had happened. They hadn't answered their cell phones or the house phones. She left messages.

She'd half expected Garrett to rush down there, if only for Ryan's sake. But there was no sign of him.

Covered in soot and smelling of smoke, Ryan's handsome face had defeat written on it. "It's gone. It's all gone. I tried to get in and save some of the memories, the awards and older papers my parents put out. All of it was gone."

Maggie put her arms around him, and he rested his head against hers.

"Did they say what caused it?" She was still thinking about Albert.

"The fire chief says it was probably faulty wiring, but they won't know for sure until it cools off and they can investigate. I don't see how it could be bad wiring, Maggie. I had everything checked a couple of months ago. It couldn't have gone bad that quickly."

She didn't say anything. He needed her comfort now more than her curiosity.

"Did you see my dad?" Ryan lifted his head. "I called him. He didn't answer. I left messages. I didn't see him anywhere."

"No," she said. "But it's dark and there are a lot of people here."

"This was everything my parents built over forty years." His voice trembled in the dark car. "It was everything I've worked for. My heritage and legacy."

"No, it wasn't. It was a building," she reminded him. "*You're* the *Durham Weekly*. You can go on. You were already thinking of ways that you could continue when you thought you had to sell the place. You'll find a way."

He smiled at her. "How did I get so lucky and find you?"

"I think it was because you believed in me when I said I didn't kill my ex-boss." She brushed the blond curls back from his forehead. "That kind of thing sticks with a woman."

He kissed her. "I couldn't imagine you hurting anyone."

"And you stayed with me through all of that. I'm here for you too."

Ryan kissed her again and then looked around as the firemen were starting to pack up. There was almost nothing left of the old building.

"I don't understand why Dad isn't here." He called Garrett again, but there was still no answer. "One of the most important things that could happen, and he's nowhere to be found."

"Aunt Clara frequently forgets to charge her

phone or turn up the volume on it. He probably isn't paying attention either since they're together."

"I'm sure you're right." Ryan grabbed his camera out of the backseat. "I'm gonna take a few pictures of what's left—for me and for the insurance company. I'll be back in a minute."

Maggie squinted out of the car window. Albert Mann was still sitting in his car on the side of the street, looking at the ashes of the old building. Maybe she didn't feel right bringing it up to Ryan yet—and maybe Albert wasn't involved at all—but she was going to find out.

She got out of the car, carefully avoiding firefighting equipment that was still on the sidewalk. Strolling to Albert's car, she knocked on the window.

He rolled down the glass with a quick touch of a button. "Yes?"

"Did Ryan tell you he'd found a way to keep from selling you the building, or did you hear it from someone else?"

Albert's homely yet compelling face seemed astonished. "I hope you aren't suggesting what I think you are. I won't tolerate slander, Maggie. I'm a businessman. I don't set buildings on fire because I can't have them. If that were the case, your pie shop would've already been replaced by a five-story medical office building."

"I'm glad I'm not the only one who thinks it's

suspicious that the *Weekly* building was destroyed after Ryan said you couldn't have it."

He smiled in a tolerant way, as though Maggie were a small child. "First of all, Ryan didn't tell me the building was no longer on the market, unless you count that emotional outburst at his home. Garrett assured me that he would talk the boy around."

"So you didn't know about the college small business project? I thought you always had your ear to the ground."

"Thank you for your faith in me. While I try to stay on top of what's happening in our city, I'm not a mind reader. I was on my way home from a meeting tonight and saw the terrible fire. I won't dignify your unspoken accusations with denials of my involvement. If Ryan thinks I was here setting a fire, he can tell the police. Good night, Maggie. Give Ryan my condolences."

He rolled the window back up between them. Maggie walked back to Ryan's car.

He was leaning against it, waiting for her. "What's up? Was that Albert Mann gloating over the fire?"

"I don't know about gloating." She sighed, knowing she was going to have to tell him what she'd been thinking. "I kind of accused him of setting the fire."

He nodded. "That occurred to me too before I even saw him here. I also thought about my father being responsible."

"Ryan!"

"I know. I reined it in. Albert is a jerk, but he's never so obvious. This would raise too many questions. As for my father, he loved this place as much as I do. He couldn't hurt it."

"I'm so sorry. You've been through a lot tonight. Do you have enough pictures? Are you ready to go home?"

He put his arms around her. "I think so. There's nothing else I can do here. What really makes me mad is that this will hit all the other media in the city tonight and tomorrow. I won't be able to report the destruction of my own office until it's old news. It's the story of my life."

"I know you. You'll have some kind of inside scoop that the other outlets won't have thought of. Besides, think of the sympathy you might be able to turn into subscribers." She smiled at him. "Will the insurance cover building something new?"

"No. We only carry what we had to on the place. The land is worth something—Albert will still be interested in that, no doubt. Between the two, maybe I can find a place to rent for a while."

"Well then, I think we should go and tell your dad and Aunt Clara what happened. It's probably still going to be a long night. You know the police and fire departments are gonna want to figure out what happened."

He agreed, and the two of them got in the car.

They headed for Aunt Clara's house. Ryan told Maggie he was glad his laptop was still in the car. At least he hadn't lost whatever information was on it.

"I think I even have copies of the older, original pictures that were destroyed in the fire. It won't be everything, but it will be enough to start over with."

Maggie kissed his cheek as he swung over to park behind his father's car outside Aunt Clara's house. "Looks like I was right. Garrett probably didn't even hear his cell phone."

Ryan turned off the engine and opened the door. "It might be better this way. I know Dad talks tough sometimes and he was ready to sell the office, but only because he's afraid of losing the house. It'll still be hard on him, seeing what's left. Maybe not as hard as watching it burn."

They went up to the house. Maggie frowned as she noticed that there were no lights on inside. "That seems weird."

Ryan laughed. "My dad is old. He's not dead."

"You mean they're in there, in the dark—"

"What do *you* think?"

"I kind of thought it was cute—until now." Maggie got ready for finding her aunt and Garrett on the sofa in the parlor. "Aunt Clara said she wasn't ready for another relationship right now."

"My dad can be pretty persuasive."

The front door was open when she touched the handle. "They didn't even have time to lock the door."

Ryan pushed the door open and almost stumbled over something large left in the doorway. "What's going on?"

Maggie switched on the lights in the foyer and on the front porch. She gasped when she saw Garrett lying on the floor at their feet.

Twenty-two

"Dad!" Ryan lifted his father's head and tried to get him to respond.

Maggie dialed 911 as she ran through the downstairs area of the house, calling for her aunt, and switching on lights as she went. "I can't find her," she yelled back at Ryan. "She's not down here."

"Try upstairs." Ryan was still trying to revive Garrett. His father's head was limp and white-faced on his lap. "There's a lot of blood, Maggie. I don't know if he fell and hit his head or what."

Maggie was going through the bedrooms and

bathroom upstairs. There was still no sign of Aunt Clara. Had she run out to look for help when Garrett fell? Why didn't she use the house phone? Where was she?

She ran back downstairs and noticed as she looked out the side window, that there was a light on at the Walkers' house next door. Scratching sounds at the back door got her attention. She opened the door, and Fanny shot into the house.

"I'm glad you're okay." She stroked the cat as she ran to her babies. The tiny kittens made their usual meowing sounds as they realized she was back. "I wish you could tell me what happened."

Fanny pushed her head against Maggie's hand and purred loudly.

"I'm going to find out if David saw her," Maggie shouted to Ryan.

"Wait," he called back. "I think there may be more to this. Don't go until the police get here."

Maggie heard him, but ignored his warning. She ran out the back door, heart pounding. She rang the doorbell and then pounded on the sturdy wood portal when no one answered immediately.

David finally came to the door and turned on the porch light. "Maggie? What are you doing here? Is something wrong?"

"Aunt Clara," she blurted out. "She's missing. Did she come here? She might've wanted to use the phone. Have you seen her?"

"I've been here all night working on my laptop. I haven't seen or heard anything. When did you see her last?"

She briefly explained that her aunt should've been in the house with Garrett. "He was unconscious in the foyer. That's why I thought she might've panicked and come here for help."

He pulled on a jacket and went outside with her. "Let's ask the other neighbors. She might be at someone else's house. Don't worry, Maggie. We'll find her."

• • •

Aunt Clara wasn't at any of the neighbors' houses. Maggie went tearfully from house to house with David at her side while Ryan waited for the ambulance to come for his father. Where the houses had all been quiet and settled in for the night, suddenly lights were blazing in every window as police officers arrived on the scene.

"Where could she be?" Maggie asked David as a light, freezing rain began to fall. "Could someone have taken her to the hospital? She couldn't simply disappear."

David put his arm around her as they started back toward her house. The ambulance was arriving. Some of the neighbors got out of their beds to help look for Maggie's aunt. They arrived with radios, cell phones, and flashlights, ready to do what they could to help.

Officer Jack Harding joined them and took Maggie's hand in his. He was a regular at the pie shop—a slightly older, rounder version of Frank, dressed in his uniform. Maggie ran to him when she saw his familiar face in the crowd.

"We've looked everywhere," she said. "I don't understand where she went."

"Come in and warm up," he told her. "You're chilled to the bone. Let's talk about this."

The paramedics were taking Garrett's vitals in the front doorway. Maggie and Jack walked around to the back door and went inside.

"Is he going to be okay?" Maggie asked him.

"I haven't heard yet, but it seems obvious to me that his injury is involved with what happened to your aunt."

Maggie sat on the edge of the sofa with David beside her. She only half noticed that he'd taken her hand in his. It didn't matter—she was focused on what had happened to Aunt Clara.

"This is the way we see it right now," Officer Harding said. "We think someone came up behind Mr. Summerour and hit him with a rock we found on the porch. There's some blood on it. Do you know what I'm talking about?"

Maggie nodded. "It's that stupid decorative rock

that holds the front door key. Like anyone couldn't tell that's what it was. I've asked her a hundred times to get rid of it. We each have keys to the house. We don't need a spare on the porch."

"That's it," he agreed. "Mr. Summerour went down in the doorway. We believe that whoever hit him has taken your aunt."

"Someone kidnapped Aunt Clara?" Maggie couldn't believe it. "Why? You can tell we don't have much money. What would someone hope to gain?"

"I don't know all the answers right now. We'll have crime scene take a look around and see what they can find. After that, we'll wait for a phone call. It may not be about money. Sometimes people are kidnapped for reasons other than money. Can you think of anyone who might have done this?"

"Kidnapped Aunt Clara?" Maggie's mind raced. "No. She doesn't have any enemies. You know her. I can't even imagine why anyone would do such a thing."

There was a commotion near the front door. Ryan, appearing shocked, tears in his eyes, told Maggie that he was riding in the ambulance with his father.

"They think it's a concussion," he told her. "I'll let you know what happens."

"Stay strong," David remarked.

Ryan glanced at him—and at his hand linked with Maggie's. He turned away without another word.

"Good luck, Summerour," Officer Harding returned.

Frank walked carefully through the doorway a short while after Ryan had gone. Crime scene techs were already looking for prints, and whatever else they could find, to figure out what had happened and who might be responsible.

"I came as soon as I heard," Frank said to Maggie. "What's going on? I leave you alone for a couple of days, and everything falls apart."

Officer Harding explained what he'd said to Maggie and David. He walked Frank through what they thought had happened. Frank sat down with them after the explanation.

"I take it Ryan is with his father." Frank gave David a significant look—his eyes focusing on his hand, which was still holding Maggie's. "And you are?"

David got to his feet and shook Frank's hand. "David Walker. I live next door. Maggie and I go back a long way. I want to do whatever I can to help."

Frank's raised eyebrows spoke volumes about what he thought of that statement.

"Listen, Maggie, I don't want to point any fingers, but there are a lot of people who have grudges against Garrett. Ryan too. It goes with the territory. Newspapers aren't always popular. It basically happened at the same time that the *Durham Weekly*'s office was torched," Frank said. "I know I'm a suspicious man, but what are the odds?"

"Are you saying Aunt Clara might not have been the target?" Maggie asked. "That she might've been kidnapped because she was with Garrett?"

"I'm saying it's one possibility. Garrett has been shot at, almost run down, and threatened because of his newspaper. Someone might have taken Clara as a warning to him."

Maggie put her hands to her head. "We both know the only controversial thing Ryan has been writing about lately is Donald Wickerson."

"That's right. Sometimes I feel like I'm chasing my own exhaust." Frank patted her hand. "I think we should let the crime scene investigators do their job. Let's see what they turn up. Arson investigators will probably start on the office tomorrow, or the next day. In the meantime, keep your phone handy. If you receive any kind of unusual message, let us know. It could be as innocuous as a note left at the front door. Just stay focused."

Maggie scrubbed her eyes with her hands. She wasn't sure how to stay focused on something like this. Just the idea that someone was out there with Aunt Clara made her want to run into the night screaming.

"I'll do my best. Thanks, Frank. You too, Jack."

"What about surveillance?" David asked. "Shouldn't

you set up to record and answer all of Maggie's calls until this is resolved?"

Frank chuckled, and Officer Harding joined him.

"This isn't TV, son, or some thriller novel," Frank said. "There's no FBI—no money for that kind of thing, at least not until we have some real clue about what happened to Clara. Right now, for all we know, she called a friend and went to her house because she was upset. Anything is possible."

Maggie accepted everyone's condolences and convinced David that she didn't want him to stay with her. She tried to stay positive. Aunt Clara was going to be fine. She tried not to think about what had happened, but it took on a nightmarish quality in her mind.

Long after the police cars had left, and the crime scene people had packed up, Maggie lay in her bed, thinking about her aunt.

Ryan had called from the hospital. After an MRI and other tests, the doctors had determined that Garrett had a hairline skull fracture. He'd regained consciousness. Ryan planned to spend the night with him.

"I'm so glad your dad is all right," she replied. "Take good care of him tonight. I'll talk to you tomorrow."

"We'll figure out where Aunt Clara is, Maggie."

Fanny and her kittens joined Maggie upstairs on

her bed. Both doors were securely locked. Maggie still felt uncomfortable in the house. Tossing and turning, she finally moved herself and the family of cats into Aunt Clara's bed. Maggie kept her cell phone in her hand to wait for daylight.

She didn't know why, but it made her feel better to be in the old bed her aunt and uncle had shared for so many years. She wished Uncle Fred were there to help find her aunt. She wished that there was something more she could do. Patience and waiting to see what was going to happen were driving her crazy.

• • •

Everything was covered in a thin layer of ice the next day. Trees, power lines, cars, and rooftops were frozen in place. Power outages were reported all over the city. Icicles hung from the gutters and the doorways as Maggie looked out at the world.

The long night was finally over. It was still dark, but it was time to get up and open the pie shop.

She wanted to stay in bed all day with her phone tucked against her ear, waiting for information about Aunt Clara. She felt helpless and angry that she couldn't do anything to make a difference. She had to rely on the police. It was harder than anything she'd ever done.

She was up and awake. Spending the day in bed was out of the question. She didn't know what to do except what she would normally have done. Aunt Clara wouldn't want Pie in the Sky to close because she was gone. Maggie made herself get out of bed to do this for her.

Maggie got up, took a shower, and got dressed in warm clothes. She made toast but couldn't eat it. She fed the cats. Fanny wasn't interested in going to the pie shop that day. Maggie didn't blame her. It was a cold, dark morning. Why not stay home where it was warm, and snuggle in her box with her kittens?

She watched Fanny clean her babies meticulously, even holding one of them down with her paw when he resisted his bath. Maggie wished she could climb in there with them and hide from the world. They were lucky to have their mother.

Maggie put on her boots, jacket, and scarf and pushed herself out of the house. She put one foot after another on the frozen sidewalk. The Christmas lights were gleaming red and green through the ice that covered them, illuminating the early morning. Traffic was lighter than usual. Most people either went in late or stayed home on a day like this.

The power was still on in the block with Pie in the Sky. She went inside and switched on the lights to begin the morning rituals she normally performed with her aunt. She didn't let herself think about how much she missed Aunt Clara's nonstop conversation and her sweet smile.

Mechanically, she made a few fresh apple pies

and put them in the oven. She started the coffee in the big urn and then mopped the floor and wiped everything down.

The shop wasn't dirty—she and Aunt Clara had cleaned up before they left last night. It was more having something to do than anything else. She needed to get her mind off the fact that there had been no phone calls, no messages about her aunt. There was no word from the police on where Aunt Clara had gone or if someone had taken her.

What was she going to do? How was she going to greet her customers and act as though everything was fine when her whole world was wrong?

Maggie was ready for her customers by six. The pie shop was so quiet and she felt so alone. There was a new batch of pumpkin pies in the oven. She made herself a double-shot mocha and switched on the Hot Pie Now neon sign on the window.

She was looking out at the dreary, nearly empty streets outside as the gray light of morning crept up on the city. *Where are you, Aunt Clara?*

She'd already called the police desk several times to ask for information. She'd left messages for Frank too.

The phone finally rang after the last time she called, startling her. She answered with a quiet, fearful voice. It was Ryan telling her that he was leaving the hospital.

"I'm at the pie shop." Her voice was wooden. "That's great news. No word yet on Aunt Clara."

"Frank is here talking to Garrett about what happened last night. He said he'll bring me by your house to get the car."

"I'm glad you two have made up."

"Me too. All it took was my newspaper office burning to the ground, my father being attacked, and your aunt disappearing."

"Does Garrett remember anything about what happened?"

"He remembers everything, Maggie. He said he thought it was a woman who attacked him and took your aunt. Maybe that isn't too surprising."

"Why?"

"Because the police had to let Debbie Blackwelder go last night."

Twenty-three

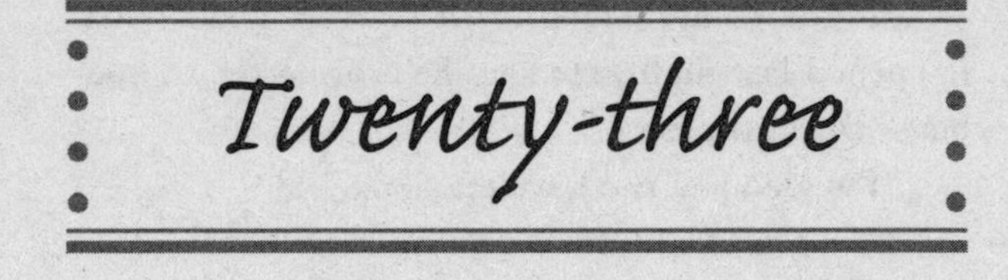

"What?" Maggie couldn't believe they'd let the only real suspect in Donald's murder go free. "Why?"

"The DA refused to prosecute the case. He said there wasn't enough hard evidence."

"So we're thinking that Debbie may have attacked Garrett and taken Aunt Clara?"

"That's what Frank thinks. I was up all night thinking about it. My brain feels like scrambled eggs. The police sent someone to Debbie's house, and the salon. There was no sign of her, or Aunt Clara."

Maggie saw her first customer drive up and park in front. "I have to go. Are you coming here after you get your car?"

"I need a quick shower and a change of clothes. I'll be there as soon as I can. Do you think you should be at the pie shop today? Maybe it would be better if you stayed home."

"Too late. Professor Simpson is here, and he's got his newspaper with him. It's just another day."

"Don't worry, Maggie. I'll come and help out. We'll get through this."

"Thanks, Ryan. I'll see you in a while."

Professor Simpson was followed by several police officers. They all wanted coffee and warm apple pie. Maggie took their orders and brought their pie and coffee. She wondered if Aunt Clara's disappearance was in the newspaper or on TV this morning. She hadn't heard anything about it.

She wasn't sure if that was good or bad. The more people who knew to look for her aunt, the better—like when they issued Amber and Silver Alerts.

On the other hand, if Aunt Clara had been kidnapped, the person who took her might not like the notoriety, and that could be dangerous.

The usual group of early-morning customers came in. Some stayed and ate there, talking about the bad weather, and classes at the university that had been canceled or rescheduled because of it.

Some left right away—trying to get to work before they were late.

Angela came in and filled up her oversized coffee mug from the urn. She also asked for a whole mincemeat pie in a box to go. "Where's your aunt this morning?"

Maggie had considered earlier what her response would be if someone asked. "She's a little under the weather today. It was hard, but I convinced her to stay home with the cats."

"I heard about the police picking up that other woman for Donald's murder. I know Clara must be very relieved."

"Oh, she is. She could hardly sit still last night. You know how excited she gets."

Angela smiled. "I'm glad to hear it. I don't know if you'd stay here without her. I didn't like to think about my favorite pie shop closing down."

"You don't have to worry about that." Maggie handed her the white pastry box. "Is that it?"

Maggie rang up Angela's order first, and then the two police officers' orders. Four firemen came in, talking about a frozen pipe that had burst in one of the main roads. There had also been a fire in downtown Durham that had blazed through most of the night.

Feeling sorry for the firefighters with their exhausted, sooty faces, Maggie gave them coffee on the house, and they bought a whole cherry pie to split.

Ralph Heinz came in as the firefighters took over one of the small tables and four chairs. The older lawyer glanced around the pie shop, his eyes finally landing on Maggie.

"Can I get something for you, Mr. Heinz?"

"I was hoping to talk to Clara. Is she here this morning?"

Maggie quickly took him into the kitchen and, in hushed tones, told him what had happened. She could see the expression of shock and horror on his face. It probably looked a lot like her own.

She'd needed to talk to someone about it. She hoped he was a good choice.

"That's terrible. The police have no leads on her yet?"

"No. Not yet. It's possible the suspect the police had in custody is responsible. They had to let her go last night."

"I'm so sorry. I wish there was something I could do to help."

Maggie took his hand. "Thank you so much. I'll let you know when they find her."

"Thank you. Please be sure to keep me posted."

"I will."

They went back into the dining area, and Ralph ordered a latte to go. Maggie made it, and the aroma enticed two new customers to try lattes too. Ryan arrived as a line had formed at the cash register while Maggie was making lattes. He threw on an apron, started taking money and putting pies in boxes.

They exchanged glances as Maggie took the two lattes to her customers. She was so glad to see him. She could hardly wait until they could sneak a moment alone in the kitchen.

When they could, she threw her arms around him and cried into his shoulder. "I thought she'd be back by now. I thought someone would've seen her."

Ryan kissed her and smoothed her hair back from her face. "We're going to find her. The police have everyone out looking for her."

"It wasn't on TV or in the papers that she was missing."

"Captain Mitchell is keeping this quiet until they have some idea about what happened. She hasn't been gone forty-eight hours yet. Normally they don't even look until it's been that long."

"I guess that's good." She wiped her eyes and dried her face. "I feel like I should be doing something, Ryan. Standing around here, selling pies, seems stupid. What if she's hurt or lost? We don't know that she wasn't hit in the head too."

"My dad said she went with the woman. He said she wasn't hurt. We have to remember that right now."

The door to the pie shop chimed. Ryan kissed Maggie, and told her he would take care of the front. "I can do everything else but make pies."

She laughed, thinking that was exactly what she'd told Aunt Clara when she first came back home. It had turned out not to be true. She needed her aunt. Until she thought about facing life without her, she hadn't realized how much she needed her.

"Thanks. I can handle the pies."

"And the lattes," he reminded her. "That coffee thing scares me."

Maggie made ten Elegant Eggnog pies in rapid succession. She and Aunt Clara had pre-made some filling. She'd wanted to make a few of those since the last one had been taken out of the front refrigerator case. She and Aunt Clara had worked on the filling together because it was tricky and could be difficult to thicken.

There was pounding on the back door. It was Mr. Gino.

"I have those quotes for you," he told her. "Where is Clara? Does she want the ingredients for the chicken potpies today? How about that ice cream freezer? Are you gonna have enough room in the refrigerator for the potpie stuff?"

"We aren't talking about having ice cream until summer. I want the ingredients for the chicken potpies today. We'll see about the refrigerator."

They had a small discussion about using canned carrots. Maggie knew Aunt Clara wouldn't like that. Mr. Gino had some fresh carrots on the truck. His price was a little high.

"I can get them for cheaper at the grocery store."

Mr. Gino slapped himself in the forehead. "You're putting me out of business. You and your aunt take advantage of the fact that I can't say no to ladies like yourselves. I'll give you the carrots at cost."

Maggie put aside the estimates for the ice cream and freezer. She signed the invoice for everything Mr. Gino had left for them.

"So where's Clara?" His large, drooping mustache twitched when he asked again.

"She's a little under the weather. She'll be back soon."

"That's good. I'm glad she has you now, Maggie, for these days, you know?"

Maggie nodded, afraid to say anything more for fear that she'd start crying again. Mr. Gino hugged her and left through the back door, whistling as he went.

"Everything okay back here?" Ryan peered through the open doorway from the front.

"Fine." She sniffled a little. "I got everything to make twenty potpies for the library fund-raiser. I know Aunt Clara would want to go on with that."

"I know you're right." He smiled at her. "There's a man out here who wants to talk to you about one of the shops Clara rents."

Maggie took off her apron and hung it on the

hook by the door. She glanced in the tiny mirror at the corner to make sure there was no flour on her face. She hoped it wasn't anything complicated. She didn't know if she could handle much more.

The man waiting for her was Artie Morgan. He and his friend Rick Russell were both recent Duke graduates. They ran the X-Press It store two doors down in the same shopping center.

Aunt Clara owned the property and leased the store to them. She called them the twins because they were almost the same height and weight. Both the young men had brown hair and brown eyes. Her aunt could never remember which was which.

"Nice to see you, Artie." Maggie sat down with him. "Where's Rick?"

Artie shrugged. "He moved to Alaska. I know, right? Who does that kind of thing? His brother offered him a good job, something to do with the oil pipeline. He isn't coming back. I can't run the shop without him—and his money. Our lease is up in January. I wanted to let you and Clara know that we won't be renewing."

"I'm sorry to hear that. What will you do?"

"I don't know. Get a job or something. It's a crazy world out there, like that guy getting shot right out here. What's up with that, huh?"

"I'm sure you'll do fine."

"I'm not so sure, but thanks. Where is Clara? Will she be okay with this?"

"She'll be fine. She's a little under the weather today. She'll be back before you leave." Maggie wondered how many more times today she'd have to lie about her aunt.

"Okay. Well, thanks. I'll arrange to have everything moved out. It's all leased."

"Sure. That's sounds great."

He got up to go and looked back at her. "You know, I felt really bad when I heard the police were going after Clara for killing that dude out there. Like she could do anything like that."

"Thanks. The police are after someone else now."

"You know, I told them the person I saw out there was taller and bulkier." He made gestures with his hands to indicate the bulkiness. "Clara is much smaller, and kind of dainty, you know what I mean? Besides, I've never seen your aunt wear hot boots like that."

"Hot boots?"

Twenty-four

You know, the kind with the ten-inch heels and the chains—well, at least one of them had chains. Nothing against your aunt. It would just surprise me to see her dress that way."

Maggie took no offense at his remarks. She stared at him as he left, her brain mulling over his words.

"Losing a tenant, huh?" Ryan had been listening in, of course. "That's too bad. I might know someone who's interested."

"That would be a great solution! You could move into that space and run the *Weekly* from there."

"We'd be a lot closer for coffee breaks!"

"I love it. I'll talk to Aunt Clara. I'm sure she'll be thrilled too."

Ryan put a few notes into his phone, already thinking about the story again. "I wonder if he told the police that part about the ten-inch heels."

"Could be Debbie. She was wearing heels at the salon."

"Maybe." Ryan's phone rang. The fire chief wanted to talk to him about the fire at the *Weekly* building. He gave her a hug good-bye and then turned to leave. Maggie hated to see him go, but she knew it was important. It would be slower as the day went on. Mornings were always their busiest time.

She went into the kitchen and started making the chicken potpies. She cooked the diced chicken with the stock and vegetables. She needed the base to be as thick as possible. She tried to remember everything Aunt Clara had done when she made the dish at Ryan's house.

A few students came in wanting Coke and some day-old pieces of pie. Aunt Clara always kept some on hand and sold it for half of what a fresh piece brought. She primarily did that for the students. Sometimes it was all they could afford.

Maggie made ten piecrusts and tops for the potpie mixture. The students in the front were studying, not making any noise. She kept pushing herself to keep her schedule. If she baked ten potpies today and ten tomorrow, she'd be ready for the library event.

She prayed that Aunt Clara would be back by then. If she wasn't, Maggie would take them to the library in her place. It was all she could do right now. If she couldn't help Aunt Clara, she'd at least keep her reputation going.

The door chimed, and Maggie glanced through the service window. It was Albert Mann. She closed her eyes and shook her head. Maybe when she opened them again, he'd be gone. She really didn't want to talk to him today.

"Feeling all right?" he asked from the doorway.

Note to self: Get a door on that space to keep people from popping in.

"I'm fine. Thanks. Something I can do for you?"

His eyes searched the kitchen. "Where's Clara?"

"She's under the weather. I hope she'll be back in a few days."

Albert's face took on a sly expression. "So it's true. Your aunt *has* been kidnapped."

Maggie set down the bowl of chicken filling harder than she'd meant to. "Why are you here? Did *you* kidnap her? The police don't know what happened to her. How do *you* know?"

"My dear, when you've been listening to people—ferreting out their weaknesses—as long as I have, you learn a lot of things you're not supposed to know."

"Are you ferreting out my weaknesses?" She was ready to throw the potpie filling at his head.

"No. Actually, I went by the police station earlier to see what I could find out about Garrett's building being burned—obviously arson. Instead, I learned that he was in the hospital after being attacked while with your aunt. Maybe the police don't want to call it a kidnapping as yet, but I think we both know a skunk when we see one."

"Go away," she said wearily. "I don't want to talk to you."

"I hope she's all right. She's a wonderful person. I would hate for anything to happen to her, despite what you may think, Maggie."

She took a deep breath before she turned to face him again. She didn't want him to see her cry. "Thanks." Maybe he wasn't sincere, but she didn't have the heart to press him on it.

"I know we've had our differences, but I hope we can still be friends. Believe me, I only have your aunt's best interests at heart."

He left her with a smile, and tears in his eyes. Maybe he really did care about what happened to Aunt Clara, she considered as she continued working.

A surprise birthday party group occupied her time for the next two hours. There were ten yelling, running children in the dining room, trying to do as much as they could in the small space.

The two mothers who'd accompanied them sat and drank coffee as though they were out by themselves. Neither one looked up when the napkin holders were thrown to the floor or the children used filling from their slices of pie to draw on the front window.

Maggie was glad to see them go. Why did mothers even think of bringing a group that size to Pie in the Sky if they couldn't handle them? It wasn't a pizza restaurant with games and slides.

She spent the next hour wearily cleaning up the mess. Had they eaten any of the pie at all? It all seemed to be on the windows and the floor. At least they'd left a good tip.

The chicken potpies smelled wonderful baking in the kitchen. It was such a different aroma from what people were used to smelling at the pie shop. She knew they were going to have some twitching noses and eager customers once the word got out.

It was five thirty when Maggie sat down at a clean table. No one else had come in as the day was ending. The weather had been clear but cold all day. No doubt everyone was worried about ice forming again that evening as the sun went down.

There was no word about Aunt Clara. She didn't know what to think. With each passing hour, she grew more worried.

How long could someone keep her aunt without anything worse happening to her? The stakes were getting higher too. If she had been kidnapped, the longer she was held, the more trouble the person holding her would be in.

All Maggie could do was pray that Aunt Clara was okay.

The potpies were scheduled to come out of the oven at five forty-five. Even though she longed to close early and go to the police and ask for word about Aunt Clara, it would be six before the pies were cool enough to put away. Her phone rang. It was Ryan, updating her on everything that had been going on.

"I'm taking my dad home. The doctor said he should be fine as long as he rests. He wanted to come and see you. I told him he'll have to wait a few days unless I can convince you to come to my place. You shouldn't be alone, Maggie."

"I'll be fine. I've got Fanny and the kittens. I want to be there in case Aunt Clara comes home. I don't want her to find the house empty."

"You've been at the pie shop all day," he reminded her.

"She'd expect that. She would've looked for me here first."

"Okay. I'll try again later. I wish you'd come to my place. I don't have anyone to stay with my dad. I hate to leave you alone this way."

"There's nothing wrong with me. Garrett needs you, Ryan. I'll be fine. Did you hear anything else about Debbie?"

"No. Frank said it's like she's fallen off the map. The police are watching the roads, bus station, and the train. She hasn't used a credit card, tried to get in her house, or use her bank account."

Maggie nodded. "And what about the fire?"

"The fire chief says it was definitely arson. Someone started a fire in a trashcan. They think it could have been a homeless person trying to stay warm. But the investigation isn't over. I can't do anything else until the chief makes his determination. So the paper will probably be homeless next week. I'll have to figure out what to do."

They said good night on the phone. Ryan promised to call her later, and asked her to call him when she got home.

"I will. Take care of your dad. I'll talk to you later."

Maggie closed her phone, and felt close to tears again. The timer in the kitchen buzzed. It was time to take the pies out of the oven.

By the time the potpies had cooled and she'd put them away, it was a little after six. The whole afternoon seemed like it had gone on for weeks. Time was dragging as her mind wrestled with the questions about Aunt Clara. Was she warm and comfortable? Was someone treating her well? Was she scared and begging for her life?

She tried to keep positive thoughts in her head. Garrett had said she seemed to go willingly with the other woman. Maybe it was someone she knew. She was going to be fine. She *had* to be fine.

Maggie put on her jacket and scarf, switched off the lights in the pie shop, and opened the door to leave. To her surprise, Debbie Blackwelder was on the sidewalk outside.

A little nervous at finding her there—not sure if she had killed Donald and kidnapped her aunt—Maggie tried to handle it carefully. She didn't want to be Debbie's next victim.

"I'm sorry. The pie shop is closed." Maggie smiled and waited, hoping she'd leave.

"Do you recognize me? You and the newspaper reporter came to visit me at my salon. I was wondering if we could have a cup of coffee and talk for a while."

Maggie didn't know what to say. If she told Debbie she was on her way home, the woman would want to go there and talk. Maggie felt safer at the pie shop. She was closer to the police, and could possibly find a way to call for help as she was making coffee.

"Sure. Come in."

Debbie stepped inside as Maggie held the door for her. She looked at Debbie's boots—definitely the type Artie had described, except without a missing chain. She was also "bulkier" than Clara, as Artie had said.

She could have replaced the missing chain on the boot.

"I'm sorry about this." Debbie sat down at a table as she removed her coat and put down her handbag. She set down a thick folder. "I was hoping the reporter would be here. I have to get my side of the story out. I'm out, but my lawyer says they could haul me back in at any time if they get fresh evidence. I didn't kill Donald Wickerson."

That caught Maggie's attention. She wanted to hear the story. Maybe she could convince Debbie to do the right thing if she knew where Aunt Clara was.

"It would be easier for me to make a couple of lattes, if that's okay. The coffee urn is huge."

"Anything is fine. Any chance of getting the reporter over here? I have a feeling the police might find me before morning. I've been one step ahead of them all day."

Maggie paused as she started to make a latte. She had to know. "Do you know where my aunt is? Did you kidnap her?"

Debbie's face was a mask of surprise and anguish. She bit her lip. "Of course not! Why would anyone kidnap her? Why would you think I could do such a thing?"

Maggie turned her head toward the latte machine. "I know you were arrested for Donald's murder."

"So if I'm capable of murder, I could do anything?" Debbie shook her head. "All I wanted to do was find out what happened to my mother. I guess everything that happens now is going to be blamed on me. I didn't kidnap your aunt. I haven't done anything wrong, except to try and get justice for my mother."

Maggie's first impulse was to believe her. She seemed sincere. On the other hand, she might only be a good actress. All of the puzzle pieces fit together, implicating her in Donald's death.

But Maggie had been on that short list for wrongdoing once too. Timing and proximity had made her appear guilty, but it wasn't true. It might not be true for Debbie . . . Fran . . . either. Aunt Clara would definitely give her the benefit of the doubt, if she were there.

"Sorry. I had to ask. You know who Aunt Clara is because of your research on Donald, right?"

"Yes." Debbie snorted. "I know who she is. He went after her, and every other woman in Durham who had a little money and no husband. He didn't mind bragging about it at the salon. I would've liked to cut his throat right there in the chair for what he did to my mother—and those other women—*and* what he planned to do again."

Maggie acknowledged the truth of her words. "The police were looking at my aunt for Donald's killing before they set their sights on you. She wasn't guilty, but someone went to a lot of trouble to make it look like she was."

"That's exactly the kind of information I need."

Debbie opened the thick folder. "I've been following Donald for a year, trying to get a bead on him. I *know* he killed my mother, and probably those other women too. I think I have enough to prove it now."

"Did you tell the police?" Maggie looked through all the information she'd gathered.

She had hundreds of photos of Donald with dozens of women, as well as crime scene information. She'd interviewed people from Atlanta and throughout North Carolina who knew anything about the deaths Donald had been accused of.

"The police!" she spat. "I've given them concrete proof that Donald was responsible for my mother's death. They ignore me. They won't even look into it. They have fingerprints, motive, and opportunity. I can't get anyone to pay attention. It's like they want to ignore what he's done because it would be too much trouble to follow through."

Maggie didn't understand why no one took Debbie seriously either. She had more real information against Donald than the police had on her, or Aunt Clara, for his murder.

"They said believing he killed my mother gave me motive to kill him." Debbie shrugged. "Maybe it does. I don't know. Mostly, I wanted everyone to know the truth so it couldn't happen again. I didn't want him dead. I wanted to hear him admit what he'd done."

"You said you've been following him. Is there

anything you've seen that could help us find his killer?"

"I don't know. I didn't kill Donald. If your aunt didn't kill him, I'm not sure who did. Probably one of those other women in town that he played fast and loose with. I fit the composite the police have thrown together for his killer—and I own a gun I can't find. But I don't know who did it. I wish I did."

"I'm sorry. The police might be looking at you for kidnapping my aunt too."

"Like I said—I'm guilty of everything now."

"Are you sure Donald didn't say anything about one of his ladies getting violent, or beginning to doubt him?" Maggie tried to concentrate.

"There were only two women actively in his life, as far as I know." Debbie took pictures out of her file. "Your aunt—and *this* woman."

"Lenora, my aunt's friend." Maggie looked at the photos.

"Yes. I think Donald had made his choice right before he died. Something spooked him about your aunt. He was circling Lenora. She was lonely. She had money. I'm sure, if he'd survived, she would've been his next victim."

The lattes were finished. Maggie gave one to Debbie/Fran and then sat down at the table with her coffee. "Ryan—the reporter—can't leave his father—another victim of my aunt's kidnapping last night. I was thinking we could use my phone to Skype with him, if that's okay?"

Debbie was fine with that. Maggie called Ryan using Skype. He answered right away, his face grainy and almost comical on the small screen.

"What's up?" he asked. "Are you home yet?"

Maggie explained the circumstances. "I thought we could talk to Debbie this way."

Ryan was clearly upset about this idea. He didn't come right out and ask if Maggie was in any danger, but he hedged all around it.

"Look." Debbie stopped him. "I'm not here to hurt anyone. I'm scared to death. You should've heard the incredible story they were creating about me killing Donald. I don't stand a chance against that."

"Did you kill him?" Ryan asked.

"No. I wanted to find my mother's killer. That's all. I got caught up in Donald's newest scheme. I thought I could use it to my advantage, but it backfired on me."

"Yeah. Sorry. I have to ask the hard questions too. Go ahead. Tell us what happened." Ryan waited to hear what she had to say.

Debbie and Maggie were sitting with their heads close together so they could both be on the screen.

"I moved to Durham about six months ago to follow him around." Debbie shrugged. "He's always on the move. I have skills that make it easy to get a new job quickly. I didn't waste any time getting a free coupon to the salon into his hands. I did everything I could to keep him coming back."

"And he didn't know you, didn't recognize you?" Ryan asked.

"No. I used a different name. I left Fran Belk behind. I was a kid when he was married to my mother in Georgia. He didn't have a clue who I was."

"So you started following him around?" Ryan nudged her story along.

"Yes. How else would I get information about him? He didn't spend all of his time at the salon. That's why I signed up at Durham Singles after he told me that he had signed up, looking for a lucky lady. He said the woman he was dating wasn't working out. He was looking for someone new."

Ryan glanced at Maggie. "Probably not Aunt Clara. He hadn't been seeing her that long."

Maggie agreed. "So far it sounds like he was following his familiar pattern."

"Yes." Debbie sat forward, eyes alert. "I was afraid he was going to get married and kill someone else again. I started chasing him. I ate lunch with him a few times. I thought maybe I could distract him, throw him off course. I was hoping he'd come after me. That would have been sweet! But he wasn't interested."

"Betty's Subs." Maggie nodded at Ryan.

"You probably weren't old enough or dependent

enough," Ryan agreed. "I'm assuming you don't have an alibi for the time Donald was killed?"

Debbie shook her well-kept mane of hair. "I should've been at work, but I had this awful headache. I sent email messages to my clients, and I stayed home that day. I know. Not much of an alibi, but it's true."

"I believe you," Maggie told Debbie.

"Thanks. I'm so sorry about your aunt. I hope you can find her."

"I hope so too."

"Hold on a minute. Debbie knew about Pie in the Sky, Maggie," Ryan argued. "She was following us around at the winter carnival. I don't know how much harder it would have been to set Clara up for Donald's murder—or to kidnap her."

"If you'd take a look at my files," Debbie urged him, "you'd see that wasn't what I was going for."

"I'm afraid it's not that simple now," Ryan told her.

Debbie put everything back in her file. "Please. Can we meet somewhere? I have more information that you can put into your newspaper as a follow-up to your other stories. If I don't get it to you now, the police could call it evidence, and you'll never see it."

Maggie sat back in her chair. "I know Frank thinks he has the right person, but I think he's wrong. I know she seems guilty, but it doesn't feel right. I still think whoever killed Donald knew Aunt

Clara personally. They need to take another look at Lenora. She fits the bill."

"We don't get to make those decisions," Ryan said. "You should get her out of there."

"Since when don't *you* make decisions on who you think is guilty?"

As Maggie spoke, two police cars pulled in front of the pie shop, their blue lights flashing.

"Sorry," Ryan said.

Maggie couldn't believe it. "You called the police?"

"Clara is already missing," he argued. "I didn't want anything to happen to you too."

"How am I ever going to prove I didn't do this if I'm in jail?" Debbie shoved the file into Maggie's hands. "Keep this for me. If they take me in, I'll lose it."

"All right." Maggie hid the file behind the counter. "There's a way out the back. Come with me."

Maggie could hear Ryan yelling out warnings at her from Skype. She quickly shut off the phone and ushered Debbie out the back door, closing and locking it behind her.

Two police officers knocked on the front door. Maggie answered, trying to appear bewildered about why they'd been called there.

"We got a tip that Debbie Blackwelder was here." Jack Harding looked around the dining room. "Have you seen her this evening?"

"No," Maggie lied. "I was just closing up."

Her phone rang persistently. She knew it was Ryan. If he was going to warn her not to go out on a limb for Debbie, he was too late.

The officers carefully searched through the pie shop. When they were satisfied that Debbie wasn't there, Officer Harding thanked Maggie.

"Any word on Aunt Clara yet?" she asked him.

"I'm sorry, no," Officer Harding said. "Captain Mitchell wanted to question Ms. Blackwelder about your aunt's disappearance."

"Are you *sure* you haven't seen her?" the other officer asked, eyeballing the dining room again.

"Yes." It was all Maggie could do not to rush over and cover the two coffee cups on the table.

It's okay. You told them you were closing up. You weren't finished cleaning yet.

"Take care." Officer Harding tipped his hat to her. "Someone will notify you if we hear anything about your aunt."

Maggie thanked them. She didn't take a breath until they were gone. She wondered if Debbie had gotten away. She hoped she'd made the right decision to help her.

She didn't waste any time getting out of there. The sidewalks were becoming icy again, so she walked home carefully. She tried not to think about Aunt Clara, thinking instead about the pie shop, and the new line of potpies that their customers were going to love.

It didn't really help, but it was a small distraction from her worries and fears. Ryan kept calling her until she finally turned the phone off and stuck it in her bag.

Exhausted, more by the emotional upheaval of the day than the physical exertion, Maggie was glad to see her home come into view. As she reached the bottom of the stairs, David surprised her, reaching out to grab her arm.

"Someone was looking for you," he said. "You'll never guess who's waiting in my kitchen."

Twenty-five

"Aunt Clara!" Maggie ran to her aunt's side. "Are you all right? Should we call an ambulance? Where were you? When did you get back?"

Wrapped in a blanket, Clara looked smaller and more fragile than ever. Her hair was a complete mess, standing up in little orange tufts all over her head. She had a cup of tea in one hand.

"For goodness' sake, I'm fine," she assured her niece. "I was sitting out on the steps, waiting for you to get home. David found me and brought me here. I seem to have lost my keys. I couldn't even get in my own house. It's a good thing I'm not very old yet. People would start thinking I was losing it."

Maggie hugged her tightly, refusing to let go, as she sobbed all over her. "You should probably see a doctor. Do you know what happened to you?"

"Would you like some tea or coffee?" David asked her.

"No, thanks." Maggie's mind was a whirl. She wasn't sure what to think or do next.

Did someone take Aunt Clara, or did she just wander off? Had she been hurt too, contrary to what Garrett had said? Should she bundle her into a taxi and take her to the hospital? Or maybe David would take them.

"Of course I know what happened to me," Aunt Clara said with some irritation. "Someone kidnapped me. I've already bored David with this story. Can we go home now?"

"You're sure you're okay?" Maggie helped her aunt up. She didn't seem like someone who'd been kidnapped. She didn't seem scared at all. Aunt Clara took David's arm. "Thank you for your help. It was getting a little cold out there. The tea was delicious."

"I'll be glad to help you to your house," David volunteered. "I could probably carry you."

Clara took a step back. "That's fine. I can walk. I'm not a cripple, you know. Good night, David."

Maggie muttered another quick thanks to her

childhood friend. She and Aunt Clara left David's house and carefully went to their own.

"Do you need help getting up the stairs?" Maggie asked her.

"Why is everyone treating me this way? I can get up the stairs. I do it at least once every day. Your uncle used to say it was good for you. Can we get inside now? I really want a hot bath and my bed."

Maggie walked up with her aunt anyway. She opened the front door. Fanny and all the kittens were waiting for them. Her aunt stopped to talk to them for a moment, and stroked them until they were all purring and rubbing her ankles.

"How was it at the shop today?" Aunt Clara asked. "Were you very busy?"

"Okay. That's it. You were kidnapped, and you're asking me how my *day* was?" Maggie was angry and frustrated.

Aunt Clara blinked. Her mouth trembled. Tears formed in her eyes.

"I'm sorry." Maggie hugged her. "I'm so sorry. I've just been so worried about you, I could hardly breathe. And now you're acting like nothing much happened. I don't understand."

"I can explain."

Maggie took a deep breath and looked down at her. "Let's do that. Before you take a hot bath or anything else. Let's sit down in the kitchen and talk, okay?"

"All right." Clara's tone was long-suffering. "I'm a little hungry. Do we have any of that soup left from last week?"

Maggie heated up the soup and put some in a bowl. Aunt Clara had removed the blanket. Outside of looking tired and a little smudged, her aunt seemed to be all right.

"*Mmm.* Good." Aunt Clara had some of the soup. "I'm sure you know that Garrett and I were coming in the house when we were attacked. Someone stepped out of the shadows on the porch, and hit him in the head. I hope he's all right. I hadn't even thought to ask."

"He's fine. What happened next?"

"I didn't see the person. Whoever it was put a hood over my head in the dark and held something to my back—maybe a gun. I'm not sure. We went down the stairs and got into a car. We drove around for a while and finally stopped. We got out of the car and went into another house."

"And you couldn't see anything at all?"

"No. It was totally dark. And the hood smelled bad. I was too terrified to even move. I kept wondering who would do this sort of thing to me. And I was worried about Garrett. It was awful, Maggie. I kept thinking about you and Fred. I didn't know if I was ever going to see you again."

Maggie could see where Clara's calm demeanor

simply masked her fear. She'd been brought up that way. A lady didn't give into her fear. She faced it, stuck out her chin, and pretended she wasn't afraid at all.

"I sat alone in a room for a long time, tied to a chair. I think they used stockings to tie me. The knots felt tight but didn't chafe. I heard voices arguing, but they were muffled. I think they were in another room. I can't be sure. I don't know how long I was there."

Maggie watched as her aunt finished her soup. "Were they mean to you?" It was as close as she could come to asking if the person had done anything really bad to her.

"Oh no. Not at all. I used the restroom, which was completely embarrassing knowing there was another person with me. I went back and sat in the chair again. I wasn't tied up after that."

"How did you get away?"

"I didn't exactly. Someone came and put me in a car again. They dropped me off here. I tried to get the hood off fast enough to see the car, but they were gone by the time I was able to focus."

"And you don't know who it was?"

"No. Can I have more soup?"

"You're not hurt?"

"No. Just hungry."

There was something wrong with her story. Maggie couldn't put her finger on it. She knew her aunt was lying, but she couldn't imagine why. She ran through her words in her mind as her aunt ate.

"What happened when Garrett was knocked down?"

"I panicked, of course. I couldn't see a thing. I turned around, and the hood went over my head."

"And you didn't put up a fight? Just went along with someone you knew could hurt you? That doesn't sound like you."

"May I have some crackers now?"

Maggie got the crackers for her aunt. "I have to call everyone. The whole neighborhood—not to mention the police—have been looking for you."

"I'm sorry. I didn't mean to cause so much trouble."

Maggie called Ryan first.

She called Frank too, not wanting any officers out on a raw night like this looking for her aunt. It didn't take long for him to knock at her door.

"Frank."

"Maggie." He took off his hat and gloves. "Where is she?"

"She's upstairs changing clothes and having a bath. She seems fine, just a little hungry and thirsty."

"Any ideas on who did this?"

"Not that I could tell from what she said." She tried to decide if she should tell him that she was convinced her aunt was lying. But for now, she decided to keep quiet to protect her aunt, at least until she found out why she was hiding the truth. Aunt Clara could get into trouble if the police felt as though the kidnapping didn't really happen—or she knew who'd taken her.

That was it!

Aunt Clara *knew* who had taken her, and she didn't want to tell anyone.

Who could she be protecting?

Frank nodded, his narrow face serious. "Sounds like you two dodged a bullet. I'll have to talk to her myself. I'm glad she's okay."

It was as good a time as any to talk to Frank about Debbie. Maybe she could throw him off the trail of whatever Aunt Clara was hiding until she could get to the bottom of it.

"I know you're invested in the idea that Debbie killed Donald," Maggie said. "And I know if I can change your mind, we'll be right back to Aunt Clara being in the hot seat. But I don't think Debbie did anything wrong."

Frank and Maggie sat down at the kitchen table. Fanny was asleep in her box with her kittens again. Maggie made Frank a cup of instant coffee.

"She's got plenty of motive, and no alibi for when Donald was killed," Frank said. "She might even be involved in what happened to Clara. What have you got that could change my mind?"

"You said yourself that it looked as though someone was trying to set Aunt Clara up for Donald's murder—the flour, the gun at the back of the shop, and waiting until she wasn't in the kitchen. I don't think Debbie could have set that up as well as someone who really knows us and our routines."

"I thought that made sense. But the circumstantial evidence is overwhelming against Ms. Blackwelder. I can't ignore it." He stared at her with canny eyes. "What aren't you telling me? Why do you want her off the hook?"

Maggie swallowed hard. "I don't think she did it. I think it was someone we know."

"Like who? If you have a suspect in mind, please share."

"I don't," she admitted. "I wish I did. I have this gut feeling—"

"Gut feeling?" He shook his head. "You were talking to her at the pie shop today, weren't you? I thought it was odd that Ryan called in a tip on where to find Ms. Blackwelder. What's going on?"

"Nothing. I only want to make sure the right person goes to jail."

"And you think I don't?" He sipped the last of his coffee. "Maggie, a good sob story about a murdered mother doesn't make someone innocent—it gives them the greatest motive in the world: revenge. Don't be so softhearted. And if you see Ms. Blackwelder again, call the Durham Police."

Frank would've said more, but Aunt Clara joined them. "Hi, Clara. I understand you've had an adventure."

Maggie sat at the table and listened again as her aunt explained everything that had happened to her, and to Garrett. The slight hesitation was there in her aunt's voice again. She told the same tale she had earlier. There was still something off. Aunt Clara definitely knew who'd taken her, and was covering for her.

"And you're sure you can't remember anything else about the woman that kidnapped you?" Frank was finishing up with Aunt Clara.

"Only what I told you. At first it was all Shalimar, you know. Then something smelled like goulash, and I realized I was hungry. How odd is that?"

Shalimar?

Maggie knew at once who had kidnapped her aunt. Lenora had reeked of the strong, spicy perfume both times at the pie shop. Aunt Clara had kept her story amazingly straight, but she'd given Lenora away.

Why would Lenora kidnap her? It didn't make any sense. Once Frank was gone, she intended to get to the bottom of this.

Frank put away his little notebook and pen. "If anything else occurs to you, let me know. I'm glad you're back safely."

"So am I. Thank you, Frank." Aunt Clara hugged him and then went to check the cats' food bowl.

"Can I talk to you a minute, Maggie?" Frank muttered as he walked by her to the door.

She followed him, glancing back into the kitchen. "What's up?"

"She's been through an ordeal, especially at her age. You should think about getting her counseling. That's what it says in our public relations handbook. She's a tough old lady. I think she might be hiding something. She might be afraid of what will happen if she tells the truth, you know? The kidnapper might be someone she knows, someone who threatened to hurt her, or you, if she tells the truth."

Maggie was stunned by his perception. "Thanks, Frank. I'll check into getting her some help, and I'll be sure to call if she remembers anything else."

"Good night, Maggie. Let's celebrate this last week before Christmas peacefully, huh? No kidnappings, murders, muggings, or fires."

She agreed, and said good night. She watched him get into his car and drive away before she closed and locked the door.

Frank had seen it too. Was he also right that Aunt Clara was afraid to say what had happened? Had Lenora threatened her? How was she going to reassure Aunt Clara that everything was going to be all right and that Lenora would never be able to hurt her again?

"I'm off to bed now." Aunt Clara started up the

stairs. "Good night. Sleep well. I can't wait to get back to work tomorrow."

Maggie didn't want to upset her aunt, but she knew she had to ask her again about what had happened to her. This time, she didn't mince her words.

"Lenora kidnapped you, didn't she? She hit Garrett in the head, and you were afraid she might hurt him again, so you left with her."

Clara's head popped up like a small bird's as she turned to face Maggie. "I don't know what you mean, dear."

"I know you too well. And you gave it away—Shalimar. The only person I can think that you'd protect this way is Lenora."

Her aunt sank down on the stairs. Maggie sat beside her and put an arm around her.

"Yes. She hit Garrett in the head. I wasn't afraid for him, though I suppose I should have been. I was afraid for *her*. I was troubled by the look in her eyes, Maggie. I was afraid she might hurt herself. That's why I went with her."

Maggie drew a deep breath. "So Lenora took you to her house, right? What happened?"

"Pretty much what I told you, except I wasn't tied to a chair. I sat in her kitchen while she ranted and raved about her whole life. I guess she wanted to feel safe in her own home going off that way. I can't think why she went to such an extreme. I felt so sorry for her. She has always been miserable, poor thing. I didn't realize how much she loved Donald. She saw him as her last chance for happiness."

"What happened then?"

"Alice finally came home. She argued with her mother and then brought me home. She was so apologetic. She knows her mother needs help now. I hope she gets it for her."

Maggie hugged her aunt. "I knew it. Anyone else would have had to fight to get you to leave the house."

"I guess you *do* know me well." Aunt Clara sighed. "I feel so bad for her. I can't tell the police what really happened. I know Garrett will be angry and probably want to prosecute her. She doesn't need jail, though. She needs a doctor."

Not knowing what else to say now that she knew the truth, Maggie walked with her aunt up to bed. "You should stay home tomorrow, you know. You've been through a lot."

"Whatever!" Aunt Clara waved away her sympathy. "I've worked with a broken leg before. Your Uncle Fred came back to work three days after gallbladder surgery. I want to see how the potpies turned out."

"We'll see how you feel in the morning." Maggie insisted on tucking her aunt into bed. She hugged and kissed her. "I love you. I was so scared I'd never see you again."

Aunt Clara smiled and lightly touched her face.

"You can't get rid of me that easy. I'm not going anywhere until you and Ryan make me a happy grandmother. Not technically, I suppose, but the next best thing."

"We'll talk about *that* later too. I love you. Next time, call, and tell me what's happening."

"I do heartily swear to call you the very next time someone kidnaps me, Maggie. Good night, dear."

Twenty-six

Maggie went to her room, where she cried happy tears of relief that her aunt was finally home. She couldn't sleep thinking about Lenora, and what could have happened. She understood her aunt wanting to protect her old friend, but there was a place where a person had gone too far.

It occurred to Maggie at about 2:00 a.m. that it was distinctly possible that Lenora had killed Donald. Aunt Clara refused to believe Lenora could hurt anyone. This proved she was wrong.

Lenora knew their routines at the pie shop. She was desperately afraid of losing Donald to Clara. If Lenora could conceive of kidnapping her aunt, what else could she think of?

Maybe Frank was right that the same person who killed Donald had also kidnapped her aunt—he just had the wrong person.

Maggie wasted no time calling Ryan. He was awake. She knew he would be. She told him about Lenora. "What should we do?"

"Let me check and see if she has a nine-millimeter pistol registered to her. That could be the deciding factor. I'll call you when I know."

Maggie fell asleep waiting for that call. It never came, but Aunt Clara was at her bedside, fully dressed, urging her to get up just before 5:00 a.m.

"What? What is it? Is everything okay?"

"Everything's fine, dear. The alarm will go off any minute. I'm so *excited* to go back to work. Let's go early."

Maggie dragged herself out of bed. Of the two of them, maybe she was the one who should stay home. Aunt Clara seemed better than fine. She was ready to go.

When Maggie got downstairs, Aunt Clara shoved a slice of toast into her hand and gave her a sip of orange juice. "Sorry. We shared the last of the juice. *Someone* was supposed to pick some up yesterday. The cats have already eaten. It looks like Fanny is staying home today. I think she's finally used to it here. Isn't that wonderful?"

Maggie grunted something. She wasn't sure if it was intelligible. She chewed and swallowed a single bite of toast and threw the rest away. "You know, I was a *little* preoccupied yesterday."

Aunt Clara was pacing and impatiently standing at the door while Maggie put on her scarf and coat. She wasn't sure if she was going to survive Aunt Clara's kidnapping if it only made her more energetic.

When Maggie reached her side, she noticed a blotch of red lipstick on her aunt's coat. She thought about what Ryan had said about matching the lipstick to the brand found on Donald's lapel. "Just a minute. Let me wipe off that lipstick for you. Is that the kind Lenora wears?"

"I'm not sure." Clara watched as she carefully wiped off as much of the lipstick as she could. "I want to forget that happened. Isn't it lovely outside this morning?"

Maggie ran back to the kitchen to get a plastic bag and sealed the lipstick-stained paper towel into it. Aunt Clara was going to have to have her coat cleaned. It wouldn't all come off. In the meantime, that evidence might be what Frank needed.

She knew her aunt was going to be angry if she helped prove Lenora had killed Donald, but it couldn't be helped. She wasn't willing to take a chance that Lenora might not be such a *nice* kidnapper next time.

Aunt Clara took in a big breath of cold air as Maggie closed and locked the front door. "We're going to have to get our Christmas tree up soon. I'm so glad we decorated at the shop this year. It's such an exciting Christmas."

Maggie followed behind her aunt after a caution about the frozen sidewalks. Aunt Clara talked nonstop all the way to Pie in the Sky. The morning was cold, but the temperatures were already warming up from yesterday. They got to the pie shop twenty minutes early—a new record for Maggie.

Aunt Clara opened the door and rushed inside, switching on all the lights as she went. She took off her coat and put on her apron in one quick movement. She went to check the refrigerator and laughed out loud.

"Maggie, you baked enough to feed an army yesterday! I hope we have a crowd today."

"And I hope there's enough coffee in the shop to keep me awake all day." Maggie yawned.

They went through their normal routines but didn't bake any of the regular pies. Clara felt confident they didn't need to make those yet. They worked on the potpies instead.

Maggie went in at six and started the coffee. Aunt Clara looked over the figures Mr. Gino had left for them yesterday.

"What do you think we'll have to charge per scoop to make money on the ice cream?" Aunt Clara figured as Maggie wiped down the tables before customers started coming in.

"I'm not sure yet. He said he'll let us have the freezer for free—if we buy the ice cream from him."

"We'll have to see if that's a good deal or not. We still have time to consider it before summer. Now tell me about the twins. I can't believe they're leaving."

Maggie explained about Rick leaving, and Artie not being able to carry on without him.

"Oh, that's too bad. I'm going to miss them. I hope we'll be able to find another tenant."

From that moment, they were hopping. Aunt Clara started baking the chicken potpies. The mouthwatering aroma filled the shop and wafted outside into the frosty morning each time the door opened. Everyone who came in demanded to know what the delicious new smell was. When they found out, they wanted either a slice or a whole pie.

There was such enthusiasm that Maggie convinced Aunt Clara that it was all right to sell them the day before the fund-raiser. They sold five pies in the first hour. Maggie called Mr. Gino for more supplies. At that rate, they would use up what they had and have to bake fresh for the library event.

This could be what Maggie had been looking for to boost their lunch crowd. That could make a huge difference in their bottom line.

Ryan came in early too. He'd left his father with the housekeeper for the day. He hugged Aunt Clara and kissed Maggie good morning before he took his coffee and sat on the stool in the kitchen.

"I'm so glad Garrett is doing better," Aunt Clara said. "I'll have to stop by after work and take him a pie and some flowers. He was very gallant trying to save me from the kidnapper."

"He's very happy you're home too," Ryan told her. "I'm sure he'd be glad to see you tonight."

"You know Garrett and I are just friends, don't you?" Aunt Clara looked concerned that he might think otherwise. "It's too soon after losing Donald to commit to anyone again."

Ryan smiled. "I'm sure he'll be willing to wait for you."

Maggie and Aunt Clara took orders and baked pies, as they always did. Ryan finally sat down in the crowded dining room with a piece of potpie for breakfast.

"Wow!" he said loudly as new customers came into the shop. "This new chicken potpie is awesome. I can't wait to take one home with me." He winked at Maggie when several of the customers around him inspected what he was eating more closely.

It helped—the potpies kept selling.

When the early rush began to die away, Maggie sat with Ryan and had a soft drink with a piece of potpie. "You're right. This is going to be good for us.

We have a chance to offer something besides sweets. Thanks for the promo. Two of the people who were sitting close to you bought whole pies."

"Now all we have to do is keep up with the demand," Clara squawked from the service window. "What are we going to call them?"

"I'm not sure." Maggie hadn't considered it, but she knew her aunt liked all the pies to have names. "I'll start a contest on the whiteboard out here. That will help advertise when Ryan isn't here."

Ryan watched Maggie write on the whiteboard after Clara had returned to the kitchen. "I was worried about you after you cut me off last night. What made you decide to help Debbie get away from the police? She could be Donald's killer. She might have kidnapped your aunt."

"It was my gut," she said with a smile as she finished her note to their customers about the new potpie. Ryan used that excuse all the time for unexplained feelings he had.

"You don't have a gut." He laughed. "It takes years to develop a gut. Believe me, you don't have one. What you did last night was impulse."

"Maybe. But I think I was right, now that we know about Lenora, don't you?"

"Oh yeah. That's right." He glanced at the service window. "Lenora Rhyne doesn't own a gun of any kind."

"What? Are you sure?"

"You can look it up yourself. It's public record. She's never owned a gun, at least not one that she registered."

"Maybe she's got one that's unregistered. Maybe that's why the police couldn't find anything on it."

"That's always possible. Where do you want to go from here?"

Maggie handed him the plastic bag with the lipstick sample in it. "I got this from Aunt Clara's coat, the one she was wearing when she was kidnapped. Could you give it to Frank?"

He nodded. "This could clinch it if it matches. How is your aunt going to feel if Lenora is arrested for murder?"

"Let's not discuss that right now. When we know about the lipstick, I'll talk to her."

Ralph Heinz came in and spent a few minutes with Aunt Clara, telling her how happy he was that she was safe.

He was no sooner out the door than Albert Mann came striding in. He removed his hat and gloves. "It's good to see you back, Clara. You know, we never discussed the possibility of you and I having dinner."

Clara's face turned pink, but her voice was harsh when she said, "And we're not going to, Albert. I didn't join that dating service—Maggie did. Maybe you should ask *her* out for dinner!"

Maggie felt as though she deserved that. She glanced at Albert. "Pie and coffee?"

There was a chorus of disappointed groans from customers who'd been watching the show.

Albert played into it. He put his hat on and faced his audience. "I tried. That's all a man can do.

"Ryan Summerour!" Albert hailed him before joining him at his table. "I'll have coffee, Maggie, and a slice of whatever smells so good."

Ryan had been on his cell phone. "It's the new chicken potpie, and it's great." He lowered his voice. "What do you want, Albert? I don't want to hear you gloating about getting my property."

"I'm not here to gloat. I'm here to offer you the same deal I would have when the building was still on the property. I'd say that's a good offer, wouldn't you?"

"Not really. I know you only want the property. This way you have less to get rid of. I think you should offer me more."

Albert laughed and slapped Ryan on the arm. "I knew you were the one I should have been doing business with from the start. You know, your mother was always the one with the head for money. Your father, not so much." He named another sum that was twenty percent higher than what he'd originally offered.

"That sounds better." Ryan got to his feet. "But the fire is still being investigated as arson. I can't do anything with the property until the fire chief says so. See you around."

Ryan smiled as he heard Albert hit his fist on the table and utter an obscenity.

"That made my day," he told Maggie when he was in the kitchen. He hugged her. "I have to go. I'll talk to you later."

Maggie let him out the back door, as she had Debbie the night before. She wondered if Debbie had made it out of Durham, and away from the police. She believed something would break soon that would exonerate her.

Aunt Clara was furiously making piecrust. Maggie took a few minutes to put some chicken filling into the crusts before she went back out front to take Albert his pie and top off coffee cups.

The morning went quickly. It was sliding into the slack time right before lunch when the pie shop lost the entire early-morning crowd. Business didn't pick up again until the late-afternoon customers. It was a time when they didn't make much money, but Maggie and her aunt enjoyed the break.

But Maggie remained hopeful that the potpies would change all that, although it might mean hiring someone to help if they got much busier.

The woman from the library fund-raiser called late that morning to make sure everything was in order. Aunt Clara told her they'd come up with something special. She didn't say that she meant to kill any competition from Lenora's pies, but Maggie could hear that between the lines.

"Have you and Lenora *ever* really been friends?" Maggie asked her aunt after she was off the phone.

"Of course. We've always been the jealous, underhanded kind of friends that you read about and see in the movies. I should've broken it off long ago, but that would mean being the first one to admit defeat."

"If you wait much longer, it won't matter." Maggie laughed.

"I suppose you're right. I don't know if I can make the first move—especially after this latest affront. I know it wasn't her fault. She couldn't help herself."

Maggie helped her take out a tray of pies and put them on the cooling rack. Mr. Gino knocked at the back door with their much-needed supplies. He hugged Aunt Clara and spent five minutes telling her how much he'd missed her.

Maggie was wondering if Mr. Gino was going to be the next one dating her aunt when her cell phone rang.

Twenty-seven

"Thanks for the lipstick sample," Frank said. "This could help with the case. I take it Ryan told you about the lipstick on Mr. Wickerson's jacket lapel."

"He did."

"Don't clean that coat that you got this from. I'll send someone over to pick it up. How's Clara this morning?"

"I couldn't keep her home." Maggie bit her tongue before she said anything about Lenora. "Thanks. Let me know how it goes."

She was going to have to find some excuse about Aunt Clara's coat going missing. She took it from the hook in the kitchen when her aunt wasn't looking and put it near the front door of the pie shop. A police officer came in a short while later and picked it up with gloved hands, dropping it into a large plastic bag.

Aunt Clara didn't notice.

"I'm going to get lunch at the sub shop," Maggie told her aunt. "I thought I'd go while it's slow. The way those potpies are selling, we may be busy later today."

"I've thought of a name," her aunt said. "Chubby Chicken potpies. That's if no one else comes up with something better."

Maggie scrunched up her face. "I guess that could work. I'm hoping people will write down other suggestions on the whiteboard. It may take a few days."

"Okay. We'll see."

What was she going to do about her aunt's missing coat? It wouldn't matter until it was time to go home tonight, but it would really matter then.

Straining her brain on how to explain the loss of the coat, Maggie walked to the sub shop. She saw Ryan talking to the fire chief in front of what was left of the *Durham Weekly* building. He glanced her way and then shook the fire chief's hand before starting toward her.

"I hope you're on your way to get lunch," he said. "I'm starving."

"You're in luck. I thought I'd get *you* something for a change."

"Maybe I should go home and shower first." He looked down at himself. "Walking through a burned-out building isn't as exciting as it seems."

"You can get washed up at the pie shop, if you want. Or I'll save your sandwich for you. Did you find out anything else about the fire?"

"Not much. Even if a homeless man did it, the building is still gone."

Maggie gingerly touched his arm. Flecks of soot and ash flew off of him. "Maybe I'm wrong about the shower thing. Or you should at least change clothes. I don't know if I want you dragging all this ash and stuff into the pie shop."

He brushed off his jacket and sneezed as debris went everywhere. "I think you're right. I'll drop you at the sub shop and go home for a shower and a change of clothes. It'll give me a chance to check up on Dad too. I'll be back soon."

He bent his head as though he planned to kiss her.

Maggie stepped back. "I know you're not trying to kiss me with all that stuff on you, right?" She sneezed just thinking about it. "I think I'll walk. It's not that far." She waved to him, and darted toward the sub shop.

"Fine," he yelled after her. "Just don't eat my sandwich."

Betty pumped her for information about the fire and Donald's death while Bobby made her sandwiches. Maggie didn't want to give away any information until the police had verified it. Betty wasn't happy about being left out of the loop, but she understood.

The pie shop was still almost empty when Maggie got back. One customer was eating what looked like a whole potpie. Maggie went into the kitchen with their sandwiches and asked Aunt Clara what was going on.

"I don't know. He wanted a whole pie. I gave it to him. He said he liked it. Let's eat!"

Maggie took out their sandwiches and got them each a glass of sweet tea before they sat down to eat. "I took your coat away to have it dry-cleaned while I was out."

"Oh?"

"You know—the lipstick?"

"Of course." Her aunt's brow furrowed. "What am I going to wear home tonight? Is it one of those new twenty-minute dry cleaners?"

"No. You can wear my jacket home. I'll be fine. I didn't want the lipstick to set."

A few new customers came in. They'd already heard about the hot potpies and were looking for something different for lunch. Maggie was happy to oblige them. Aunt Clara took her sandwich and went into the kitchen.

By twelve thirty, they were swamped. Aunt Clara couldn't keep up with making enough potpies to keep the crowd happy. Maggie served dozens of their regular customers, and many more new ones who'd heard about their new lunch special.

"The potpies are a hit!" Maggie proclaimed as she went back to help put more pies into the oven. "I think this is it!"

"Good." Aunt Clara took a deep breath. "I hope we can stand being so busy all the time."

Ryan finally got back after the rush had died down. He'd showered and changed clothes. "Dad is doing fine. He still has to take it easy the next few days. I think he's out of the woods anyway."

Maggie told him about giving Aunt Clara's coat to the police. "I don't know what I'm going to say to her if the police think Lenora is guilty of killing Donald."

"You'll think of something. She'll understand that her friend can't be out on the street killing people. She's not stupid." Ryan sipped his coffee and asked for a slice of cherry pie for dessert.

"I hope so."

"I'll swing by this evening and pick you two up so you don't have to worry about the coat problem." He sighed. "I'm giving up the battle, Maggie. I have a doctor's appointment to get glasses this afternoon.

Or maybe contacts. How do you think I'll look in glasses?"

He made circles with his fingers and put them around his blue eyes.

Maggie laughed. "I think you'll look like a writer—which you are. You may even look more intelligent."

He grinned. "In that case, I'll definitely get glasses. I'm receiving an award from the Business Owners' Association too, so I guess I'm doing okay."

She kissed him. "Well, at the very least, you need to see what you're doing."

As a few new customers came in, Maggie shot to her feet.

Ryan stood too and stopped her as he put his arms around her. "Thanks for being there with the fire—and everything else. I love you, Maggie."

"I love you too." She closed her eyes and inhaled his distinctive scent of ink, aftershave, and fresh air. "Thanks for being there for me too. I wouldn't want to be anywhere else."

"Me either."

She watched him leave for another city meeting, thinking how lucky she was to have him and Aunt Clara, and then she went to greet her customers.

The afternoon was very busy. Kids of all ages were out of school and stopped in for hot chocolate. Some had pie. Some wanted cookies. Maggie kept her smile in place for even the most annoying of the customers.

David came in again for pie and coffee. Maggie thanked him for his help with Aunt Clara, and made an effort to be especially kind to him. She hoped, even though they'd gotten off to an awkward start, that things would smooth out between them now that he was going to stay.

They talked again about things they did when they were children and about teachers they hadn't liked, wondering if they were still teaching.

"Remember Mrs. Fossick, the science teacher?" David whistled. "I hated that woman. Nothing I did was right for her."

"I know what you mean."

"She said I was 'troubled.' My parents grounded me for a month."

Maggie laughed. "I remember. I had to sneak comic books and snacks into your house."

"And I came down after my parents went to bed and got them." He smiled at her. "Those were good times. It was fun being a kid with you."

"I know. We do have some great memories. Have you found a job yet in Durham?"

"I think so. I'm definitely staying. After seeing what a hard time my parents are having, I can't leave them again. If nothing else, maybe you could hire me to make pies."

"I could do that. If these potpies keep selling,

I'm gonna need someone." She knew they were both joking around.

"Well, don't fill that position until I go through this next interview." He sighed. "Why does everyone require you to come back for so many follow-up interviews nowadays? My first job, they hired me on the spot."

"I know what you mean. Good luck, David."

"Thanks." He paid his bill, and left her a hefty tip in the jar before he went to his interview.

• • •

Ryan picked up Maggie and Aunt Clara promptly at 6:00 p.m. They went to his house to have dinner with Garrett, who was happy to see them.

The mood was a little somber since the police had arrested a homeless man for starting the fire at the *Durham Weekly*. Ryan had gone to see him at the jail. He'd told Maggie that he probably wouldn't press charges against the old man.

"He was so pitiful," Ryan explained. "He was just trying to stay warm. It was an accident."

Maggie felt bad about it too. So did Aunt Clara and Garrett, but there was nothing anyone could do about the charges being leveled at the man. The fire could have burned more than just the newspaper office, and might have killed someone.

It made for an odd, melancholy mood as Maggie

helped Ryan take his family's old Christmas decorations out of the basement.

"I can barely do this after everything that's happened," Ryan said.

"It won't make anything better to sit around and mope about it." Maggie encouraged him with a kiss and a smile. "You help us with our decorations, and we'll help you. Okay?"

He nodded. "Yeah. I guess that's all we can do, right?"

Garrett moved into the foyer to sit and watch. Ryan set up the tree and put a new set of LED lights on the branches.

Aunt Clara put on garland and ribbon while Maggie and Ryan hung the ornaments. One of the ornaments was a baby in a basket being carried by a stork. It was Ryan's first Christmas ornament. It was a little tarnished. Some of the blue paint was gone. Still, it was a special moment. Maggie thought he looked as though he might cry.

There was also a bride-and-groom ornament that Aunt Clara coaxed Garrett into hanging on the tree.

"My wife had that made from the top on our wedding cake." He chuckled, thinking about it. "It was a long time ago."

There were almost too many memories stored in those boxes. Garrett had to ask to be excused, saying he had a headache. Aunt Clara kissed him on the cheek. Ryan briskly hugged him.

It wasn't long after that that Maggie and Aunt Clara called it a night. Ryan took them home and walked them to the door. He kissed Maggie good night under the porch light.

"That was odd," she said. "You never kiss me goodbye outside the door. You always come in to say good night to me."

Ryan smirked, and glanced at the Walker house next door. "That was for your new neighbor."

Maggie started to protest, and Ryan put his lips on hers, holding her tightly. His hands supported her back as he pressed her closer. Maggie's heart fluttered, and she felt warm all over, despite the cold.

"I–I think he gets the point," she said breathlessly when he released her.

"Then my job here is done!" He skipped down the stairs, whistling a Christmas tune.

Maggie went inside, slamming the door hard behind her, but a smile lingered on her lips. *Men!*

Aunt Clara and Maggie took down their Christmas decorations from the attic. Maggie remembered each and every glittering glass globe and shining star. There were homemade ribbons and ornaments she'd made in school too.

"Look!" Aunt Clara held up a little ornament made to look like a storefront that said "Pie Shop."

"Your uncle got that for us the first Christmas we opened Pie in the Sky. We had such dreams and hopes. It was a wonderful time in our lives. Not as wonderful as that first Christmas with you, but exciting and special."

There were several ornaments shaped like slices of pie, and whole pies too.

"What do you think happened to Lenora that made her snap?" Maggie asked her. "I know she lost her husband, but so did you. She has a lot of money and a nice house. She has Alice. Why is she so unhappy?"

"Even when we were children, it was hard to satisfy Lenora. There was never enough of anything for her—money, boys, clothes. Nothing was ever as she wanted it to be. I think it made her crazy. And she's scared of dying, Maggie. Scared of being alone. We all are, I suppose. She doesn't think she can depend on anything, or anyone, to be there for her. It's a sad state of affairs."

Maggie hugged her, a little sorry that she'd sent the lipstick and the coat to Frank. Maybe if Aunt Clara was satisfied with how things had turned out, she should be too. She just didn't want her aunt to be hurt anymore by Donald and Lenora.

They sat with Fanny and the six kittens by the fireplace, drinking hot cocoa. Aunt Clara named them all after pie fillings: Coconut, Chocolate, Raisin, Pecan, Cherry, and Key Lime.

"Isn't Fanny going to feel a little odd since she has a nonedible name?" Maggie asked with a laugh.

"I think she'll be fine with it," her aunt said. "Tomorrow, we'll get a Christmas tree from that nice man on the corner. And by next week, our pot-pies will be famous! I can't wait to see the look on Lenora's face!"

Maggie hoped that "look" wasn't going to be as bad as she feared.

Twenty-eight

Pie in the Sky was closed for the fund-raiser. It was such a big event for the library that Clara had justified it as a day off for the shop.

Maggie found it hard to believe that there could be so many people at a fund-raiser that it would be worthwhile closing the shop. She'd offered to stay at the shop and keep it open while her aunt went to the event. That way they wouldn't be letting down their regular customers, and they could make income from both places.

Aunt Clara wouldn't hear of it. "It gets very hectic there. I had to hire someone to cashier for me the last two years. Now I have you. We make money at the event, you know."

"But forty percent of it goes to the library," Maggie argued, though she knew it was a lost cause.

"A *worthy* cause. I hope you can keep up with the money while I dish out the pie."

Now that the event was at hand, Maggie was glad she'd finally agreed to accompany her aunt. Maybe it would be busy enough to warrant both of them being there—maybe it wouldn't. She certainly didn't want Aunt Clara and Lenora there together without her and Alice to intervene if necessary.

The kidnapping, and the fact that Lenora may have killed Donald, put a whole new spin on things. Maggie realized she might have to be there to protect her aunt. She hoped it wasn't from a gun.

Maggie wanted to call Frank. She wanted to spill the whole story to him and hope that he'd arrest Lenora without any other proof. That would mean Aunt Clara being willing to tell him what had really happened. What were the chances?

Even for her own safety, her aunt wasn't willing to turn Lenora in. Maggie didn't understand her reasoning—she'd never had a friend she was willing to sacrifice this much for.

They got up early the next morning and headed out the door as quickly as possible to warm the potpies at Pie in the Sky before they went to the library.

Once the potpies were ready, they slipped them into boxes. Mr. Gino had let Maggie borrow some insulated bags from him—no charge—that would keep them warm for a few hours. She hadn't wanted to buy them. Who knew when, or if, they'd need them again?

"It's going to be chaotic when we get to the high school gym," Aunt Clara explained like a general marshaling her army for a battle as Maggie drove Garrett's car.

It had still been parked outside their house since the night of the kidnapping. Ryan had given her the keys. She planned to drive the car to his house when the event was over.

"It can't be more hectic than the pie shop some mornings," Maggie commented as she drove to her old high school.

Clara laughed. "Imagine the pie shop during the morning rush, but there are *hundreds* of people wanting pies and slices. They're all waving their money and checks at you. You don't have a cash register so you can't use credit."

That was where Maggie planned to surprise Aunt Clara. She'd invested in a credit card-reading app for her phone. It wasn't expensive, and if it *was* as busy as her aunt made the event sound, she'd be ready.

"Do you know where our table is?"

"Someone will tell us when we get there. It's a

different table every year. The best ones are slightly to the back of the gym. People seem a little stunned when they first walk in. I had a table right at the door a few years back and I was so pleased. Then I realized the customers couldn't get a good look when they first came in. It was my worst year ever. The next year, I asked for a table near the back."

Maggie pulled into the crowded parking lot at the school. The old, red-brick building seemed almost the same as when she'd gone to school here. There were a few additions—a dozen double-wide mobile classrooms that were attached to the school by covered walkways.

"I'll get out here and check in." Aunt Clara opened her car door before Maggie had even parked. "Find a close place. I'll see if I can get someone to help us bring in the pies."

Garrett's car was stuffed full of potpies. They'd made an extra dozen after their warm reception at the pie shop. Aunt Clara had been afraid they might run out before the event was over. Maggie liked that idea better than having to bring dozens of potpies back home. They wouldn't be salable, not even discounted.

"I found our spot." Aunt Clara came to the car with a young man whose dark hair hung down across most of his face. Maggie recognized him from the pie shop, where he hung out almost every day. "Zack is going to be our helper today. He's a student at Duke. He helped me last year."

Zack nodded. "Where are the pies?"

"Let's get the pies out of the trunk first." Maggie made an executive decision. "We can get the ones in the backseat later."

The inside of the car smelled like chicken potpie. Maggie hoped Garrett didn't mind.

They'd stamped Aunt Clara's name for the potpies—Chubby Chicken—on each of the boxes. Maggie had hoped for something a little catchier, but no other suggestions had shown up on the whiteboard yesterday. They could always change it later.

Zack carried a dozen pie boxes in with him. Aunt Clara carried three. Maggie had ten. They walked into the bustling gym and looked for their table. As per Aunt Clara's request, the Pie in the Sky table was near the back. All around them, vendors were setting up their tables with every kind of food imaginable.

"Hey! Clara! Maggie!" Betty called out from the sub shop table. Her daughter, Betsy, and son, Bobby, were both with her. Bobby had a huge metal cash box he was working on setting up.

Maggie and Aunt Clara waved back at her.

Raji and Ahalya were also there at a table. They looked nervous and uncertain. Maggie realized it was probably their first time at the event too. She'd have to go over, when she had some free time, and talk to them.

Alice and Lenora were also setting up their table. Maggie wondered why a consignment shop was there selling slices of apple pie. All the rest of the vendors seemed to be people who owned restaurants and food trucks. She realized it was probably because Lenora was on the library board, like Aunt Clara. They were probably just glad to have as many board members as possible at the event.

"There's Lenora." Aunt Clara surreptitiously glanced at her old friend from across the room. "I hope she doesn't come and speak to me. I really don't know what to say to her. I think we need a little more time apart."

Maggie spoke her mind. "I still think we need to call the police and tell them what happened. I know she's your friend, but she could've hurt you. She *did* hurt Garrett. We don't know if she's lost control before and hurt someone else."

As Maggie had known she would, Aunt Clara disregarded her suggestion. "She's not going to hurt anyone—at least not on purpose. She didn't mean to hurt Garrett. It was an accident."

"I can't do this without you," Maggie told her. "The police won't listen to me. You'll have to tell them the truth. If you're wrong and she hurts someone else, can you live with yourself, knowing you could've stopped it?"

Aunt Clara's green eyes met Maggie's. "*Pish!* I know that woman. I think you're overreacting. Let's get these pies out before the crowd rushes in."

The double doors opened at 8:00 a.m. A stream of people trickled in. That stream widened to a flood within a few minutes. By ten, Maggie felt as though she'd been washed away by a tsunami of hungry customers.

"I hope we have enough pie," Aunt Clara yelled to her as she handed slices of potpie to customers on paper plates. "I wish we'd invested in the heavy-duty plates. I'm afraid someone is going to drop pie all over the floor."

Maggie was busy taking cash and checks, and scanning credit cards. She was amazed at how many people could fit into the gym. Aunt Clara hadn't exaggerated the event at all. There were hundreds of customers, some familiar faces, waiting in line to reach her.

Her aunt refused to even look at the portable scanner Maggie's phone had become. "I don't like the way they've put computers into everything. Look how it's messed up my cash register! I couldn't even use it until you showed me how."

"What a crowd." Maggie observed the people flowing into the gym. "I'll plan differently next year."

"That's my girl."

At ten thirty, Maggie had to take a break. She couldn't wait any longer to go to the restroom. That meant Zack had to hand out pie while Aunt Clara took money.

"I won't be able to do this phone credit thing," she fussed. "It's all I can do to make a call on one of these gadgets. We'll have to do things the old-fashioned way until you get back. Cash and checks only. Hurry!"

Maggie wasted no time getting to the restroom. There was a line there too. Why was there never a line going out of the men's room?

"Hi," Alice greeted her. Maggie hadn't even noticed she was ahead of her in the bathroom line. "How are things going for you all?"

"We're slammed," Maggie said. "How about you?"

"We're almost sold out. I don't know if people even look at what they're buying here. I guess because it's for the library, they don't care. It's a wonderful event, isn't it?"

"I'm sure it helps that it's Christmas too. Who wants to cook?"

Alice laughed. "I know what you mean. Of course, my mother always fills the house with cookies and homemade candy. She baked three Bundt cakes last night. I'm on schedule to gain my usual fifteen pounds over the holiday."

They moved into the restroom at the same time. Even though it was crowded, Maggie hoped to have a word with Alice about the kidnapping.

They were at the sinks washing their hands. "I wanted to thank you for helping my aunt."

Alice didn't pretend not to know what she was talking about. "I'm so sorry about that. My mother went off the deep end that night. I couldn't believe she'd brought your aunt to our house. I hope that man she hit on the head is okay."

"He's fine *now*." Maggie dried her hands on a paper towel. "But what about next time? Your mother needs help. I won't lie to you—I've encouraged Aunt Clara to tell her story to the police."

"Oh no! Please don't do that. I agree that she needs help. Her sister will be here over the holidays. I can't talk my mother into anything. I'm sure my aunt will be able to take care of the problem. Can you imagine my mother going to jail? It would be terrible."

Alice reached out to put her hand on Maggie's, dropping her paper towel on the floor. Maggie bent down to pick it up for her—and noticed Alice's boots. They were exactly the same kind Debbie had been wearing—clearly they were a trend this year.

But one of the chains was missing from the left boot.

Heart racing, Maggie stood up and really studied Alice. She had dark circles under her sunken eyes. The rest of her face was chalky white except for the bright red lipstick she was wearing.

Could it be true? Did Alice kill Donald?

That didn't make any sense. Alice certainly wasn't involved with him. She couldn't be related to anyone he'd killed. What would her motive be? Was she so worried about him taking everything from her mother that she put an end to the relationship? She'd just admitted that she couldn't talk her mother out of anything.

On the other hand, the missing chain on her boots and her shade of lipstick didn't necessarily make her a killer.

Maggie tried to rein in her imagination, and threw her paper towel into the trash. Maybe if Alice believed her mother might go to prison, it would move her to tell the truth. It was worth a try.

"So far, Aunt Clara won't budge on turning in Lenora," she told Alice. "What makes me even more worried is that the police think your mother may have killed Donald."

If it was possible, Alice's face got even whiter. "W-what makes you say that? Why would anyone think my *mother* would do such a thing? You saw how much Donald meant to her. She'd never hurt him."

Maggie accompanied Alice out of the restroom, her brain buzzing with questions as she tried to put it all together. "Whoever killed Donald knew our routine at the pie shop well enough that she could plan to kill him when Aunt Clara was outside in the alley. She put flour on his clothes and hid the gun behind our trashcan. No other suspects the police have talked to have that knowledge."

Alice's eyes filled with tears. "Why do you think a *woman* killed him?"

"The owner of the shop close to where it happened saw what he described as a bulky woman wearing high-heeled boots with chains on them. There was also lipstick on Donald's lapel. The police are researching the brand. They're checking the lipstick that I found on Aunt Clara's coat too. It was stained when she was kidnapped."

Maggie and Alice were standing in a small, dark alcove outside the women's restroom. Dozens of people walked by without noticing them. Maggie could see Aunt Clara glancing frantically at the bathroom. The line in front of her was even longer than when Maggie had left.

"'Bulky,' huh?" Alice snickered. "I guess that's as good a description as any."

Maggie frantically tried to think of what she could say that would push Alice into a confession. She seemed nervous, vulnerable, and about to crack. She may never have the chance again.

"As you can see, the description fits your mother. I'm afraid she may have lost it before she kidnapped Aunt Clara. You can understand why the police should be involved. There's another woman out there who lost her mother to Donald. The police think *she* killed him. We both know that's not true, don't we?"

Twenty-nine

Alice pushed her dark bangs out of her face. She peered at the crowd going by. She was crying when she turned her gaze back to Maggie.

"You don't understand. Donald drove my mother *crazy*. She was so afraid of losing him to another woman. There wasn't anything she wouldn't do for that man. She even signed over the deed to our house . . . the house that *I* was supposed to inherit one day. Can you imagine? She gave him her savings. She planned to marry him and give him everything else we had, including the consignment shop."

"And that's why you killed him."

Alice nodded, sobbing now. "She was leaving me with *nothing*. She didn't care what happened to me anymore. It was all about *him*. You're lucky your aunt didn't fall for him that way. The man was a leech. He used women, and killed them. He would've killed my mother when he was done with her. I took care of the problem. I protected both of us!"

The two women stood together for few more minutes. Maggie knew her aunt and probably Lenora were likely getting worried about how long they'd been gone. Clara and Lenora needed them, depended on them.

What would Lenora do without Alice?

Maggie was relieved to finally know the truth. But at the same time, she liked Alice. She hated to think that she'd killed Donald, no matter how much she feared what he'd do to her and Lenora. The man had ruined too many women's lives. It wasn't fair.

"What happens now?" Alice asked Maggie in a soft voice. "Are you going to turn me in? My mother doesn't know anything about what I did. She's not responsible."

"I have a friend with the police. I'm not sure, but I think it would be better for you if you got a lawyer and turned yourself in."

"I don't know if I can do that."

Maggie put her hand on Alice's arm and smiled at her. "You can do it. It's for the best. Get it out in the open, and get past it. I'm sure a jury will be sympathetic when you tell them what you just told me."

She walked across the gym to the Pie in the Sky table, where her aunt was about to pull out what little hair she had left.

"What in the world took so long?" Aunt Clara changed places with Zack again. "We need pies out of the car. Zack said he'll go get them. He needs the keys. I was beginning to think you weren't coming back."

Maggie watched Alice walk out of the gym. Lenora was also watching her daughter. When the door closed behind her, Lenora sat down behind her table and cried.

Maggie knew then that Alice had lied to her. Lenora knew what she'd done, though probably not until after the crime had already been committed. Alice was protecting her mother again.

Epilogue

They all supported one another through the terrible things that had happened before the holiday.

Ryan had gone through the arraignment that day for the homeless man who'd started the fire at the newspaper office. Maggie worked hard to keep him from getting dragged down by what he thought of as an injustice when the man wasn't released.

She also kept smiling for Aunt Clara after Alice's arrest and Lenora's confinement to a psychiatric hospital.

Maggie was happy that she and Aunt Clara had

decided to share Christmas with Ryan and Garrett. Dozens of presents were heaped under the Christmas tree at their house.

Aunt Clara had also invited David because she was worried about him being alone on the holiday. David's parents had made a surprise decision to go on a cruise to the Bahamas over Christmas. No one was more surprised than David.

Maggie was glad that David and Ryan seemed to have resolved their jealousy over her. Ryan and David had nicely refrained from any loaded barbs while they were getting dinner on the table.

Christmas dinner included a roasted turkey (Garrett's favorite), a ham (Ryan's favorite), spaghetti with meatballs (Aunt Clara's choice), and Maggie's favorite—macaroni and cheese. Of course, there were cranberries and two different kinds of stuffing as well as cheese, wine, and homemade bread.

Aunt Clara doted on Garrett—filling his plate and admonishing him to eat more. Maggie believed there was a future between the two, even though her aunt still said he was just a friend.

They moved to dessert (coconut cream and mincemeat pies) and coffee before opening the gifts.

"Is Frank going to ask you to testify against Alice since she confessed to you at the high school?" Ryan asked after the huge dinner. "I heard he found the gun. I couldn't believe it was constructed by a 3-D printer. That's a first for me to write about. Those are rare. No wonder Frank didn't recognize what it was."

"It probably wouldn't have happened if some student wasn't playing around with that printer that belonged to the university," Garrett protested. "Too much time on his hands."

"Is this my boyfriend asking out of weird curiosity, or the reporter for the *Durham Weekly* who recently moved into one of our shops?" Maggie stared hard at him.

"I'm not sure." Ryan smiled and adjusted his new glasses for the umpteenth time that evening. He was having a hard time getting used to them. "Maybe that question should wait until tomorrow when I'm setting up my new office in the aforementioned newly leased space."

"And we're happy to have you there," Aunt Clara added with a wink at Maggie.

"You're working the day after Christmas?" She kissed him. "I don't see any rush to that response. The paper just came out."

"You're right." He put his arm around her as they walked into the parlor, where a fire was blazing in the hearth. "Merry Christmas, Maggie. That's from me. You might get a card from the paper too. I think I sent one here since your aunt is a subscriber."

David turned back from using the iron poker to stoke the fire. He was roasting chestnuts—or trying to. So far, there were no popping sounds, despite the heat from the flames.

The doorbell rang. Maggie couldn't imagine who would be there that late on Christmas night. She left Ryan in the parlor to answer it.

"Sorry to bother you, Maggie," their UPS man said with a grin. "I found this at the back of the truck last night. It has your address, but the name on it is Ryan Summerour. I guess someone screwed up. I didn't want someone not getting a gift today. Merry Christmas!"

Maggie thanked him and gave him a tip and a slice of mince pie. She took the box to Ryan. Everyone was seated in the parlor. She sat beside him on the sofa. "Looks like you get to open the first gift."

Ryan looked at the box, which was wrapped in red paper. It had no return address. "Is this your way of giving me a surprise gift?"

Maggie laughed. "I'm not that clever."

"Besides, she'd never expect some poor UPS man to deliver something on Christmas." Aunt Clara had Fanny and the six kittens on her lap. "Maybe you have a secret admirer. Open it."

Ryan pulled off the red paper and carefully opened the box. Inside was a doll that looked passably like him, even down to his new glasses. The curly blond hair looked real, and the blue eyes were brilliant.

There was also a noose around his neck, and a tiny wood stake through his chest.

"Looks like someone doesn't like you, Summerour," David said with a laugh.

New Pie Recipes from
Pie in the Sky

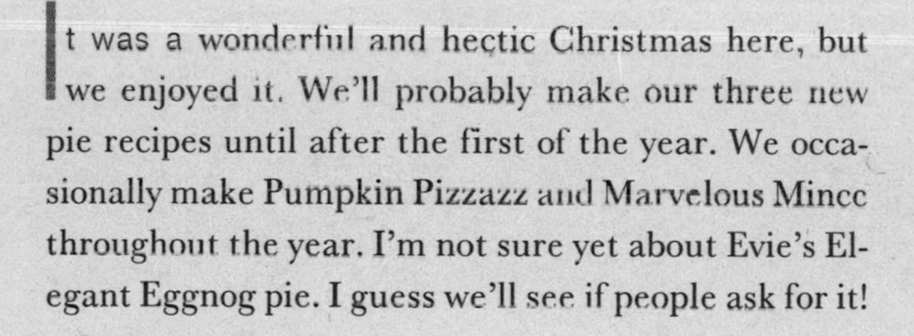

It was a wonderful and hectic Christmas here, but we enjoyed it. We'll probably make our three new pie recipes until after the first of the year. We occasionally make Pumpkin Pizzazz and Marvelous Mince throughout the year. I'm not sure yet about Evie's Elegant Eggnog pie. I guess we'll see if people ask for it!

Flaky Piecrust

• *Makes 1 nine-inch piecrust*

1 cup vegetable shortening
2 cups flour
1½ teaspoons salt

1. Chill all mixing utensils and ingredients first.
2. Work the shortening into flour and salt quickly until the particles are as small as possible.
3. Sprinkle in cold water, only enough for the dough to stick together in a ball. It should be dry, not moist. Chill for at least 30 minutes.
4. After the dough is chilled, place it on a pastry board or another flat, nonstick surface. Dust surface lightly with flour. Flatten the dough a little, then use a lightly floured rolling pin to make smooth, even strokes from the center to the edge of the dough.

5. Turn the dough frequently to keep it round. Use an ungreased metal pie pan for flaky crust. Don't turn the crust over when putting it into the pan. Leave rolled side up. Use your fingers to lightly press any cracks in the crust together. Flute crust, if desired.
6. For pies with unbaked fillings, bake the crust at 350 degrees for 10 minutes before adding filling. Otherwise, bake the crust with filling.

Pumpkin Pizzazz Pie—an old favorite

Did you know the original "pumpkin pie" consisted of eggs and milk mixed with sweetener and baked on a fire inside a pumpkin shell?

1 fifteen-ounce can of pumpkin
1 fourteen-ounce can of sweetened condensed milk
2 large eggs
1 teaspoon ground cinnamon
½ teaspoon ground ginger
½ teaspoon ground nutmeg
½ teaspoon salt (optional)
1 nine-inch unbaked piecrust

Mix pumpkin, condensed milk, eggs, spices, and salt in medium bowl until smooth. Pour into crust. Bake at 350 degrees for about 40 minutes or until a toothpick inserted comes out clean. Be sure to cool before you cut!

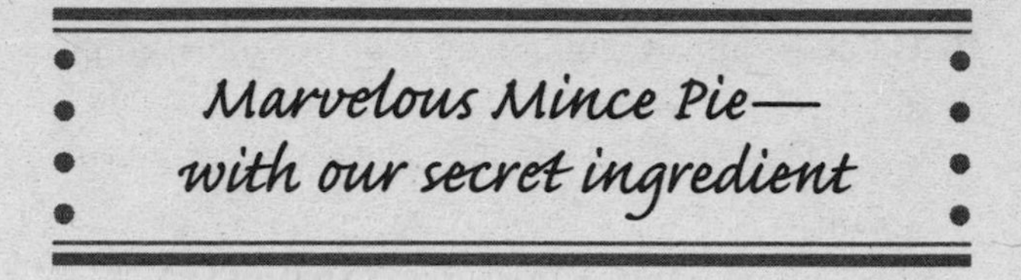

Marvelous Mince Pie—with our secret ingredient

Our secret ingredient is a whole lemon and juice. Our pie is also a "mock" meat pie, as it doesn't contain beef or pork.

- *Makes two pies.*

1 cup chopped apples
1 cup raisins
¼ cup lemon juice
¼ cup orange juice
1 small lemon, peeled and cut into tiny pieces
1 small orange, peeled and cut into small pieces
¼ teaspoon salt (optional)
½ teaspoon ground cloves
1 teaspoon ground cinnamon
1 teaspoon ground nutmeg
1 cup white sugar
½ cup molasses (in place of sorghum)
1 cup apricot juice
4 nine-inch unbaked piecrusts

1. Combine all ingredients and fill two unbaked pie shells. Cover with second shells and pinch at edges to seal. Prick several holes in the tops to release steam.
2. Bake for 1 hour at 375 degrees.

Evie's Elegant Eggnog Pie

This is a nice, light pie that is easy to make!

1 small box vanilla pudding mix, cooked variety

¼ teaspoon ground nutmeg

1½ cups eggnog

2 teaspoons rum (optional)

2 cups heavy cream

1 nine-inch baked piecrust

1. Combine pudding mix, nutmeg, and eggnog. Mix well. Cook over low heat, stirring constantly, until thick. Remove from heat, and stir in rum (optional). Move ingredients to a large bowl, cover, and refrigerate until cold.
2. Whip cream into soft peaks. Remove the cold pudding from the refrigerator and fold in whipped cream. Spoon the mixture into a baked pie shell. Refrigerate 2 hours or until set.
3. Enjoy!